GUARDING YOUR HEART

BAYTOWN BOYS

MARYANN JORDAN

Cover Design by: Graphics by Stacy

Cover and model photography: Eric Mcinney

ISBN ebook: 978-1-947214-36-1

ISBN print: 978-1-947214-37-8

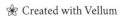 Created with Vellum

The small Coast Guard Station at Cape Charles, Virginia was my muse for the Baytown's Station.
This book is dedicated to the courageous members of the U.S. Coast Guard. Thank you for your service.

AUTHOR'S NOTES

I have lived in numerous states as well as overseas, but for the last twenty years have called Virginia my home. All my stories take place in this wonderful commonwealth, but I choose to use fictional city names with some geographical accuracies.

These fictionally named cities allow me to use my creativity and not feel constricted by attempting to accurately portray the areas.

It is my hope that my readers will allow me this creative license and understand my fictional world.

I also do quite a bit of research on my books and try to write on subjects with accuracy. There will always be points where creative license will be used to create scenes or plots.

Four years ago, my husband and I discovered the Eastern Shore of Virginia and fell in love with the area. The mostly rural strip of land forming the peninsula originating from Maryland has managed to stay non-commercialized. The quiet, private area full of quaint towns captured our hearts, and we rushed to buy a little place there.

It has become our retreat when we need to leave the hustle and bustle of our lives. I gather ideas, create characters, and spend time writing when not walking on the beach collecting sea glass.

The summer sun blasted down on the beach, scorching the sand, but that did little to deter the people on the public beach in Baytown. One of the few public beaches on the Eastern Shore of Virginia, the Baytown beach was long, and deep, and filled with pristine white sand. It afforded families plenty of space to spread out their colorful blankets and umbrellas as well as the multitude of children's sand buckets and shovels. Children and parents alike, not used to the hot sand, ran from their blankets to the water and back again, hopping along to keep the soles of their feet from burning.

The sleepy little coastal town brought visitors from May to October as they filled the rental houses and, subsequently, the beach. But for the kids who were lucky enough to reside in Baytown all year around, the crowded beach only meant that they had more people to dodge as they chased each other, their feet used to the hot sand.

A group of boys, having earned the nickname

Baytown Boys, weaved amongst the visitors, laughing and playing tag. Nine-year-old Callan Ward raced along the sand chasing his friends, Grant, Aiden, Zac, and Philip. Brogan and Mitch were a year older than the others, and the seven boys were inseparable. The townspeople knew that if you saw one boy, you would find them all.

Today, their gang included some of the local girls as well. Younger than the boys, they were determined to keep up. Jillian, Tori, and Katelyn were fierce competitors in the game of tag. Philip's younger sister, Sophie, was not as fast. She was never able to catch the others and almost always ended up as *it*.

Tearful, she stopped running and dropped her chin to her chest as the others ran off. Her blonde corkscrew curls had escaped her ponytail and whipped about as the wind blew.

"Come on," Brogan called to the other boys. "I'm tired of playing with the girls. Let's go to Callan's house."

The boys instantly agreed, loving the old shed in Callan's backyard that his parents had allowed them to turn into a boys-only clubhouse.

Callan nodded but ran over to Sophie first. He held out his hand and said, "Here, Sophie. You can tag me."

She lifted her tear-stained face upward and cocked her head to the side.

"It's okay. Tag me. I know it sucks to be the littlest one and always get stuck being *it*."

Her small hand reached out tentatively, and she tapped his wrist.

"Come on...say it," he encouraged.

Sucking in her lips for a few seconds, she whispered, "Tag. You're *it*." Callan grinned and ran off to follow his friends.

Philip ran to his sister and gave her a hug. "Aw, don't worry, Squirt. One day you'll be older, and you won't always get tagged."

She smiled up at him, adoration in her eyes. "I'm okay, Philip," she promised, wiping the rest of her tears away. "Callan let me tag him." She knew her brother would not tease his best friend but was not sure about the others.

Brogan called out to his sister Katelyn and said, "We're leaving. Boys only now, so you can't come!" He turned and led the boys as they disappeared over the dunes after grabbing their sneakers.

Katelyn, a fierce expression on her face, stood with her fists on her hips. "Boys stink!" she yelled.

Jillian and Tori walked over to Sophie. "It's okay, Sophie," Tori said. "It's not your fault you're the youngest and can't keep up."

She sniffed and wiped her nose. Her eyes followed Callan as he ran off with the others. She wanted to tell the girls that he was now *it*, but she did not want to share what he had done. *They might tease me.* So, she remained silent and waited to see what game they wanted to play now.

Katelyn turned and walked over to Sophie as well. "Well, at least your brother is nice most of the time. Sometimes Aiden and Brogan make me so mad."

"That's because you play just as hard as they do," Jillian said. "They're just jealous."

The girls fell into giggles at the thought of the boys being jealous of them. They ran off toward the Sea Glass Inn, the bed and breakfast that Tori's grandmother owned. They were sure cookies would be waiting, and they did not have to share them with the boys.

Later, that afternoon, Sophie walked to the back of her yard where she could see the shed in the corner of Callan's yard. She could hear the boys laughing and recognized Philip's voice. That did not surprise her considering they were best friends.

Their houses were separated by only a small dirt alley that delivery or garbage trucks used. Many of their neighbors had erected fences, but their parents kept the back open. She knew it was because the Wards and the Bayles were friends even before Callan and Philip had been born. But especially now that the two boys were best friends, their parents kept the back yards open so the kids could run between the houses easily.

"Philip!" she called out. "Mom says it's time to come home for supper." The grumbling from inside the boys' not-so-hidden hideout could be heard. In a moment, she spied them all tumbling out into the yard. Aiden and Brogan waved to the others and jogged down the alley toward Main Street where their grandfather's pub was. Mitch and Grant called out their goodbyes and walked toward the front, heading to their houses.

Philip and Callan were the last to come out, and after their goodbyes, Philip ran to her, calling out, "Hey, Squirt."

She looked up and smiled in return. "Mom's got some cookies from the Sea Glass Inn for you. I brought them home."

Giving her an affectionate pat on the head, he said, "Thanks." He took off, and glancing over her shoulder, she watched as Philip headed into their house, the back screen door slamming behind him.

Once all the boys were out of sight, she turned to the Wards' yard and saw Callan still standing by the shed in his yard. She crossed the alleyway and stopped just a few feet in front of him. Sticking her hand into her pocket, she pulled out a napkin and opened it. Two chocolate chip cookies rested in her palm, and she held it out for him.

His eyes widened at the offered gift, and he asked, "What's that for?"

"Tori's grandma made them, and I wanted you to have some."

He reached for the cookies, mumbling, "Why?"

She lifted her small shoulders in a little shrug and replied, "Cause you're nice to me."

He grinned a chocolate chip grin and said, "Thanks. These are good. "

She met his grin with a shy one of her own and whirled around to run back to her house. Just as she was almost to her back door, he called out, "Hey, Sophie."

With her hand on the doorknob, she stopped and turned around.

He waved and said, "I think you're nice too." With

that, he darted around the shed, out of sight, heading to his house.

Another grin slid across her face, and she giggled as she ran inside for dinner.

Callan stood next to Philip, the rest of the Baytown Boys forming an imposing semi-circle behind them. Furious, he stared at the vacationing teenage prick who had been teasing Sophie. At thirteen, he and the rest of the gang had grown by leaps and bounds, their young bodies hard from sports and their loyalties fierce.

"You come near my sister again...you say anything to her...you even breathe in her direction, I'll come after you so fast, you won't know what hit you," Philip growled.

The other boy gave off an air of false bravado, but Callan noted his gaze moved through all of them and fear flickered in his eyes. *Good...be afraid, asshole.*

The boy's gaze jumped back to his, and Callan realized he had spoken out loud. Lifting his chin slightly, he emphasized the threat.

"This is a dumbass little town filled with a bunch of dumbass people," the other boy grumbled, his squeaky voice giving away his fear. He turned and ran down the street, leaving the Baytown Boys laughing at his retreating form.

Turning back to a wide-eyed, tearful Sophie, Philip was the first to get to her side. She looked up at him and said, "Thanks."

"Aw, Squirt, don't you know that I'm the only one who can tease you?" Philip joked, giving her a hug.

She nodded, a small grin playing about her lips. As the others agreed, Brogan joked, "Good thing we got here first. If Katelyn had heard about that dick, she'd have kicked his ass."

The others broke into laughter before they jogged back toward the beach. Callan stayed back for a moment and walked over to her. Her wild, blonde curls were pulled back from her face, and her wide, aqua eyes stared up at his.

She glanced down the road at the others before turning her gaze back to him. A blush rose over her cheeks, and she said, "Thank you, Callan."

He moved to her and gave her a little hug. "Don't worry, Sophie. I'll always guard you."

He watched the blush deepen and he grinned before running after the others, his heart strangely light with her smile pressed into his memory.

At twelve years old, Sophie Bayles sat in the bleachers next to her parents watching the Baytown Boys first game of the season. The people in the stands all around her were cheering for the hometown team, her mother cheering the loudest.

Philip and Callan were in ninth grade. While she hoped her brother performed well, it was Callan who captured—and held—her attention. *But then, he always did.*

All of the Baytown Boys were cute, but Callan was the cutest of all. Dark black hair and dark eyes. Even at the age of fifteen, it looked like he was almost ready to shave. Grant, Philip, and Aiden still had cute but youthful looks. Aiden and Mitch were tall, and Brogan was not only tall but big with muscles.

But Callan was it for her. While her girlfriends would ooh and aah over the rest of them, Callan had held her interest for as long as she could remember. *Maybe today he'll notice me.* She sighed, knowing it would not happen. While he had always been nice to her, as soon as he went into high school, he had entered a different world. A world where he had captured the attention of girls who had boobs. Boobs and bras. Makeup and cute haircuts. Halter tops and cutoff shorts.

As her parents jumped up and down from their seats, cheering with each homerun Philip and the others made, she sat, dejected, watching the teenage girls standing by the fence. Glancing down at her preteen body, she wanted to cry. Her long curls were braided to keep them from exploding wildly in the breeze, and she felt every bit twelve years old.

She had middle school friends, but her closest friends were already in high school. By now, Jillian had captured Grant's attention, and Katelyn only had eyes for Sophie's brother, Philip. Tori lived in Virginia Beach, but whenever she came to visit her grandmother, Sophie had noticed that Tori and Mitch always stared at each other. *It sucks to be the youngest in a group.*

Her mother jostled her to the side as she jumped up

again, and Sophie's attention moved back to the playing field. Callan had hit a home run, and as he rounded the bases, Philip, Grant, and Mitch had each made it home. Despite her morose musings, she could not help but cheer for Callan as well. She stood and watched as he hopped onto home plate, his hands thrown into the air in a sign of victory. Her gaze never left his face, and his smile widened at the cheers from his teammates and everyone in the stands.

He seemed to walk with an extra swagger as he headed to the fence and was soon surrounded by a group of girls. Girls with boobs and bras. Makeup and cute hair. Halters and cutoffs.

"Are you okay, honey?"

She looked up toward her mother and nodded as she blinked back tears. "Yeah, I think I just got something in my eye. Probably some dust."

"I'm going to go on and head home," her mom said, "so I can put out the food for the cookout. You want to come with me?"

The different Baytown Boys' parents had each agreed to host weekend cookouts during baseball season, and tonight was the Bayles' turn. Sophie had planned on hanging around the ball field with her friends and walking to her house with them, hopefully finding a chance to tell Callan that she was proud of him. But, seeing him surrounded by the teenage girls, she no longer wanted to witness that.

With shoulders slumping, she nodded toward her mom and said, "Yeah, I'm ready to leave."

She walked along beside her mom toward the car,

lost in her dejected musings. Her mom nudged her shoulder, and asked, "You okay, baby?"

She twisted her head up, seeing her mom's soft gaze staring at her. "I just wish I was all grown up, like those girls in high school."

As usual, her mom did not laugh at her ridiculous statement but instead said, "It's hard being twelve, I know."

She nodded and replied, "It's a dumb age, Mom. I'm too old to play with dolls and too young to have a body that any boy would notice."

Her mom wrapped her arm around Sophie and gave her a hug just before they climbed into the car. "When you get to my age, it feels like the years passed so quickly," her mom said, pulling out into the street. "It seems like just yesterday that Philip was a toddler and you were a baby. But I know that when you're a preteen, the months seem to crawl by."

"Exactly!" Sophie agreed.

"Any particular boy you wish would notice you?"

Shrugging again, she mumbled, "No. Well, kind of." She did not know why she hesitated because she could always easily talk to her mom. Feeling like she would burst if she could not get it out, she blurted, "Callan. It's always been Callan."

Her mom nodded in understanding and said, "He's always been a nice boy."

She felt her mom's gaze boring into her as she stared out the front windshield. Finally daring to glance to the side, she could see her mother's worried expression. "I know he's too old for me, Mom. It's just hard being this stupid age."

Baytown was so small that it only took a couple of minutes to drive from the ballfield to their house. Not wanting to talk any more about Callan, she jumped out of the car and hurried into the kitchen. Glad that her mom could sense she was over the conversation, they began to pull the platters from the refrigerator.

Her father had driven separately and was already in the backyard firing up the grill. She took the platter of hamburgers and hotdogs from her mom and walked toward the back door to take them outside. Before she had a chance to push open the screen door with her hip, her mom called out, "Sophie?"

She looked up expectantly, watching her mother approach.

"You were an adorable baby, a cute little girl, and a pretty preteen. Give life a chance, sweetie, and you'll find that before you know it, you'll be a beautiful young woman."

She sucked in her lips, thinking, and asked, "But what if he's gone by the time I blossom?"

Her mom bent and kissed her forehead and replied, "He'll notice." Smiling, she added, "I'm sure he'll notice."

Her mom gave her a nudge, and she hurried out the back door to give the platter of meat to her dad just as the other cars were parking in the alley, their occupants spilling into the yard for the cookout.

Hours later, she was much more relaxed since the cookout was just for the Baytown Boys and their families, all friends for years. Not feeling self-conscious since the gang of teenage girls was not around, she found herself sitting in a lawn chair next to Callan.

Feeling tongue-tied, she managed to mumble, "You did really good today."

He grinned in return, and her tummy felt weird but in a good way.

"Thanks, Sophie."

"Squirt, you didn't tell me I did a good job," Philip quipped, hugging her and rubbing his knuckles over her curls on the top of her head. He walked away, grabbing another plate.

The heat of blush hit her cheeks, and she was glad that the evening hid the color on her face. As soon as everyone's attention was diverted, Callan leaned closer. "Don't worry, Sophie. I like that you noticed that I played well."

Her lips curved into a smile, and the flip-flops in her tummy increased. He finished his meal quickly and jogged off with the other boys who were congregating across the alley in his backyard. The moms were already cleaning up, and the dads were hauling the lawn chairs back to their vehicles.

Sophie said goodbye to Jillian, Tori, and Katelyn as they were leaving with their parents. The backyards were soon empty, but she sat under a tree by herself, watching the fireflies and listening to the crickets.

"Sophie?"

She scrambled to her feet and looked around in fright, relaxing her stance as she saw Callan standing in the dark. "Yeah?"

"I found this the other day and thought you might

12

like it. I didn't figure I'd give it to you in front of anybody because they'd just laugh. You've always been really sweet to cheer for me, so I wanted to give you something in return."

She looked down at his extended hand and saw a beautiful piece of blue sea glass resting in the center of his palm. "Oh, it's beautiful. It's for me?"

"I know you like to collect sea glass." He jerked his chin up toward the back of her house and said, "I see the jars on your windowsill." He ducked his head down before lifting his gaze back to hers. "It reminds me of the color of your eyes."

She reached out tentatively and took the sea glass from his hand, fingering the smooth edges. "Thanks," she said. Unable to think of anything else to say, she watched him flash another grin before he tossed a wave her way and jogged through his backyard and into his house.

Her heart began to sing at the knowledge that he had looked at her window and seen her collection of sea glass. *And he noticed my eyes.* It might not have been a declaration of love from him, but she vowed at that moment that he would always be in her heart.

2

The game was over, the Baytown Boys won, and the crowd was still clapping. Callan, a high school junior, stood in the middle of the field of victory, the team members all gathered around cheering each other. As they slowly dispersed and headed toward the dugout, he looked over to the fence. Jillian, in her cheerleading outfit, was still waving her pom-poms for Grant. Katelyn had just high-fived her brothers, Aiden and Brogan, and was on her way running toward Philip, her arms wide for a hug he knew his best friend would offer readily.

Aiden and Brogan had already moved into the gathering of girls that were swarming around them. Tori had come from Virginia Beach to watch the game and now had Mitch's complete attention.

Taller than most of the gathering, Callan looked over to the fence where one lone cheerleader was left. Her mass of curly blonde hair was braided intricately along the sides of her head and then spilled out in a curly ponytail. Her eyes, the most brilliant aquamarine color he had ever seen, were staring back at him. Sophie. Sophie Bayles.

He knew he should wave and turn away, but his feet were not listening to his brain, and he walked toward the fence. Never coy, her interest in him flared bright. Now, finishing her ninth grade year, her beauty had blossomed, and it was easy to notice her in the halls of their high school. He could not remember when she had just gone from Philip's little sister to a young woman that had definitely captured his attention. *Philip's little sister. Philip's little sister. I can't go there.* The chant he repeated inside his head helped him remember why he needed to keep her firmly in the friend zone, but it was harder to tell his heart that. She may have only been a ninth grader, but she was more mature than most of the juniors in his class.

Her gaze had never strayed as he walked toward her, her shy smile widening as he neared. Stopping just on the other side of the fence, he grinned.

"Hey, Sophie. I watched you cheering. You were good."

She blushed deeply and replied, "Thanks, but you're the one who was great today."

Before he had a chance to say anything else, a hand clapped him on the back. Twisting his head around, he saw Philip with his arm around Katelyn. Callan was almost certain there was a slight questioning in Philip's gaze before his attention focused warmly on his sister.

"Hey, Squirt. You cheered good today. Jillian says you're the best ninth-grade cheerleader we've got."

Callan watched as Sophie blushed again, staring adoringly toward Philip, the pom-poms in her hands rustling as she fiddled.

"Thanks, Philip. Congratulations on winning again."

Philip reached out and tugged her ponytail before turning his attention back to Callan. "Since this was Mitch and Brogan's last game, some of us were going to head out to the old shack. See you there?"

Nodding, Callan said, "Absolutely." He watched as Philip and Katelyn ambled away, their arms wrapped tightly around each other. Turning back toward Sophie, her wistful expression, so easy to read on her face, tugged at him. Unable to think of anything else to say, he just grinned as he waved goodbye. "Well, I better go. See you around, Sophie."

Sophie lifted her hand to wave goodbye, but Callan had already turned and was jogging toward the other guys on the team. She sucked in her lips, afraid that anyone around would be able to see how excited she was. *He noticed me. Of all the girls out here, he noticed me.*

Giddy, she turned and ran back to the other cheer-leaders.

The sun was setting over the Eastern Shore, and Callan sat with his friends around the bonfire on the beach. The small, one-bedroom, one-bathroom shack was an old fishing cabin that Mitch's grandfather had owned for many years.

He never minded the boys using it as their more grown-up clubhouse, making each of them promise that they would never drive away from it after drinking. Not that they were old enough to drink, nor drank often, but Zac was easily the master at sneaking alcohol.

The Baytown Boys had hauled fallen logs from the woods and placed them around the bonfire providing a place to sit, or if they were sitting in the sand, a place to lean back.

Now, they each held a beer and watched the sun set. The mood was somber at best. The winning baseball game from earlier had been pushed to the background as they each pondered the changes on the horizon.

Mitch and Brogan would soon be graduating from high school, and both had made their announcements to the group. Mitch was leaving in two months for the Army. Brogan, the same, only to the Marines.

Callan cast his gaze around the others, inwardly acknowledging that this group had been his close friends since he was in preschool. They had played together, fought together, celebrated each others' triumphs, and held each other up when life was tough.

Callan remembered standing with his brothers at a couple of funerals of grandparents. He remembered welcoming Zac into his home numerous times for sleepovers when Zac's dad was too drunk to take care of him. He remembered Mitch's father, the Police Chief, calling them in to give them a lecture when he caught them drinking the first time.

Scrubbing his hand over his face, he shook off the morose feelings of life changes and cleared his throat, gathering the attention of the others. Lifting his beer high, he said, "Here's to friends. Here's to your brothers. Here's to Mitch and Brogan, getting ready to flee this little backwater town. Here's to the Baytown Boys."

The others followed suit, and shouts of *'Hell yeah'* were called out, floating into the evening sky. Later, they climbed into sleeping bags inside the shack, and the next morning said their goodbyes as they headed home. Since he and Philip lived across the alley from each other, they drove together.

Parking in the alley, Callan reached for his door, but Philip's words halted him.

"Callan, I don't suppose it's missed your notice, but I think my sister has the hots for you."

He jerked his head around, hearing the strange tenor in his friend's voice. "Philip, I've done nothing—"

Philip lifted his hand and said, "I know, I know. I'm just saying that I've noticed. But you know you can't go there, man. She's only fourteen."

Nodding, he said nothing, strangely hurt that his best friend did not trust them. Before he could think of anything to say, Philip continued.

"But, Callan? I just want you to know that if there was anybody good enough for my sister, it would be you."

A warmth spread throughout him, hearing that his best friend had just given him the greatest compliment he could have received. But he agreed...the time was not right. "You don't have to worry, Philip. I get it."

The two climbed from his old truck, and with chin lifts and slight waves, they parted company, each jogging into their own houses.

Sophie sat on the bench in the locker room, her heart pounding so loudly she had to strain to hear what the girls on the other side of the lockers were saying. She recognized Stacy Usher's voice and held her breath so they would not know she was in the room.

"He may have asked Jillian to the prom, but I have no doubt I could've gotten him if I wanted," Stacy said.

Another girl replied, "Dream on, Stacy. You know Grant only has eyes for Jillian."

"Stacy, I thought you were going to go through all the Baytown Boys?" another girl said.

"Well, I've had Aiden," Stacy replied. "Philip is stuck on Katelyn, so he's out of the running. But there's always Zac or Callan."

Hearing Callan's name, Sophie pressed her fingers to her lips to keep from crying out. *No, no, Stacy. Please stay away from Callan!* In truth, Stacy was such a bitch to everyone, Sophie did not want her around any of the Baytown Boys, but especially not Callan.

The girls' voices faded away as they walked out of the locker room, and Sophie breathed easier. Mitch and Brogan had graduated the year before and were now both overseas in the military. As a sophomore, she had gotten closer to Jillian and Katelyn, and the three girls hung out all the time with the remaining Baytown Boys.

And while Zac was a sweetie, it was Callan who continued to hold her heart.

She left the locker room and wandered down the hall, her thoughts turbulent. Everything was changing. Life was moving forward at a rapid pace, and she wanted to reach out and snatch on to moments, holding them close to her. Zac, excited to get away from Baytown, had enlisted with the Navy and would be leaving right after graduation. Aiden, always wanting to do what his older brother did, had signed with the Marines. Callan's father had been in the Coast Guard, and, determined to follow in his footsteps, Callan had just announced that he, too, had enlisted. And Philip had announced to the family that he had joined the Army.

Her parents did not seem surprised, but she simply could not imagine life without Philip. *No one to watch over me. No one to chase away the bullies. No one to call me Squirt.*

Overwhelmed, she leaned her back against the lockers lining the hall and dropped her chin, staring at her feet. She had not heard anyone approach, but suddenly, she blinked as a large pair of shoes stopped right in front of hers, toes to toes. Her head snapped up, and she saw Callan staring down at her, concern in his eyes.

"Hey, Sophie. Is everything okay?"

She peered into his dark brown eyes and felt him reaching deep into her soul. His thick hair was trimmed short but dark and lush. The slight evidence of a beard was on his face, and she could only imagine how handsome he would be if it grew out. Her gaze dropped to his lips, and it was all she could do to keep from lifting on her toes to see if they were as soft as they appeared to be.

"Sophie?"

Startling, she realized that she had never answered his original question. "Yes, yes. Sorry...I guess I was just lost in thought." She looked around and did not see anyone else in the hall. Shifting her gaze back to his, she asked, "What are you doing here? Isn't there practice?"

Nodding, he smiled, and her breath caught in her throat at the beauty.

"I was looking for you," he replied. "There was something I wanted to ask you, but I needed to clear it with Philip first."

Curious, she remained quiet, but cocked her head to the side, waiting to see what he wanted.

"I know the prom is for juniors and seniors, and you're only a sophomore. But you can go, as long as you're with someone who's a junior or senior. And I wanted to know if you'd like to go with me."

She gasped, her eyes widening. "You're...you're asking *me*? To the prom?"

He chuckled and reached out to take her hand, giving her fingers a little squeeze. "Yeah, if you'd like to go with me."

She sucked in her lips, thinking on something he said. "You had to clear it with Philip?"

Two red spots appeared on his cheeks, and he ducked his head. Shrugging, he said, "Well, yeah. Philip is my best friend, and you're his little sister. I really like you, Sophie, but I wanted to make sure it was okay with Philip."

"And what did he say?"

"Well, obviously, he told me it was okay for me to ask you to the prom." She remained quiet, and he added, "Actually, it was kinda cool. He told me that I was the only guy he would allow to take you to the prom." Squeezing her fingers again, he asked, "So, what do you say?"

The butterflies in her stomach fluttered wildly as her heart threatened to pound out of her chest. "Yes. Of course, I'll go with you, Callan."

With one last squeeze of her fingers, he said, "Cool. Thanks, Sophie." He leaned forward and kissed her forehead before letting go of her hand and jogging down the hall.

She felt lightheaded, almost like the time she passed out after having her blood taken. But this time, instead of fear, it was because the man of her dreams had asked her to the prom. Twirling, she ran down the hall to find Jillian and Katelyn.

3

He did not care about the streamers draped from the ceiling nor the twinkling lights strung from the basketball goals. The table with platters of food and a punch bowl hawked over by the assistant principal held no interest for him. The DJ's choices of songs were a little outdated, and the teachers moved about the room, prodding apart couples that were plastered together.

But prom had filled every hope Callan had. Sophie had danced in his arms all night. The emerald green dress hung off her delicate curves. The heels she wore gave her a few inches, but she still just barely reached his chin. Her hair, tamed into soft curls, was pulled back from her face and hung in a blonde curtain down her back.

She had been in his sights for as long as he could remember. While Jillian and Katelyn often talked too much, giving the boys a reason to escape their constant chatter, Sophie had always been the calm one.

Even as a child, he used to wonder what filled her

head. When the others ran and played, screaming and shouting, he would sometimes find her standing alone, just staring out over the Bay. Or her eyes would always be on him.

He knew that her parents and Philip would never have agreed for her to go to the prom as a sophomore with anyone except him, and he took that responsibility seriously. They danced, and laughed, and hung out with their friends. Philip even pulled her away for a dance, twirling her around until she laughed dizzily. But it was the last slow dance of the evening that gave him a chance to lead her over to the side and hold her in his arms.

He could tell she was nervous, uncertain in the high-heeled sandals she wore, occasionally wobbling. She constantly checked to make sure her dress was hanging just right. His cock twitched and he counted to ten, tamping down his hard-on, knowing Philip would kick his ass.

"I don't know if I told you that you're beautiful tonight," he said, staring down at her, his gaze devouring her.

Her blue-green eyes widened, appearing larger with the mascara she was wearing, and her glossy lips opened slightly before curving into a grin.

The way she was staring at his lips had him throw caution to the wind, and with their arms circled around each other, he dipped his head and kissed her lightly. Her lips were soft and pliable even as her body jolted. She was by no means his first kiss, but he felt something move through him that he had never felt before.

Lifting his head, he smiled down and asked, "Was that your first kiss?" He felt certain he knew the answer but wanted to hear her say it.

Her head jerked up and down quickly, her breath coming in pants, and she whispered, "Yes."

He grinned widely, and with one hand banded around her back and the other one tangled in her thick curls, he pressed her head against his chest. Whispering, he said, "I wanted to be your first." *And I'd like to be your last.* Those words moved through his mind, but he dared not say them out loud, knowing it was not fair. He would be leaving in two months for the Coast Guard, and she would be starting her junior year in high school. *Way too young for either of us to make promises.* But that did not keep him from hoping that down the road, she would be in his future.

The hot July sun beat down, but to the teenagers on the beach near the shack, they barely felt it. Hotdogs on the grill, sodas in the cooler, and brightly-colored towels spread out on the logs around the bonfire.

Behind her, Sophie could hear the laughter and shouts of her friends celebrating the next group of Baytown Boys' last nights of freedom. She knew if she looked over her shoulder, she would see Aiden and Zac surrounded by giggling girls, Jillian and Grant either kissing or fighting, both something they did often. Of course, Philip would be off with Katelyn, planning their future. That last thought made her smile, knowing that one day she and Katelyn would be true sisters, in marriage if not of blood.

But it was the thought of Callan that kept her staring out over the water, afraid to turn around and lay her eyes on him. They had become closer since the night of prom, but just like with her brother, the knowledge that he was leaving for a long time hung over her. She felt a chill despite the sun's warmth. She watched the gentle lapping of the waves and closed her eyes, focusing on the sound of the seagulls more than the noise of the party behind her.

"Hey," came a deep voice from behind her.

She startled, recognizing Philip. Turning, she grinned at her brother and said, "Where's Katelyn? I don't think there's been an inch of separation between you two for months."

"Aww, Squirt, you exaggerate." He moved to stand beside her, staring out over the water as well, throwing his arm over her shoulders. "Okay, maybe you don't exaggerate."

She laughed and wrapped her arm around his waist, laying her head on his shoulder. She was not sure when she went from pesky sister to something more like a friend, but she relished the closeness they had. Suddenly tears stung the back of her eyes, and she blinked, unable to hold back the sniffle.

"Oh, no, Squirt," he said. "You're not allowed to cry when I leave."

She swallowed deeply, but the words she had held in her heart came bubbling forth. "I'm going to miss you, you know. But I know we're lucky." She felt his gaze boring into the side of her head, but she refused to turn and look at him, afraid the tears would not stop flowing if she did. "Lots of siblings don't like each other, but I was given the best big brother in the world." A sob broke loose, but she choked it back, and added, "You'd better come back safe and sound to me, Philip. I don't know what I'll do without you."

He pulled her in for a hug, and she felt his lips on the top of her head. "Don't you worry, Squirt. I'll stay safe, and one day I'll come back to this little town so I can watch you and my best friend get married."

She glared up at him, her face scrunched, and fussed, "Don't tease me, Philip Bayles!" She blinked through teary eyes, but instead of bursting out into laughter, his expression softened.

"I'm not teasing, Sophie. I once told him that he's the only guy I ever thought was good enough for you. I still feel that way. I know it's going to be hard having both of us leave at the same time, but don't worry...we'll come back to you."

With his promise ringing in her ears, she gave him a squeeze before letting him go, watching him jog back to the bonfire where Katelyn was waiting.

As though he had been giving them a moment to themselves, Callan now walked toward her. She quickly swiped the tears from her face, offering him a smile as he approached.

"There's so much going on," Callan said, "with everyone getting ready to leave. I just wanted to make sure I had my chance with you."

"I hope you won't forget me," she ventured, her voice softer than normal even to her own ears.

He wrapped his arms around her, but instead of the sisterly feeling she had with Philip, Callan's embrace made her heart race. "I'll come back," he promised. "I'll come back, and we'll all be together again."

Two days later, she stood with tears streaming down her face and watched as Callan, Philip, Zac, Aiden, and Grant climbed aboard a Greyhound bus that would take them to Virginia Beach. From there, they would each go their own ways, bound for the various boot camps they would attend. The gathering was large, with parents and siblings waving goodbye.

The dads beamed proud, the moms wiped a few tears as they hugged each other, and Jillian and Katelyn clung to each other, sobbing. Moving off by herself, Sophie watched the bus roll down the road until it was no longer in sight. A strange emotion swept over her, chilling her as her stomach clenched. The fear threatened to choke her, and she wrapped her arms around her middle tightly, praying she was wrong. But for some reason, the idea that they would never all be together again shook her to her core.

4

TWO YEARS LATER

The sun was barely able to peek through the clouds, casting shadows on the large gathering below. Just on the outskirts of Baytown, people stood in tight groups, surrounding the folding chairs underneath the white tent. A strong breeze blew, carrying the sniffles from those present, tissues fluttering as tears were wiped.

Sophie sat next to her parents in the front row, her grandparents on the other side. Katelyn and her parents filled the chairs next to them. Her mother kept a wad of tissues in her hand, constantly bringing them up to dab her eyes, but Sophie had no tears. For a week she had cried incessantly and now was wrung dry.

Her eyes focused on the scene in front of her as the casket was carried by a military honor guard, each man in the uniform of his service. Aiden and Brogan MacFarlane. Mitch Evans. Grant Wilder. Zac Hamilton. And Callan Ward. The strange thought slid through her mind that if it were not for the reason they were gathered there, she would have thought they each looked resplendent in their dress uniforms. Instead, her eyes fell back to the flag-draped coffin.

The service had already been delivered in their church, so the minister's graveside words were simple. She watched as the honor guard lifted and folded the flag, the intricate triangle of red, white, and blue presented to her mother, who clutched it to her breast.

Her numb heart could barely take it all in when she watched as the former Baytown Boys all knelt in unison at the side of Philip's casket, their hands placed on the smooth, polished surface. With heads bowed, they each whispered their goodbyes.

Her chest heaved, each breath more ragged than the previous one. It was Callan's ravaged face that captured and held her attention, causing the tears to finally spring forth once more. He dropped his gaze to her, and she could see his inner battle to contain the tears that streamed down his face.

Her parents stood at the minister's signal, and she forced her legs to stand as well. Following them, she walked to the casket to lay a single white rose on top. Sucking in air again, she felt as though her lungs would never fill. Her knees buckled, but before she hit the ground, she was pulled tight against a tall, hard body.

"I've got you," she heard Callan say as he whispered into her hair, his lips at the top of her head.

Just the way Philip used to. And would never again. Nothing would ever be the same again.

A few hours later, the Bayles' house had emptied of most of the visitors after offering heartfelt sympathy to Philip's parents, Tonya and David. The Baytown Boys' moms were in the kitchen with Tonya, their voices low and soft as they helped her put away the many casserole dishes. David was still in the living room with the dads, their voices also murmuring.

Sophie walked through the den and stared out of the sliding glass door leading to the back patio. Brogan and Aiden hovered around Katelyn. Sophie knew that Philip had asked Katelyn to marry him when he got out of the military. He had not given her a ring yet, but it did not matter, Sophie had known that Katelyn was going to be her sister. And now that dream was ripped away.

Mitch, Grant and Jillian, Zac, and Callan stood off to the side of the patio. Torn between wanting to be alone and wanting to be with her friends, she hesitated until Callan turned and stared at her through the glass. He immediately moved away from the others and met her at the door as she slid it open.

Wordlessly, he reached down and took her hand, maneuvering her over to the side of the patio. Neither spoke for several minutes, and then he finally said, "I want to ask how you're holding up, but I know that's so stupid. I know how much I'm hurting...I can't imagine how you feel right now."

She lifted her shoulders in a slight shrug and shook her head, no words coming forth. Grateful he did not seem to expect any, he simply wrapped his arms around her and tucked her in tightly to his chest, resting his chin on the top of her head.

She reveled in his warmth, glad for the respite from the chill she had felt since they had received the news.

Hearing the sliding glass door open, she turned to

see her mother in the doorway, her father standing right behind with his hands on her shoulders. They stepped out onto the patio, and her father said to the gathering, "Boys, your folks have all left, and Tonya and I are going to go upstairs to rest for a little bit. We just wanted to say..." He stopped, a sob choking him, and pulled Tonya in closer as he swallowed hard to maintain control. "We just wanted to say what an honor it was to have each of you be friends with our son. We've watched you grow and mature into men, and your duty today was the greatest gift you could have given to him and to us. I know most of you will be leaving in the morning, but we didn't want the day to end without letting you know that as far as we're concerned, you're in our hearts and still Philip's friends for life."

Sophie began to quiver as silent sobs wracked her body, and Callan's arms tightened in response. Through watery eyes, she watched as each of the Baytown Boys stepped up to hug her parents. Before going inside, her mother looked over at her. With an imperceptible nod, her mom and dad walked back into the house.

Brogan and Aiden walked over, their arms still supporting Katelyn, and they hugged Sophie. The others, just like with her parents, came by to hug her as well before they left. At the end, it was only she and Callan left standing on the patio.

"Let's take a walk," Callan suggested, "unless you're too tired."

She was exhausted but nodded and said, "I could use the fresh air."

Their houses were only a few blocks from the town

pier, and they walked silently out to the end. Leaning her elbows on the rail, she sucked in a deep breath of salty air and closed her eyes to the setting sun.

"I can't imagine this place without him," she said, her words barely heard over the breeze. "Not just my house, but every part of this town has Philip imprinted on it."

"I know," Callan agreed, his arms on the railing, touching hers.

They fell into another silence, both seemingly lost in their thoughts. The warmth of his arm began to seep into her, and just as she opened her mouth to tell him how glad she was that he was here, he spoke suddenly.

"I leave tomorrow."

Her head jerked around, and she asked, "Back to base?" His silence stretched, and renewed fear begin to claw at her heart. "What? What aren't you telling me?"

"I'm being deployed," he said, turning to face her, his hands on her shoulders. "I didn't want to tell you because I didn't want you to worry. But we're being called up under the Department of Navy."

Her mouth opened, but the words halted in her throat.

"There are a lot of oil rigs in the water of the Middle East," he began. "I can't tell you much, but we're needed to help protect that."

The fear in her heart began pounding, but she could barely feel it over the roar in her ears. "You're going over there? You're going to be in danger?"

"It was always a risk, Sophie," he said, anguish in his voice. "I don't want to hurt you, but I wanted you to know. I wanted us to—"

She stepped backward, out of his reach, her head moving slowly back and forth as she whispered, "No. I can't do this...not again. I can't risk this...not again. I'm sorry...I've got to guard my heart."

Before she gave him a chance to speak, she whirled around and ran back down the pier as fast as her legs would carry her. Once she reached the sidewalk, she did not slow down, running all the way back to her house. By the time she made it, she was gasping but stayed downstairs long enough to slowly catch her breath, not wanting to wake her parents. Her heart had belonged to Callan but now was broken with Philip's death...she could not risk it again.

Callan followed Sophie, keeping his eyes on her until he was sure she made it home safely. *Oh, Sophie...I would have guarded your heart.* He walked into his house, hugged both of his parents and went upstairs to his room. His heart was splintered with grief for his best friend and agony for his best friend's sister, the girl he knew he loved...and now, would never have.

5

TEN YEARS LATER

The waves of the Chesapeake Bay lapped against the side of the boat, but the three men on board were sure-footed as they moved about their duties. This call for distress had been easy. Callan, Jarrod, and José maneuvered their RB-S vessel to the side of the stalled boat.

A group of five men had rented a boat, taking it out into the middle of the Chesapeake for a day of fishing. As Callan looked over from the deck of his Coast Guard response boat, he was not sure if the men were doing more drinking or fishing. Empty beer cans scattered the deck, rolling back and forth as the boat moved, and two of the men hung over the far side, throwing up.

The man who seemed steadier on his feet yelled over, "I think we ran out of gas."

Callan, holding the Coast Guard boat steady, gave Jarrod the command to board the other vessel. Jarrod easily made the transfer and within a moment came back out onto the deck and gave a quick nod. José and Jarrod, working together, quickly added enough gasoline to their fuel tank for the fishermen to be able to get back to the marina.

Jarrod took over the controls of the Coast Guard boat while Callan talked to the man who had called in for help. Getting his name and information as well as who he rented the boat from, he wrote up his initial report.

"Are we in trouble?" the man asked, pulling his cap off and rubbing his forehead. "I could've sworn the guy at the boat rental company said we were starting out with a full tank."

"No, sir, you're not in trouble. But you might want to look your contract over carefully. Many contracts start out with the boat having a full tank and, obviously, they charge more. Some people want to start out with less than they pay for initially and then fill it up themselves."

Shaking his head, a hound dog expression on his face, the man replied, "This was our first time out, and Charlie kept saying that he wanted to keep it as cheap as possible. Damn fool probably went for the cheapest, which meant we didn't have a full tank."

"Well, what we've given you will get you back to the marina. Don't make a mistake now in thinking you have enough to continue to stay out here for hours." Callan nodded to the two men who were now slumped on the deck, their sunburned faces obvious, and said, "Have you got enough drinking water for your partners over there? If they've been out in the sun all day doing nothing but drinking beer, they're going to be dehydrated, even in this cold weather."

Nodding, the man said, "Yeah, yeah. We've got a cooler full of just water bottles. I'll make sure they start drinking it."

The man signed Callan's report and yelled to tell his compatriots that their fishing day was over, and it was time to head back to the marina. One of the men who had been hanging over the side of the boat muttered, "Thank, God!"

Callan crossed over to the Coast Guard vessel, glad to see the leader passing water bottles out to all of them. They pulled away but kept an eye on the fishing boat until it had almost made it to the marina before they turned back and headed to the small Coast Guard station at the Baytown Harbor.

Securing their vessel, Jarrod and José checked the equipment, topped off the fuel, and made sure it was ready for their next call out. Callan walked down the dock and into the building.

The tiny Coast Guard Station at Baytown consisted of a one-story brick building and several outbuildings as well as the dock. Walking down the hall, he offered chin lifts to the others that were working there, making his way past offices, training rooms, and into the workstation where Chief Jeff Monroe was sitting behind his desk.

He could not help but grin knowing Jeff hated just sitting behind his desk. The Chief looked and lifted an eyebrow as Callan walked in.

Answering the silent question, Callan said, "All good. I've got the initial report, and I'll get it entered into the log."

Nodding, Jeff asked, "Just needed gasoline?"

"Yes. Amateurs out trying to play fishermen, spending more time drinking than they were paying attention to what was really happening."

The Chief looked back down at his desk, and Callan knew he had been dismissed. He walked over to one of the desks with a computer and began entering the information into their log. Once the electronic forms were filled in, he scanned the page that had the man's signature and completed the report.

By the time he finished, Jarrod and José were walking into the room, both laughing. "I'll never understand why some people go out in a boat in the middle of the Bay to fish, and they've got no fuckin' clue what they're doing," José said, shaking his head.

"It's a man thing," Tanisha said, not looking up as she worked at her desk.

"Huh?" José said. "That's kinda sexist, isn't it?"

Callan hid his grin while finishing his report, deciding to let José tangle with Tanisha on his own. She was one of two women stationed at the small Coast Guard station in Baytown. Tall and athletic, she was as smart as she was fit.

Tanisha looked up from her desk, cocked an eyebrow, and asked, "How many times since you've been stationed here have you gone out on a rescue for a boat full of drunk women?"

"None," José answered.

"I rest my case."

"No way," José argued. "I mean, yeah, I get what you're saying, but I don't get why."

"Oh, don't get me wrong," Tanisha added. "Women can be just as stupid with some of their behavior, but generally men are the ones who feel like they have something to prove...you know, whose is bigger. Men think if they catch the bigger fish, it'll prove something about their manliness."

Jarrod laughed, slapping José on the back. "She's got you there, bro."

José slumped into a chair and said, "Well, I'm secure in my manliness. I don't have to go out in a boat and catch the biggest fish."

Tanisha threw her head back and laughed. "Glad to hear it. The last thing I'd want to do is rescue a drunk, puking José and drag your ass back to the harbor."

Callan finished his report and shut down his computer. Looking at the clock on the wall, he said, "My shift's over. Anyone else going to the AL meeting tonight?"

When the Baytown Boys made it back from their various deployments and settled into life in Baytown, the idea of having a local American Legion chapter became important. Mitch, now the Baytown Police Chief since his father retired, was instrumental in obtaining a charter for Baytown to have their own American Legion. Veterans, as well as those currently serving, were eligible for membership. Brogan, Aiden, Zac, Grant, and Callan had all taken leadership roles. He found it especially meaningful since most of their fathers were members as well, and their mothers and wives were members of the AL Auxiliary.

"I'm going," Jarrod and Tanisha said at the same time, and as he looked over, José was nodding as well.

Standing, he tossed a wave in their direction and said, "See you there." With a chin lift to the Chief as he walked past his office, Callan headed to the parking lot.

The drive home was short, and he pulled into the alley behind his parents' home, parking behind their double garage. His assignment to the Baytown station had not been a random selection. He had been overseas when his father had a mild heart attack. Medication, a strict diet, and surgery had given his father a new lease on life, and he was currently very healthy. But as soon as Callan could put in for a transfer, he did. Initially, he wanted to rent an apartment or a room in town, but sitting down with his parents and discussing the options, he realized they offered a solution that could not be beat.

While he was gone, they had torn down the old clubhouse shed and built a large, separate garage that opened to the back alley, adding an apartment on the second floor. One-bedroom, large bathroom, kitchen, and an open dining and living area completed the space. They had rented it to a teacher at the high school, but when that person transferred, it was available when Callan landed back in Baytown.

Desiring to be close enough that he could help them with anything they might need, and yet needing his independence, he rented the apartment, giving him the separation that he needed.

Climbing the outside steps, he let himself into the apartment and headed straight to the shower. Afterward, he threw a load of clothes into the washing machine before walking into the kitchen. Checking the refrigerator, he chuckled to see that his mom had placed a Tupperware container full of homemade lasagna on the top shelf.

Nuking it in the microwave, he bypassed the small dining room table and headed straight to the living room sofa. Clicking on his widescreen TV to a sports channel, he propped his feet up on the coffee table and ate his dinner.

Hearing a noise outside, he stood and looked out of the window facing the alley. He saw David Bayles waving goodbye to Tonya before climbing into his car.

Living across from the Bayles' home, he saw them frequently, and the same pang hit his heart that always did when he thought of Sophie. *And what the fuck did I think was going to happen when I moved into an apartment that faced her parents' house?*

The apartment not only afforded him the chance to be near his parents while he was stationed in Baytown but also served as a constant reminder of his friendship with Philip and the feelings he had never gotten over with Sophie. *God, we were so young.* Life had certainly moved on, but his heart had never forgotten the girl he fell in love with so many years ago. He had seen her occasionally when she visited her parents...always tossing a slight wave his way or gifting him with a small, nervous smile. It did not cut as deep as the first time, and every time it hurt a little less, but it was a pain he knew would never really go away.

Her slim figure had developed gentle curves, and her

riot of curls had been tamed slightly. As a teenager, he thought she was the prettiest girl in school, but that was nothing compared to the grown-up Sophie.

But she never stayed long in Baytown...a couple of days at the most. Sighing, he walked back to the kitchen and rinsed his plate, placing it in the drainer.

Glancing at the clock on the microwave, he realized David must have been heading to the AL meeting. Locking the door, he jogged back down the steps and saw his father walking out as well.

"Hey, Dad," he called out. "Want a ride?"

His dad grinned his reply and walked across the yard to Callan's truck. "I know you're going to Finn's Pub afterwards, but I don't think I will tonight. Can you drop me off home after the meeting?"

As the two men climbed inside his truck, he replied, "No problem." Chatting comfortably about nothing important, they drove the few blocks to where the meeting took place.

After Grant, the Commander of the American Legion chapter, rapped the gavel on the podium to call the meeting to order, Callan watched as Ginny MacFarlane closed the door and walked with her husband, Brogan, who carried the flag to the front. Ginny was one of the Baytown police officers and had served in the Army police before capturing the heart of the oldest MacFarlane brother.

Callan dreaded the next minute of the meeting,

knowing it was part of their history and yet unable to stop his heart from clenching each time. It was the POW/MIA Empty Chair Ceremony. There was always a chair that remained empty at their meetings, to commemorate those who had been prisoners of war or missing in action. But it also had a great deal of meaning for remembering those who never returned.

Every meeting, he glanced at the chair, trying to imagine Philip sitting there. At thirty-one years old, he always visualized Philip as the way he looked the last time he saw him. Would he have a beard now? Would his blond hair be just as thick as it used to be or starting to thin on top? Would he have that eternal smile that always seemed to be on his face, or would life have caused him to be more introspective? No matter how he tried to conjure him in his mind, Callan always saw Philip in his youth. Eternally young.

As Grant called for the next part of the meeting, his eyes drifted over to David Bayles, and it struck him how hard that moment of silence must be for him.

The meeting went on for a while as the various committees reported, but for the first time, Callan found his thoughts drifting. He was the only one of the original Baytown Boys that was still active duty. He knew his time in Baytown was limited. He only had six more months before he would either need to get out or re-up. He had never hesitated in this decision before, but now, having been in Baytown again, reconnecting with his family and friends, he found that the idea of leaving again to be unpalpable.

But what would I do? Working with the Coast Guard

in Baytown had given him the opportunity to work in conjunction with the Virginia Marine Police. Their duties often overlapped, and they worked together when needed. The VMP Chief, Ryan Coates, had once said that he was more than welcome to join them if he ever wanted to leave the Coast Guard. Dismissing the idea at first, he had to admit to himself that it was a serious consideration.

Glancing down the row, he grinned at seeing both Chiefs, Ryan and Jeff, sitting next to each other. Aiden, the Finance Officer, had given an update on the financial status of the charter. Zac, now speaking as the Post Service Officer, gave an update on the various activities the AL were now involved in. Everyone's favorite was the baseball teams that they created for children of all ages and all backgrounds. Since it was winter time, the teams were not currently playing but would begin again in the early spring.

"I'm pleased to announce that Mayor Banks has given us permission to host an oyster roast in February, hopefully tying it into Valentine's Day to give us more attendees. Because we won't know what the weather will be like, we're looking at having it at The Sunset Restaurant's Conference Center. I'm still working out the details, but I'll let you know what I find out at our next meeting."

Valentine's Day. The only holiday where it's great to be in a relationship and sucks when you're not. And...I'm not. The last of the single, original Baytown Boys. Oh, there were certainly other friends that were still single, but he was the last of their original group that still held that status.

Mitch had left the Army to join the FBI, only to come back to become the Baytown Police Chief and marry his childhood sweetheart, Tori. They had a son last spring, and he had to admit he had never seen Mitch so happy. Brogan and Ginny had married last spring, and in the summer announced they were expecting. Aiden had just fallen for the town's new accountant, Lia, and had a ready-made family with her daughter Emily. Aiden and Brogan now ran Finn's Pub along with their sister Katelyn. It had taken years for Katelyn to finally come to terms with Philip's death, and she was now happily married to Gareth Harrison, a private investigator in town. Zac, the Baytown Rescue Captain, had fallen in love with Madelyn, and they were now married. Grant, another police officer in Baytown, had finally gotten smart and married his true love, Jillian.

Their group of friends had expanded widely once they began inviting other veterans they knew to move to Baytown if they did not have a supportive home to return to. Those men and women also filled the rows of the AL meeting, as well as most of their fathers and grandfathers who were still living.

As the meeting came to a close, his gaze shifted back to the Empty Chair, and his thoughts filled with Philip...*who am I kidding? Thinking of Philip also has me thinking of Sophie.* Many of the members would head to Finn's Pub after a meeting, and he had planned on joining them but hesitated when he saw that David had volunteered to stack the chairs. His father was involved in a conversation with the chaplain, so he grabbed the opportunity and moved over to David, offering to help. Trying to decide on a way of asking about Sophie without sounding too interested, he simply blurted, "How's Sophie?"

Well, that was smooth...

6

David turned and smiled widely at Callan, offering his hand for a shake. "Callan, good to see you, son. I know we live right behind each other, but I don't see you much. I figure you're on duty most of the time."

Nodding, he grasped David's hand, shaking it firmly.

"Sophie's doing well. She's busy in Richmond, working all the time from what we hear. She doesn't make it home as often as we'd like, but I know it's hard when you're young and building a career."

He noticed the smile David was offering was paired with a specter of sadness in his eyes. He knew Katelyn stayed in contact with Sophie and occasionally heard about her life in Richmond. It was certainly no secret that she did not come back to Baytown very often.

Katelyn had once mentioned that Sophie found it very difficult to be back without Philip around. He knew, through his mother, that both Tonya and David had sought grief counseling after Philip's death, but he had no idea if Sophie had done the same.

"She's an interior designer, I think Mom said?"

David's smile appeared more sincere as he nodded enthusiastically. "Yes, she was lucky to get a job in what she majored in. She worked for a large firm in Richmond but has now struck out on her own."

Impressed, he said, "That's wonderful."

Nodding, David agreed. "She was nervous about it and didn't go into any details as to why she decided to leave the firm when she did, but we're proud of her."

"I'm glad," Callan said, finding the sentiment to be true. While he had once held onto dreams that they would end up together, he wished her nothing but the best.

"And her mother and I are expecting to hear more news soon," David said, drawing Callan's attention back to him.

"More news?"

"I think we might hear wedding bells sometime in the near future," David said, his gaze darting up to Callan's. "She's been seeing someone, and, well, we just want her to be happy."

A strange pain struck Callan's chest, and he fought to keep from lifting his hand to rub over his heart. He had wanted good things to happen for Sophie, but news of her possible engagement obviously did not fall into that category if his heartache was any indication. Not knowing what to say, he stumbled, "Oh...well...good."

"We don't know a lot about who's she dating," David continued, a sigh leaving his lips. Standing with a chair still in his hands, his voice sounded strained as he continued. "Sophie's struggled since Philip's death. I know it's been ten years, but Sophie...well, it's been hard. Tonya and I just want her to move her forward."

Out of the corner of his eye, he saw his dad wave that he was ready to be taken home, so he shook David's hand goodbye. "Give Sophie my best when you talk to her again," he said. Walking away, he thought about his words. *I do wish her the best...It's been years, but...I just wish the best for her had been with me.*

No longer feeling sociable, he decided to forgo a trip to Finn's and instead simply drove his dad home before going up to his own apartment. Grabbing a beer from his refrigerator, he popped the top before taking a long pull. His gaze drifted around the room before focusing on the framed pictures sitting amongst the books in his bookcase. Leaving his beer on the counter, he stalked over and perused them once again, even though the images were imprinted on his memory.

One was of his family when he graduated from Coast Guard boot camp. His parents and older sister stood beside him, pride evident on their faces. The next one had been taken in high school after one of their winning games. He stood with Mitch, Brogan, Grant, Aiden, Zac, and Philip, their arms around each other as they posed proudly in their Baytown Boys jerseys. He sighed heavily at the view of their youthful faces, all excited about leaving the tiny town to see the world. His gaze settled on Philip's face, full of eager anticipation.

The last picture he stared at was taken the summer before Mitch and Brogan left, right before his senior year. It was at Mitch's grandfather's cabin on the beach, and someone had taken a snapshot of the whole gang.

All the Baytown Boys were there as well as many others, including Jillian, Katelyn, and Tori. And to the side stood Sophie. She was not looking at the camera, and knowing how shy she was, he assumed she thought she was not in the picture. But what had always captured his attention, was where her gaze held steady...*on me*.

As usual, when he thought back to those times, he could not help but wonder *what if. What if Philip had not died? Would he and Katelyn be married now?* That was a hard thought to ponder, considering how much he liked Katelyn's husband, Gareth, and now they had a child together. *If Philip had not died, would Sophie and I have stayed together?*

Suddenly turning, he stalked back over to the counter and chugged the rest of his beer before rinsing it and tossing it into the recycle bin. Pushing those thoughts to the back of his mind, he stripped and crawled into bed. Sleep, unfortunately, did not come easily. Determined to keep his thoughts from straying to Sophie, his mind bounced between re-upping or taking another job to stay in Baytown.

Finally, sleep claimed him, but it was filled with dreams of a beautiful blonde walking down the aisle in a white dress, but he could not see who she was walking toward.

Sophie stood in the kitchen of her tiny apartment, finger-combing her long, curly blonde hair up into a messy bun. She loved her apartment but wished she had more space. She had decorated it with soft yellow and green, paired with vibrant blue and peach. Beach colors always seemed to infuse all of her designs, something her former clients had loved.

The white rattan kitchen table with its round glass top and matching rattan chairs kept the small space from appearing smaller. The living room did not have enough space for a large sofa, but she had arranged a white rattan settee and chair in one corner, filled with thick cushions for comfort. Her television sat on a gray cabinet, the distressed wood giving it the appearance of driftwood.

In the other corner she had placed a small white desk, overflowing with papers and files, her laptop sitting amongst the mess.

She poured a glass of wine, continually checking the clock, wondering when Tommy was coming. They were supposed to go to dinner, but he had texted to say that he was running late. This seemed to be happening more often. *Was it only a month ago that I told my parents that maybe he was the one?* Shaking her head, she knew that had been premature...more expectation than true desire. Deciding that she had fiddled enough, she walked back over to her desk and plopped down in the white wicker chair. She had just opened her laptop when she heard the knock on the door.

Standing, she walked over, threw it open and watched him walk in, wondering what his excuse was going to be this time. Wearing his usual outfit of dark suit and white shirt, she always checked to see what color tie he was wearing since that seemed to be the only difference in his work apparel. His hair was neatly combed over, never too long and never buzzed off. Like everything else about him, it was exactly the way he wanted it to be.

Tommy stepped through the doorway, and with his hand placed on her waist, he bent and kissed her lightly. "I'm so sorry, sweetheart," he said. "We had clients that were delayed because of the impending weather. They were flying in from Boston, and their flight was held up, so we all had to shift our appointments back."

She forced a smile and said, "That's fine. It gave me a chance to straighten my apartment a little bit."

She caught his gaze drift around the room, landing on her desk.

"It looks lovely, Sophie, except for your workspace. I don't see how you can keep anything straight when it looks like that."

"It's not like I'm working in an accounting office like you," she said, trying to keep the defensive edge out of her tone. "I'm creative, you know that. I never know when the creative muse might strike, and it's fine if my desk is not perfectly straight."

"I still think you've made a huge mistake in working for yourself," he said, his lips pressed into a tight line.

She stared up at him, now battling the desire to roll her eyes. "We've been through this, over and over—"

"Yes, we have. And we'll keep going over it until you see reason."

She was beginning to hate the calm seriousness of his voice, wishing that he would show more emotion. *At least then I'd really know he was feeling something!* Before she had a chance to reply, he continued.

"You left one of the most prestigious design firms in Richmond to start your own business," he needlessly reminded her. "You had a great workplace, a boss that would be able to further your career, ready clients, benefits, and let's not forget the most important thing... a steady paycheck. And you walked away from that, determined to strike out on your own. And here you are, three months later, with only a few low-paying clients. I didn't understand your decision then, and I still don't."

"I may have had all that, Tommy, but I wasn't happy."

He stepped further into her apartment, and his gaze landed on the glass of wine sitting on the counter. Turning to her, he said, "We're going out to dinner. Were you already having wine now?"

She stared blankly at him for several long seconds, her blood beginning to boil. Tommy had seemed so safe when she first met him. No risky job. No risky behavior. Steady almost to the point of being boring. *But that's what I want, isn't it?* Quiet herself, she liked that she seemed to find her match in him. No arguments. No raised voiced.

Now? All she knew was that at that moment, she wanted to pick up the wine glass and toss it in his face. Anything to see if there was emotion inside of him.

"Forget the fucking wine, Tommy. We're talking about my job and how you're not supporting my decision."

His brows lowered, and he glared in her direction. "There's no reason to get vulgar, Sophie."

Her fists landed on her hips as she squared off toward him. "You want to talk about vulgar? I told you last year that I had a coworker who kept hitting on me. I told you that nothing I said to him seemed to stop the behavior. Did you get upset about that vulgar behavior? No. You told me that as long as he was not actually touching me, then men in the office place will often tell a coworker that they're pretty, or their legs look nice in a skirt, or they love the way a dress fits their body. I told you it wasn't acceptable then, but you kept telling me to put up with it because it was a prestigious firm."

"Yes, and what did you do? You went to the boss," he said, calm accusation dripping from him.

Rearing back, she retorted, "Yes, I did. That's what a woman should do when they're being harassed. But Mr. Holston had the same antiquated attitude that you do and did not take me seriously. I'd been wanting to spread my wings, open my own design business, and do things my way, and that's what I did."

Turning away from her, he walked over to the settee and picked up her coat. Holding it up, he said, "Let's not argue about this. You quit, and it's now going to take much longer for you to ever make it to a point to where we can have an equitable relationship. Even if you finally come to your senses and start with another design firm, you're going to have to work your way back up."

Instead of moving forward to allow him to slide her coat over her arms, she stood, numbly staring at him.

"Equitable relationship? Tommy, I don't even know what you mean by that."

His arms dropped with her coat still held in his hands and said, "Sophie, don't be obtuse. We've been dating for a while now, and I'm sure we both expected this to move to the next step. But there's no way we can get engaged and plan a marriage when you're barely making ends meet with your new endeavor."

Shaking her head slowly back and forth, she stared at him, wondering if she ever really knew him. "What does my decision to open my own design firm have to do with us getting engaged?"

"I should be making partner soon at the accounting firm," he said, staring at her as though he thought those words would make a difference. As she continued to stare at him, open-mouthed and silent, he continued, "I wanted to be able to introduce my fiancée as someone who worked for the Holston firm, but to say that she is squandering away her talents with some no-name clients hardly makes it equitable for us."

Numb cold slid through her veins. "I thought you were safe," she said, her voice barely above a whisper.

Now it was his turn to rear back, giving his head a shake, indicating he had no idea what she was talking about.

"I wanted safe," she continued, a rock settling in her stomach. Her breath ragged, she added, "Someone I could count on to come home every night. Someone I didn't have to worry about—" She cut herself off, not wanting to admit that she was going to say "dying".

Continuing, she added, "But not someone who can't be supportive and who's not truly interested in *me*."

"We don't have time for this foolishness, Sophie," Tommy said. Holding his hands up with her coat still in them, giving it a shake, he said, "Put your coat on and let's go."

Her legs felt like wood, but she moved forward, reaching out for her coat. Instead of turning and slipping it on, she pulled it from his hands and tossed it back to the settee. "You go on to dinner, Tommy. I'm really not hungry anymore. And," she looked up at him sadly, "I don't think you need to plan on any more dinners with me."

His mouth dropped open, and for a moment the awkward silence moved between them. Finally, he spoke, "You're breaking up with me?"

She nodded slowly and said, "I thought you were what I needed. I thought we were a fit. But the reality is, Tommy, we're not right for each other at all. You need a woman who can fit into the mold that you've decided is right for you. And I need someone..." Swallowing hard, she walked over to the door, and with her hand on the doorknob, stopped and turned back to him. "I want someone who would go to battle for me if they even thought that I was being harassed. I don't need to be taken care of...but I want to be cared for. I want someone who would guard my heart." A memory of those words being said years earlier caused her to gasp. Squeezing her eyes closed, she fought to steady her breathing.

Finally opening her eyes, she stared at Tommy. It

was hard to tell if he was angry or not. His face remained tightly composed. But as he walked through the door, he said, "I don't think I understand you at all, Sophie. Goodbye."

She closed the door quietly behind him, turned, and leaned her back against it. She expected to dissolve in tears, but all she felt was an immense sense of relief. The memory of wanting to guard her heart stung more than Tommy's laissez-faire attitude. Sucking in a deep breath, she let it out slowly before pushing away from the door. Walking over to her wine glass, she carried it to her messy desk, cleared a spot for it, and opened up her laptop again.

I've got my own business. I set my own hours. I can drink while I work.

7

Callan kneeled on the deck of the rocking boat, the waves higher than normal in the Bay. The distress call had come in from one of the local fishing boats, and the Baytown Coast Guard station rushed to the scene to secure and assist until the rescue helicopter from the station in Portsmouth could reach them. The fisherman's son reported the captain had been complaining of indigestion all day and finally collapsed on the deck.

Bryce, one of Callan's team members and their medic, stabilized the captain and prepared him to be transported. With Jarrod notifying him and Bryce, they watched as the helicopter approached. Within a few minutes, the Portsmouth Coast Guard was lowering two men and their basket.

"Is he going to be okay?" the son asked, hovering next to Callan as they all knelt with their heads bent against the force of the wind.

"I don't know," Callan answered honestly, "but we're doing everything we can."

"Where will they take him? I've got my brother on the radio, and he's already told my mom. She wants to head out immediately but doesn't know where to go."

Callan, trying to calm the son, pulled him back slightly, allowing the Portsmouth Aviation Survival Technicians to secure the captain into the basket. They assisted as the basket began its ascent up into the helicopter. Once the man was secure, one of the Survival Technicians went up after him, and Callan checked with the one still on the deck.

"Which hospital will you take him to?"

"Virginia Beach General Hospital," came the answer. "It's the closest and has the best cardiac unit."

Stepping back, Callan allowed the final technician to be lifted into the helicopter as well, and turned to the son, giving him the information. "Call your brother and have him get your mom safely to the hospital. You get back to the Baytown Harbor, call in some friends to come secure your boat, and make sure you get to the hospital safely yourself. You're not going to do your dad any good by putting yourself in danger trying to race down the road."

Moving back over to the Coast Guard RB-M vessel, he waved at Jarrod, and they pulled away from the fishing boat. Following behind, they made sure the boat made it back to the harbor before they docked at the Coast Guard Station.

José and Tanisha hustled out to assist in securing their medium response boat as well. By now the rain had started, hitting them sharply in the face as the wind continued to whip around.

"I hate rain in the winter," José said. "I'll take snow any day."

Callan did not say anything but inwardly agreed. Working efficiently, they quickly secured their boat and headed inside. Jarrod, Bryce, and Callan moved into the locker room, stripping off their raingear and changing into dry clothes.

"You got the report?" Jarrod asked.

He nodded and replied, "Yeah. I know you're off duty now. I'll get the report completed and see you tomorrow." By the time he finished and met with Jeff, he was more than ready to head home. Before leaving, he called Virginia General Hospital to see if he could get an update on the fishing captain. He managed to get hold of his wife and found out that her husband was still alive and in surgery. Offering them his best wishes, he hung up and leaned back in his seat, blowing out a deep breath.

He remembered his own fear when his mother had called to tell him that his father had had a heart attack. Swiping his hand over his face, he stood, shaking those thoughts out of his mind. With a wave goodbye to those still on duty, he headed out to his truck. *Another day... another rescue.*

"I'm good, Mom, I really am," Sophie said, balancing her phone between her ear and shoulder while she clicked on her laptop keyboard. "I don't want you and Dad to worry about me. I know I told you that I thought

Tommy and I had a real future together, but I finally realized that with him, I was settling. And while I want things to be safe, I don't want to just settle. I don't want to simply settle in my career, and I don't want to just settle in a relationship."

"Oh, honey, I think that's wonderful," her mom replied, and Sophie could hear the relief in her voice.

"It's true I'm not rolling in clients right now, but I have several that I have just finished interior designs for, and they love my work. So I'm hoping by word-of-mouth, I'll get more."

"I don't want you to take this in an insulting way," her mom began, "but do you need a little help while you're building up your clientele?"

Knowing her parents cared deeply but did not want to overstep their bounds, she smiled. "Thanks for the offer, Mom, but I'm fine. I had saved quite a bit of money over the last couple of years, and since I'm working out of my home, I have very few expenses right now."

Closing out the screen she was looking at on her laptop, she clicked on her email and began to scroll. Seeing one that caught her eye, she said, "Mom, can I call you later? I'm trying to get a little work done this afternoon, and I've gotten behind in my emails."

"That's fine, sweetheart. I've got to get ready for an American Legion Auxiliary meeting this evening anyway. I'll talk to you soon. I love you."

"I love you too, Mom," she said, disconnecting. Laying the phone down, she closed her eyes for just a moment, feeling the familiar pain, knowing that her mother was the only Baytown Boy mom whose son did not come home. Sighing, she gave her head a shake, then went back to work.

The email that caught her eye was from The Dunes Resort. The Dunes was in the southern part of Baytown, not in the historic town proper. It had originally been a large farm bought by a developer almost fifteen years ago who saw the property as a potential goldmine. Two golf courses graced the resort as well as a sports facility, restaurant, condos, and houses, all surrounded by lush gardens and trees.

Several years after the development began, the houses being built came to a halt when the real estate market crashed. But in recent years, a resurgence of interest had new houses popping up and a new section of condos near the golf course being built.

Clicking on the email, she saw that it was from The Dunes Resort head real estate agent, Carlotta Ventura. Curious, she began reading the email. Carlotta mentioned that she had met Sophie's mother through the AL Auxiliary and discovered that Sophie was an interior designer. Carlotta had looked at her website and was very impressed. The email detailed the resort's opportunity of having one of their houses and condos featured in an upcoming issue of Southern Living magazine, and they planned on having them professionally designed and staged. Carlotta wanted to know if Sophie would be available for a tour of the facilities so that they could discuss hiring her for the job.

The Dunes Resort! Southern Living! Oh, my God! This would be a huge job that could make my career! The idea that her work could be showcased in such a prestigious publication had her jumping up from her chair and dancing around her living room, hands waving in the air.

Catching her breath, she rushed back over to her desk and plopped into the seat, rereading the email to assure herself she had not dreamed it. *I need to respond! I need to respond right now so she knows I'm interested!*

Hands poised over the keyboard, she forced them back into her lap and took several deep breaths. This job would bring financial stability to her wobbly bank account as well as notoriety with the magazine publication of her work. *But I'd be back in Baytown for several months.* Chewing on the bottom of her lip, she thought of moving back to her parents' home. The idea of spending more time with them and her old friends called to her, but a flash of Callan's face ran through her mind and she hesitated. He had always been so polite over the last several years when she saw him but wondered if he secretly resented the way they parted years ago. *Can I face that? Can I face seeing him often, considering he lives right behind my parent's house?*

Huffing, she shook her head. *He probably doesn't think of me at all anymore. I'm just an old crush from years ago.* Biting her lip again, she dropped her gaze to her hands, noting them shaking slightly. *He may not think of me, but I've never forgotten him. They say you never forget your first love.*

Shoving those thoughts aside, she focused on the email, allowing the excitement of the job to move through her. Decision made, she typed out her response. Rereading it carefully, she continued to tweak the email until it was perfect. She thanked Carlotta for the opportunity and assured her of her excited interest. Letting Carlotta know that she was available at any time to come to Baytown, she hit send. Glancing at the clock, seeing it was late afternoon, she sighed, wishing that she could hear back today.

She walked into her kitchen and grabbed a bottle of water from her refrigerator. The cool water did little to dampen her excitement, so she decided to celebrate the possible job with some ice cream. Opening her freezer, she was thankful for the brand-new pint of chocolate-cherry ice cream she had splurged on the day before.

Carrying it over to her settee, she plopped her feet up on her coffee table and dug in. She had just taken a large bite and felt the effects of brain freeze setting in when her phone rang. Grabbing it off her desk, she choked on her ice cream as the caller ID showed The Dunes Resort Realty. Terrified to not answer, she swallowed, coughed, and grabbed the top of her head which felt as though it was going to explode. *Shit, shit, shit!* Taking a swig of water, she dimmed the brain freeze just in time to answer the phone.

"He...hello?" she croaked, then quickly cleared her throat, trying again. "Hello. This is Sophie Bayles of Bayles Interior Design. May I help you?"

"Sophie? Hello. This is Carlotta Ventura, and I just read your email response. I would be so thrilled to have a homegrown Baytown designer work on our project."

"Ms. Ventura, I was equally as excited to get your email. I would love to set up a time to come talk to you."

She could not sit still and paced the living room as Carlotta set up a time for her to come visit. "Absolutely, I can come on Wednesday," she assured. They settled on the time and disconnected the call. Once more, she twirled around the room with her arms waving in the air. She could not remember the last time she felt such elation.

Take that, Tommy and Holston Design! She felt sure that she would be able to get the contract, but quickly plopped back into her desk chair and pulled up The Dunes Resorts on her computer. Determined to spend the next couple of days memorizing everything she could about the resort, she began a portfolio of ideas to present. For the first time in months, things were looking up, and she focused on that...not the simmering worry that going home might open doors she had worked to keep closed.

"You're not going to tell your parents that you're here?" Katelyn asked, her head tilted in question.

Sophie smiled at the sight of her friend sitting across from her, holding her baby. Little Finn had just been fed, and Katelyn leaned forward to let him sit on a blanket on the floor with a few soft toys around. As much as she had wanted to escape Baytown and its memories, she had remained close to the woman she considered to be her sister.

She remembered Katelyn's wedding to Gareth, declining the invitation to be a bridesmaid. Katelyn had understood, which Sophie appreciated. She wanted Katelyn to be happy but anticipated it was going to be an emotional day, knowing that they had always planned for Katelyn to marry Philip.

"Until I have a chance to find out if I actually get the job at The Dunes Resort, I don't want my parents to know about it. I'm already nervous enough, and they would just get their hopes up. Lord knows I feel like I've disappointed them enough times."

Katelyn shook her head and said fiercely, "You've never disappointed your parents."

Shrugging, she said, "I suppose. I know they were proud of me when I started my own business, but they also knew it was a huge risk leaving a prestigious firm. Plus, the whole Tommy fiasco. I know my parents have been worried about me, and my being in a relationship eased their concerns."

Katelyn rolled her eyes. "I never met him, but from what you described, Tommy was a wimp. You're better off without him."

Little Finn clapped, and Katelyn said, "See, even Little Finn agrees." At that, Katelyn laughed out loud, causing Finn to look up at his mother and gurgle.

Sophie watched as Katelyn bent over, picked up her son and blew raspberries on his belly. Pleased for her friend, she felt the familiar pain of knowing her Baytown friends had moved on with their lives. Pushing that thought to the side, she glanced at her phone and said, "Okay, I need to go now. Wish me luck."

As they stood, Katelyn pulled her in for a deep hug. "You know I wish you all the luck in the world." Moving back, Katelyn held her gaze and said, "Having you back in Baytown, even for several months, would be a dream come true. For a lot of people."

Callan crossed her mind, but she simply nodded and headed out to her car. Driving toward The Dunes Resort, she tried to settle the butterflies in her stomach. *Time to go get this contract!*

8

Hours later, sitting in her parents' kitchen, Sophie celebrated. Her mother was beaming, and her father was nodding enthusiastically as she described the offer.

"There are three huge, beachfront homes that have just been built, and one will be featured in Southern Living. I'll have carte blanche to design each of the rooms. There are four bedrooms, each with their own bathroom. The master suite has a bayside deck with sunset views. The downstairs consists of a formal living room, dining room, large kitchen, family room, sunroom, and wide front porch."

"You get to do the interior designing and decorating for the entire house?" her dad asked. "Are you going to have enough time to do that?"

"Well, according to Carlotta, I'll have a budget large enough to handle everything. I've already started on some designs and already know companies that I can order furniture from. I don't think I'm going to have a problem getting it done. But I also have to do one of the condo designs."

"Oh, tell me about those," her mother prodded.

"They're one-floor living, each with three bedrooms, an eat-in kitchen, and a great room that includes a dining area as well as a living area. Some units are on the second floor, but they're only going to have me design one of the downstairs units. They're uncertain if Southern Living is going to include that in their article but want it staged for future publications and advertisements."

Her mom stood to clear away the coffee cups but first bent to give Sophie hug. "Honey, I'm so excited for you to have this opportunity, but I also confess that I'm excited that you'll be back in town for a couple of months."

She heard her mother's voice catch on the last couple of words and blinked at the sting of tears that hit her eyes. Her parents had been so supportive over the years…with her leaving Baytown for college, her career, her decision to work in Richmond. *But when I came home, it was always what was left unspoken that I felt deep inside.* Grateful that her parents had not spent a lot of time talking about Philip, but instead, always focused on her as though they knew the subject tormented her. *But was that fair to them?* Sighing, she had no answers but hugged her mother in return, admitting, "It'll be good to be back and spend more time with you."

"Will you be able to stay here?" her mother asked, holding her gaze.

It was obvious her mother wanted her back home

while trying to sound nonchalant. Sophie had always stayed with her parents when visiting but moving back for the first time since she left for college right after Philip's death would be different. Surrounded by memories for an extended period of time. Staring at her mother's expressive face, she felt the warm desire down to her core and could not possibly say no. Once more, a flash of Callan's face moved through her mind, and she thought about him being so close. *If I'm honest? I want to be here. I need to be here.*

Nodding, she assured, "Since I'll still be paying rent on my little apartment in Richmond, I would rather not have to pay rent here. So, unless you and Dad are going to charge me an arm and a leg to stay in my old room, I think I can swing staying here."

Her mother rolled her eyes and said, "Oh, pooh! You're just teasing me. We would be disappointed if you stayed anywhere else."

Her dad reached across the table and squeezed her hand, asking, "Are you sure you want to drive back tonight? Wouldn't you be safer if you spent the night here and left in the morning?"

"I really need to get back so that I can start making plans. I want to work on my designs, and I have a couple of furniture stores in Richmond that I have a relationship with. I'd like to go in and speak to them personally so that I can be ready to get some things ordered."

"Yes, but you can't do any of that tonight, and if you get up early in the morning you could be home in time for any of the stores to open. Plus, we'd feel better about you not driving several hours so late at night."

The excitement of the day was taking its toll, and a yawn slipped out despite her best efforts to appear awake. She giggled and said, "I think I'll take you up on that. I might as well get used to being back in my room anyway."

Hugging her parents, she grabbed her purse and slim briefcase and walked upstairs. As tired as she was, her senses were heightened with each step she took, the ache of grief always tugging at her. *How do my parents do it? Continue to live in this house where memories are in the very walls?*

She passed the room that had been Philip's, the door open. Unable to stop herself, she glanced inside, but it was dark, and she had no desire to turn on the light. Her parents' master bedroom and en suite bathroom were across the hall, and she continued into her old bedroom, flipping the light switch.

Stepping inside, she was always pleased her parents had not left it the way it was when she had been a teenager. The bed was the same, but a peach floral comforter with light blue pillows decorated it. The walls had been painted a peach hue that was so light it was almost cream. The oak dresser was the same, but all of her old jewelry and high school memorabilia had been cleaned off. She walked further into the room, turned, and sat on the edge of the bed. It was a comforting space, a welcoming room. She grinned and felt the weight on her chest ease somewhat.

Moving into the hall bathroom, she quickly took a

shower. Back in her room, she found a drawer with some clothes that she had left the last time she visited. Sliding on clean panties and a large T-shirt, she turned off the light.

Before crawling into bed, she walked to the window and pulled back the curtain looking down into the backyard. Jars of sea glass still rested on the windowsill. Her gaze naturally drifted toward the Wards' house, memories flooding her as they always did. Her mother had told her that Callan lived in the apartment above the garage, and unable to stop, she looked that way. No movement was evident, and she wondered what it would be like to live near him again. Instead of the heartache she expected to feel, a strange sense of excitement moved through her. Refusing to ponder what it meant, she forced her mind to the new job as she climbed into bed, willing sleep to come.

When Callan had parked his truck next to his garage apartment, he noticed a small car in the alley right behind the Bayles' house. *Sophie's?* It seemed late at night for her to be visiting, and he hoped everything was all right. Once inside his apartment, he got ready for bed but continually looked out his window toward the alley, noting the car did not leave. While the curtains across the way were drawn, he could see a faint light in the window of the room that had been Sophie's. He had already turned out his own lights but stood in the dark staring across the yards.

Memories, so often held at bay, flooded back. The Baytown Boys running through the alley. The clubhouse they made out of an old shed. He and Philip spending every summer evening after they came in from the beach tossing a ball back and forth. Pretty Sophie, with her mass of curly blonde hair, playing in their backyard. Then the memories turned dark as he remembered her standing there, her grief etched so deeply on her face he wondered if it would ever leave, saying her final goodbye. He wondered if she still kept her heart from taking risks.

Just as he started to move into his bedroom, a slight movement at her window caught his eye. It appeared that someone had pulled the curtain back, but in the dark, he could not see who it was and knew they could not see him either.

A tug at his heart caused his hand to move up and rub over his chest. The curtain across the street dropped back into place, and he sighed.

The next day he had a later shift, and as he jogged down his outside steps to his truck, he noticed the car was no longer there. It felt like a piece of him was once again missing.

The gathering of women in the upstairs galleria of Jillian's coffee shop pushed a few tables together so that they could all fit around them. The Baytown girls' posse had grown over the years, each welcoming new friends.

Jillian walked up the stairs and rounded the top,

her hands full of the large tray loaded with dainty cups and a teapot. One of her servers followed with a tray full of pastries. Setting them down in the middle of the tables, she thanked her assistant and turned toward Katelyn.

"Can you please tell us why you had us all meet here so early in the morning? I know you can't be pregnant again!"

Tori, Madelyn, Ginny, Jade, Lia, and Belle sat around the table, their attention riveted to the other two women. Sharing glances between each other, they all shook their heads indicating they had no idea why they were together.

Katelyn grinned and replied, "Because I've got a surprise coming...and no, I'm not pregnant."

Jillian, tossing her long blond braid over her shoulder, stood with her hands on her hips staring at her best friend. "Well? Where's your surprise?"

"I guess it's me," Sophie said, rounding the top of the steps and walking toward them.

"Oh, my God!" Jillian and Tori shouted at the same time. Jillian, already standing, got to Sophie first, pulling her in for a hug.

Tori, close behind, greeted her as well with a hug and a huge smile.

Katelyn turned to the others and said, "Sophie is Tonya and David Bayles' daughter. We all grew up together."

Belle, quieter than the others, stood and moved over to Sophie. "You probably don't remember me, but I'm Belle Simmons. Well, that's my married name. I was

Belle Gunn when you and I were friends in preschool and kindergarten."

Sophie pulled Belle into a hug and said, "Oh, my goodness. Mom told me that she had met you. I do remember us being friends so many years ago."

Katelyn, with her hand around Sophie's shoulders, led her to the table and re-introduced her to Madelyn, Ginny, Lia, and Jade. "This is Madelyn, Zac's wife. And Ginny is one of the town's police officers, married to Brogan. Jade is married to Lance, another police officer, but I'm not sure you've met him. And this is Lia, Aiden's fiancé.

"It's really nice to meet all of you," she said, her voice as sincere as her heart felt. Having spent the last several years away from Baytown with only occasional visits, it hit her how much she missed having a group of women friends.

The large gathering sat around the table and immediately dove in for the pastries and tea. Jillian, ever curious, asked, "Are you just here for the weekend to visit your parents?"

Sharing a glance with Katelyn, she grinned. "Actually, I'm moving back here for several months."

Smiles greeted her announcement, and the women appeared genuinely happy. She continued, "I'm going to be working for The Dunes Resort as their interior designer for the model home that will be in a Southern Living photo shoot."

"Oh, my goodness!" Tori exclaimed. "What a fabulous opportunity!"

Still grinning, she agreed, "Yes, it is. It could be a real

game-changing opportunity for me and my new business. I quit my other job, struck out on my own, and this should make the risk easier."

"I like running my own business," Jillian said, leaning back in her chair, taking a sip of tea.

"Me too," Tori and Katelyn said at the same time.

"It's a lot of work," Tori continued, "but I love running the Sea Glass Inn."

Sophie agreed. "It's not easy, but it's definitely better than working for a company that was more dog-eat-dog than caring about its employees."

Belle smiled, adding, "I'll bet your parents must be thrilled to have you back in Baytown."

Nodding, she said, "Yes, they are. I'll only be back for a few months, but this is such a great opportunity."

Katelyn gushed, "I was so excited when she told me, I wanted to make sure she had a chance to immediately connect with all of us, including our new friends."

They spent the next hour plying her with questions about the job at The Dunes Resort, and she learned about their lives in Baytown. Katelyn had been the only friend that she had truly kept up with, although Katelyn often spoke of the others. She loved getting to know Madelyn, Ginny, and Lia since they were married to original Baytown Boys, but she also found Belle and Jade to be delightful as well.

Looking around at the artwork on the walls and in wooden, glass-front cases, she said, "Jillian, I love what you've done here." Paintings of beach scenes, waterfowl, and boats graced the exposed brick walls. Mobiles created from sea glass hung from the ceiling. A large sea glass mosaic hung on one of the windows, the sunlight beaming through the multi-colored shards. Her design-oriented mind overflowed with ideas.

Smiling, Jillian thanked her. "I wanted to showcase the local artists." Looking back at her, she added, "If you're interested in any pieces for the house, I know the artists would be thrilled to have the possibility to be in Southern Living."

"The sea glass art is exquisite!"

"Oh, Lordy," Jade groaned. "My husband makes those, and he definitely doesn't want the publicity."

Sophie laughed, saying, "Then I might just have to make sure they're in the background, but they are definitely gorgeous."

Needing to get on the road, she stood to offer her goodbyes. Hugging each woman in turn, she thanked them for the impromptu tea party and promised to get together as soon as she arrived in town the next week.

Katelyn walked her out to her car, their arms around each other. "You have no idea how glad I am that you're going to be back in Baytown, even if it's just for a few months. And I hope this doesn't upset you, but I know your mom is going to be thrilled."

She laughed and said, "Oh, I sat up late last night talking to my parents, so I know how excited they are."

Katelyn hesitated, and she watched her friend closely. "What is it, Katelyn? I get the feeling there's something else you want to say."

"I know you might not be ready...you might not ever be ready, but while you're here, I hope you'll consider coming to one of the American Legion Auxiliary meetings. I know your mom has taken great comfort in those, and all of us belong so you know lots of people."

Expecting to feel great pain at the reminder of the loss of her brother, she instinctively put her hand to her heart, but after a few breaths, she realized that while the heartache was still there, it was not as overwhelming as it had always been. Surprised, she shook off the thought, and offering a noncommittal nod, said, "I'll think about it. We'll see."

With another tight hug goodbye, Katelyn whispered, "One more thing. I also hope you'll renew your friend-ship with Callan."

This brought another twinge to her heart, and she did not reply. Kissing Katelyn's cheek, she climbed into her car. She turned up the music, knowing she had a two-hour drive ahead of her, and the last thing she needed before her first day on the job was to spend two hours thinking about the Baytown she remembered from years ago and the boy she used to love.

9

Sitting in the conference room, Callan listened as Jeff ran the weekly meeting. The Station Chief liked to keep meetings to a minimum. He and Jeff were Maritime Enforcement Specialists. Jarrod and José were Boatswain's Mates. Tanisha was their Information Systems Technician, while Bryce and Sharon were Marine Science Technicians. A new Machinery Technician was expected to show up soon. Others filled more of the chairs, all focusing on Jeff's instructions. The station was very small, but they worked cohesively to make sure their jurisdiction of the Chesapeake Bay was safe and secure.

Turning his attention back to Jeff, Callan listened as the Chief called for a volunteer to teach cold water survival techniques to the high school Kayak Club. He knew it had been a while since he had taken on that role, so he threw his hand up to volunteer. Looking over, he chuckled as Jarrod's hand had also gone up.

With a quick notation, Jeff said, "You can both do it.

It should only take one Saturday morning, but I hear they have a very active group, and their sponsor wanted them to have the information from us."

More duties were assigned, and each gave quick oral reports on the calls they had responded to over the week. The last several days were filled with only routine calls and monitoring, for which he was glad. As the meeting came to a close and the group disbanded, Jarrod called out, "José and I are going to Finn's. You want to go?"

Nodding his agreement, the three men headed into the locker room to change out of their uniforms. A few minutes later, jeans and sweatshirts donned, they climbed into their vehicles and drove the two minutes it took to get to Finn's. Parking along Main Street, they walked through the familiar red door into the warm interior of the pub.

Jarrod and José immediately headed to the dartboard on the right, joining a group of men that were already there. Callan walked over to the bar, offering a chin lift to Aiden and Brogan who were both working that evening. The two tatted, dark-haired MacFarlane brothers were so similar in looks but opposite in personality. At least they had been. *But with Ginny around, Brogan is more laid back. With Lia, Aiden is more responsible. Hell, we're all changing.* Sliding onto a stool between Jason and Gareth, he grinned as Katelyn placed a platter of nachos in front of her husband.

"Gareth, it must be nice to get personal service," he joked. Looking over at Katelyn, he said, "You look beautiful. Motherhood agrees with you."

Accepting the beer from Brogan, he ordered a pub burger from one of the servers who walked by and then turned as Katelyn offered him a hug. She moved back to the seat on the other side of Gareth and said, "Mom and Dad wanted to babysit tonight, so I told Brogan and Aiden I'd come in for a while." Popping a nacho into her mouth, she said, "I've got news for you, but your mom might already know it."

Chuckling, he took a drink from his beer and said, "I'm never around enough to get a lot of gossip from my mom. What's up?"

"Sophie's going to move back to Baytown. Well, at least for a couple of months."

The glass of beer in his hand, on its way up to his mouth, halted. He looked her way, his brow lowered, and asked, "She's moving back here? I thought she was getting...well, her dad had mentioned that she might be getting..." The word *engaged* stuck in his throat, and all he could do was stare at Katelyn.

Katelyn was watching him closely and added, "She's not engaged. In fact, she's not dating anybody right now. Free as a bird, you might say." Her voice was lilting, drawing his attention, but she looked back down at the plate of nachos and continued popping several in her mouth.

Not engaged? Moving back to Baytown?

"So, are you gonna leave him hanging or actually explain what you're talking about?" Gareth asked, shoulder bumping her.

Wiping her hands on her napkin, Katelyn leaned forward and held Callan's gaze. "As far as who she was dating, that's not my story to tell. But as to why she's moving back to Baytown, that will soon be common knowledge. A couple of months ago, she opened up her own design company, but it's been a struggle. The Dunes Resort has just hired her to do the interior designs and staging for one of the large beachfront houses that's going to be in Southern Living. Plus, she gets to do the designs on one of the condos they want to put in their marketing material. So, she's moving back for several months while she does that."

Nodding, he barely noticed when the server set his pub burger and fries in front of him. Before he had a chance to ask Katelyn any more questions she was called to the back by Aiden.

He felt Jason's perusal as he picked up his large burger and took a healthy bite, barely tasting it. Silently chewing, he was startled when Gareth said, "Do you think she'll be able to handle being back here? I know I wasn't here in Baytown when you all were growing up, but Philip's presence is something that I've had to face since I ended up falling in love with Katelyn. Even though she and Philip were very young when they made their vows to be engaged, I had to deal with her coming to terms with her own grief before we could move forward as a couple."

Callan nodded, thinking over his words carefully before saying, "I've never told you this, but I'm really glad you came into Katelyn's life. She's a good woman and deserves the best. At one time I thought that was my best friend. But when he was taken from us, I can't think of another person besides you that I would want her to be with."

Gareth stared at him for a moment, his gaze warm, then nodded slowly. "Thanks, man. I mean it. That means a helluva lot to me."

They ate silently until their platters were almost finished. Jason tossed his napkin to the bar counter and said, "It's my understanding that you and Sophie have a past."

Callan took another long drink of his beer, aware that he had Gareth's attention as well. Swallowing before replying, he said, "Like a lot of us around here, we were sort of a high school couple. Not like Grant and Jillian, because Sophie was a few years younger than me. But it meant a lot to me, also, when Philip told me that he thought I was the right person for Sophie. But...well hell, when he died it pulled the rug out from under all of us. I lost my best friend, we all lost one of the Baytown Boys, Katelyn lost her fiancé, and Sophie lost her beloved brother. We were all young and grieving, and I can't say that any of us handled it the way we could have. The rest of us guys scattered back to the ends of the earth with our deployments. Katelyn didn't date for a long time, but," he glanced toward Gareth and said, "even though she struggled when you first came around, she finally learned to open up her heart again, which is what Philip would've wanted. Sophie had just finished high school, and I think Baytown was just too painful for her."

Swallowing past the sudden lump in his throat, he added, "A lot of things were too painful for her."

87

Catching their questioning eyes, he cleared his throat and assured them, "I understood. I really did. The timing sucked all the way around."

Shaking his head, he continued, "She went away to college, came home for holidays, and then got a job in Richmond." He paused before heaving a great sigh. "Fuck. She pretty much told me at his funeral that being around anyone in the service was just too hard...too much of a risk. She needed to guard her heart."

Jason shook his head and said, "Fuck, Callan. I'm sorry." The sentiment was echoed by Gareth.

He shrugged. "It hurt...hurt like hell. But then I was heading back overseas, and for all I knew, I wouldn't be coming back either. How could I want that for her? How could I want to tie her to someone who wasn't around?" Scrubbing his hand over his face, he added, "I wanted us to stay friends if nothing more, but I was away with the Coast Guard, and she was away with school and a job. Sometimes what we hope for just doesn't happen."

"And now?"

Shaking his head, he said, "The best I can hope for is that we can renew our friendship while she's here."

Gareth chuckled and said, "At the risk of sounding like Katelyn, I'd say you never know what the next couple of months can bring. Who knows? Maybe she's ready to come home. Maybe she's ready for something more."

Katelyn walked out and moved straight into Gareth's arms. Looking up at him, she said, "I'm done here, so if you want to go on home to baby Finn, that's fine."

Saying goodbye to them, Callan ordered another beer. Jason clapped him on the back and moved toward the dartboard. When Brogan set the beer in front of him, he said, "Aiden mentioned that you were wondering about staying in the Coast Guard or getting out."

"I'm still trying to figure everything out," he said. "I've gotten used to being back in Baytown and don't really want to get deployed somewhere else."

"You think with Sophie being back in town, that'll help you make up your mind?" Aiden asked, popping up beside his brother.

"Damn, you two. You're looking for gossip about as much as the girls do." The three of them shared a laugh, and then he shook his head slowly. "At the risk of a bad pun, I'd have to say I have no idea if that ship has sailed."

"Well," Aiden said, "a couple of months is a long time to rekindle those feelings."

The two brothers were called down to the other end of the bar, but Brogan lifted an eyebrow in a silent question. Nodding, he said, "Yeah. See you there." He threw some money down, and with a wave of his hand, walked out into the cold night air.

An hour later, a semi-circle of men stood in the Baytown cemetery. The same men that gathered every year on Philip's birthday. Callan kept his eyes on the headstone, knowing Brogan, Aiden, Mitch, Zac, and Grant were doing the same.

Simultaneously, they lifted their beer cans, popped

the top, and took a drink. "To you, Philip. Happy Birthday," they said in unison. After a moment, they headed back to their vehicles, another year marked since they lost their friend.

Thirty minutes later, Callan was back home, showered, and standing at his window looking across the alley toward the Bayles' house, where Sophie's room was now dark.

Will you be able to handle coming back, Sophie? Will Baytown finally give you the respite you're looking for or simply do more to churn up your grief?

Turning, he walked back into his bedroom, sliding under the sheets. Sleep did not come easily as thoughts of her and Philip filled his mind.

Buddy, I know the last thing you'd want would be for Sophie to avoid Baytown. If anything, you'd want her to be as happy as she could be. Maybe, just maybe, I can help with that.

One hundred miles away in Richmond, Sophie lay in bed unable to sleep. It was Philip's birthday, and just like every year, she thought of him continually. Climbing out of bed, she walked to the linen closet in the hall and looked to the top shelf. Reaching up, she pulled down a plastic tub and carried it into her bedroom. Pulling off the top, she peered inside.

Digging through the memorabilia, she pulled out a photo album. She climbed back onto her bed and turned on the light on her nightstand. She began flipping through the pages, smiling occasionally as the memories moved back through her mind.

Fishing off the pier, walks on the beach looking for sea glass, birthday parties…and in most of them were the friends that she had held so dear and the brother that meant everything to her. Jillian and Katelyn…the Baytown Boys…and Philip's best friend, Callan.

In the dark of the night, she was no longer able to pretend that the pull toward Baytown was not strong. She had let so much time pass, afraid to be in Baytown without Philip, that if she was not careful her friends were going to become strangers.

She settled on a picture in her photo album, one of Philip and Callan in high school, with their arms around each other after winning a game. Her fingers traced the outline of Philip's face, his smile wide. But then her eyes drifted to Callan, and she found herself focusing on him. Dark hair, dark eyes, already a world-liness about him.

She lay back on the bed after pulling that picture from the album and held it close to her heart. *Philip, would you have been disappointed in me, to have turned my back on Baytown?* She already knew the answer to that and sighed deeply. *I wonder if I can learn to be in Baytown without you there.*

Rolling over, she lay the picture on her nightstand, propping it so that the two men were staring down on her. As she drifted off to sleep, she thought, *Maybe, just maybe, Callan can help me with that.*

10

"Okay, let's review," Callan said, standing at the front of the classroom, looking out over the fifteen eager teenage faces. The high school classroom looked the same as when he had been there, perhaps with new, light blue, glossy paint covering the cinder-block walls. The long, industrial, fluorescent light fixtures overhead had not changed. *But some of the desks look newer.* Bringing his thoughts back to the subject at hand, he prompted, "The four stages of cold water immersion are..." He pointed to one of the girls in the front row with her hand up.

"Cold shock," she said. "That's in the first three to five minutes."

Nodding his head, he said, "That's right. And what's the most immediate response to that?"

She replied, "Panic. The person can gasp, which can suck in water. Hyperventilate. Um...and they could have sudden changes in heart rate and blood pressure."

"Good, good. In the second stage?"

This time, another member of the high school Kayak Club answered. "Short term swim failure. That's like in the next thirty minutes after you end up in the cold water. You lose your ability to grip and you can't move very well. Even if you had a flotation device, you might not maintain a grip on it."

"You guys paid really good attention," Callan commended. "Okay, who can tell me the third stage?" He looked at one of the shy members, who had not said much, and called on them, wanting to draw them out.

Her voice, hesitant at first, grew stronger. "Long-term immersion hypothermia. That happens after the first thirty minutes, and how fast it occurs depends on the temperature of the water, how much clothing the person is wearing, and even body type. It's when your body loses heat faster than it can produce it, and it affects your organs. That's usually when you lose consciousness and drown."

He smiled and nodded. "Great. And the last stage?"

Another teenage boy replied, "Post immersion collapse. That can happen during or after you get rescued. You're still in danger even when you're out of the water because your blood pressure can cause a heart attack. And if you've got water in your lungs, then that's not good. And your heart is struggling as well."

Callan looked to the side at the Kayak Club sponsor and complimented, "You got a really good group here." Turning back to the class, he said, "The best thing you can do to protect yourself is to be prepared. I know that you're taught to always have a flotation device, but you often go kayaking in the warmer weather, so your clothing is light. For cold weather, your clothing can make a big difference."

Jarrod, who came with him, moved to the front of the room to take over, dressed appropriately for cold weather kayaking. He said, "As Petty Officer Ward said, your clothing can make the difference between survival and death. You can see I'm wearing a PFD, personal flotation device, and why is this most important in the cold water immersion?"

One of the students answered, "Because you can't swim very well when you get really cold. Your mobility slows down, so if you have a PFD, then you can keep your head above the water even if your arms and legs aren't moving well."

Jarrod grinned widely and nodded. "Perfect. Also, clothing. As you can see, I'm wearing a long-sleeved thermal shirt underneath this outer long-sleeved shirt. If you layer the clothing, that will keep your body heat in for longer periods of time. Thick socks will protect your feet, and thermal pants underneath your jeans will protect your legs. The idea is to hold in your body warmth as long as possible." He reached into his pocket and pulled out a knit cap, settling it on his head and pulling it down over his ears. "Making sure your head is covered will also go a long way in keeping body heat from escaping."

The class continued for thirty more minutes as they showed a short film on how to position themselves once in the water to retain as much body heat as possible.

At the end of their time, Callan asked, "What is the

single most important thing you should always remember when boating or kayaking in cold weather?"

Several students shouted out answers, and for each one, he smiled and nodded but said, "There's still something else."

Finally, the shy girl raised her hand, and he pointed to her.

"Buddy system," she answered, her eyes hopeful.

"You got it!" he said, watching her beam. "While you may enjoy being on the water by yourself, in cold water, it's best if you go in pairs or groups. Your survival rate will be much higher if there's someone else around who can assist or call for help."

Callan and Jarrod stayed for several more minutes, taking individual questions before leaving the high school. Dropping Jarrod off at the station, he drove to his apartment, glad for the rest of his Saturday being free.

Driving down the alley between the streets, he saw a small car in front of him. With interest, he watched as it turned and parked just across from his garage apartment. He followed, parking next to the garage on his side of the alley and climbed out. Turning around, his heart leaped as he spied Sophie alighting from her car.

She turned to face him, and he found his breath halting in his throat until a shy smile spread across her face. Her long, curly blond hair hung down her back, pulled away from her face just at the top. Casually dressed in jeans, boots, and a puffy blue coat, she looked adorable. From a distance, it appeared as though she had just come home from high school, and he had to blink to keep from falling down that rabbit hole of memories.

He jogged across the short gravel alley and greeted, "Sophie, it's nice to see you. Katelyn told me you were coming back to Baytown for a while. I was really hoping to see you."

Other than seeing her at a few of their friend's weddings, they had not spent time together in years, but after a moment of hesitation, she opened her arms and moved forward, wrapping them around his waist. Thrilled she was not avoiding him, he pulled her in tightly, and without thinking kissed the top of her head. "It's good to have you home," he whispered into her hair.

She gave his middle a squeeze then stepped back. With her chin down, her hand moved to her eyes where she swiped quickly before she lifted her gaze back to his. A sheen of moisture was there, and he reached out to give her hand a squeeze.

Able to see her more closely, it was easy to tell that she had matured to the promise of beauty she had in high school. Her eyes were just as blue-green, highlighted with makeup applied with a light hand. Her cheeks were rosy and her lips slicked with pink gloss. She had been a petite teenager, but he now felt the evidence of curves on her slender frame.

The last time he had seen her was at Katelyn's wedding, where he could feel the pull between happiness for her friend getting married and sadness that it was not to Philip. Even from a distance across the reception hall, he could sense her pain. But now, staring so closely into her face, she appeared more at ease.

"It's nice to see you again, Callan," she said, her voice soft with a hint of sadness.

Determined to keep her talking, he asked, "Are you going to be staying with your parents?"

She nodded, chuckling. "Yeah, it doesn't make any sense to pay money to stay somewhere else. Being able to work for The Dunes Resort will really help my pocketbook because the last couple of months have been a little difficult. So, I guess it's back with the parents."

He immediately hated that anything for her had been difficult and said, "Hey, don't feel bad. I'm over thirty and living over my parents' garage."

Her gaze glanced over his shoulder across the alley, and he nodded. "Yep, that's my home. But, honestly, it's not that bad. I go days without seeing my parents, and the rent is cheap. They wouldn't charge me anything, but I insist."

"Well, if I know your mom, she loves having you close by," she said, her gaze moving back up to his face.

"I could say the same about you, too, Sophie. I heard the news about you coming back here from Katelyn, but as soon as I got home that evening my mom was bouncing with excitement from your mom telling her about your new opportunity here in Baytown."

Her smile widened, and she said, "Yeah, Mom and Dad are pretty excited." They stared at each other in silence for a moment, before she finally said, "It was good to see you, Callan. I suppose I should take my things inside."

He cast a glance up toward her parents' house and asked, "Are they not home right now?"

Shaking her head, she said, "I was going to come tomorrow but decided to make the trip today. Mom and Dad are at a church bazaar, helping out with some of the booths." Shrugging, she added, "It's really okay. It gives me a chance to get settled without Mom hovering."

He walked past her and said, "Unlock your trunk. I can help you carry your things in, and I promise I won't hover."

An unexpected giggle slipped from her lips, and she nodded. Pulling out her keys, she clicked the lock, and they both grabbed the suitcases. When they reached the back door, he took the key from her, unlocked the door, and held it open for her to proceed in. They entered the kitchen of the Bayles' house and moved down the hall to the stairs. Rounding the bottom, he followed as she led the way up. His gaze landed on her jean-clad ass, and he sucked in a deep breath.

She must have heard his hiss because when she got to the top, she turned and called over her shoulder, "Are you okay? I know the suitcases are heavy."

Jerking his gaze back up to her face, he said, "No, they're fine." Hoping her gaze would not drop to his crotch, the evidence of his perusal plain and growing behind his zipper, he told his dick to behave while holding her attention with a smile.

An adorable look of confusion filled her eyes, but she quickly moved down the hall to her bedroom. He knew the room they passed had been Philip's and wondered if that was why she rushed past. Before he had a chance to think on that further, he entered her room. He had not been inside her room since the days when he and Philip would be playing at the Bayles' house. It appeared that Tonya had redecorated, moving past the teenage *girlie* to a lovely guest room. "It's been a while since I've been here. Looks like your mom redecorated."

Sophie set her bags on the bed and turned, saying, "You can set the suitcases anywhere." Looking up at him, she nodded. "I told Mom several years ago to please redo this room. She actually asked what colors I would like, and I told her it didn't matter. Let's face it, after kids leave home, it's really not their room anymore in anyone's eyes except the parents." Glancing around, she smiled and added, "But, I have to admit, my mom's got good taste. Thank God! Had she put in flowered wallpaper with a striped bedspread, I might go blind staying here."

He laughed, glad to see that she did not appear upset at the changes in her parents' house. He wondered if that applied to the changes in Philip's room as well. He almost asked then halted his words before they could come out his mouth. *Right now, she seems at ease with me here. Not gonna fuck that up.*

She had unzipped her puffy jacket, pulled it off and was hanging it in the closet. Uncertain if she wanted privacy to begin unpacking, he stepped back toward the door. She looked over her shoulder at him and then turned, facing him.

Paired with her jeans and boots, she had on a thick

green sweater with a swooping neckline that managed to showcase her breasts without being tight at all. She fiddled with the bottom of it, as though uncertain what to do with her hands.

"Well, I suppose I should—"

"Would you like a cup of coffee?" she asked suddenly. "I'm sure Mom's got some downstairs. But… um…only if you have time…or um…want to—"

"I'd love to," he said. He saw the hesitant look in her eyes and repeated, "Really, Sophie. I'd love to share a cup of coffee with you."

As she led the way back down the stairs toward the kitchen, he thought, *I'd love to share so much more with you, but I'll start with a cup of coffee.*

11

Sophie found herself downstairs in her parents' kitchen popping a coffee pod into the coffee maker, suddenly very nervous. She fiddled with the sweetener packets and pulled the creamer out of the refrigerator, then realized she had no idea how he took his coffee. *The last time we spent any real time together, I wasn't even drinking coffee.*

She turned around, seeing him standing at the edge of the counter, and asked, "Um...cream? Sugar?"

He smiled, and the butterflies from many years ago that she felt when she used to look at him on the ball field returned. His dark, short hair was still as thick as ever, and a dark shadow of hair grew in a goatee around his perfect lips. But it was his eyes that captured her gaze, giving her his full attention while resting warmly on her.

"Dash of cream, one sweetener."

She startled, almost forgetting that she had asked him a question. Heat infused her cheeks, and she turned around to concentrate on fixing a cup of coffee the way he would like. Focusing next on hers, she carried both cups to the table.

It felt strange to be hosting someone in her parents' kitchen, having not spent much time there in the past years.

"So—" they both said at the same time, then looked at each other and grinned.

"You first," she said.

"I was just going to ask how you've been. I mean, I know you've got this great opportunity with The Dunes, but I just wondered how *you* were." He hesitated, as though he wanted to say more.

She tilted her head to the side, waiting to see if he was going to elaborate, and he did not make her wait.

He held her gaze and continued, "When we were outside, you mentioned that things had been a little difficult. You don't have to tell me, but I'm here if you want a listening ear."

She took another sip of coffee before setting her cup down, staring at her hands for a moment. Lifting her head, her lips curved gently, and she said, "You always were the best listener, Callan." Sucking in her lips, she pondered what to tell him and how much to tell him. It was not like she had no one to talk to, considering she had spilled her guts to Katelyn, Jillian, and the other women. And her parents certainly knew the score. But seeing Callan sitting in her parents' kitchen like he had so many times when he was growing up, she found his presence comfortable, not awkward.

Shrugging, she said, "In a nutshell, I was excited to

be hired by a prestigious design firm in Richmond after college. I felt like my life was moving in the direction that I wanted. But, after a while, things weren't so great. There were some...um...problems, and I began thinking of starting my own business. So when things became untenable, I took the plunge. It hasn't been easy, going from a decent, steady paycheck, to...well...not. I managed to snag a couple of clients, so it wasn't like I had no money coming in, but it's definitely been challenging. To get the offer to work for The Dunes, even for a few months, could be a real career boost for me."

While she had been talking, Callan's attention had not wavered at all. That was another thing she had always liked about him. Even when they were younger and the guys were around, if he had asked her a question or she was talking, his attention was riveted on her.

"I'm sorry that things didn't work out with the other design company, Sophie," he said, his warm voice sliding over her. "But I'm really proud of you for continuing to go after your dream yourself. That took a lot of guts."

Her face scrunched, and she exclaimed, "Guts? Oh, Callan, you go out every day and rescue people. I'd say you're the one who has guts."

Shrugging, he replied, "I go out and do what I was trained to do. You're stepping into the unknown, so I would say you're very brave."

"You don't think it was stupid leaving the secure job? Taking too much of a chance?"

His brows lowered, he shook his head and said, "Not at all. Why would anybody think that was stupid? If you were unhappy in the other job, then you needed to do something about it."

She could not help but compare his reaction to Tommy's, obviously finding Callan's much more comforting and less judgmental.

He drained the last of his coffee and set the cup back down onto the table. Holding her gaze once more, he said, "You took a calculated risk, and it's paying off. I think that's wonderful, Sophie."

His words had the effect of validation, and yet the word *risk* reverberated through her. *Risk. I once told him that I couldn't take a risk with him being in the Coast Guard.* The room began to feel rather small and her breathing felt shallow. Wondering if she should say something to him about what she had said to him so many years ago, she was grateful when the back door opened, and her parents came through.

"Sophie!" her dad called out, excitement in his voice. "We didn't think you'd get here till tomorrow."

Her mother hurried into the room and gave her a hug, looking over her shoulder and saying, "And Callan, how nice to see you here."

She explained in a rush, "He helped me carry my luggage upstairs." She looked up at Callan, and his perceptive gaze was pinned on her. If he had noticed her change in demeanor right before her parents came in, he said nothing.

Standing, he said, "I need to get back to my place. Tonya, David, it was nice seeing you again. Sophie, I hope we can get together more while you're here. It's good to have you back."

She stood as well and moved toward him, offering a hug. "Thanks for the help," she said.

"Thanks for the coffee and the talk," he said, mumbling into her hair.

His arms loosened, and with a wave toward her parents, he headed out the back door. She moved to the door and stared through the glass panes as he made his way through her yard, across the alley, and up the stairs to his garage apartment. When he was finally out of sight, she turned and startled, seeing her parents staring at her.

Huffing, she said, "What?"

Her dad said nothing but grinned as he made his way down the hall toward the family room. Her mom smiled and said, "I didn't say anything, sweetheart. But, I have to admit, it was nice to see the two of you talking. He meant a great deal to you at one time, and maybe you and he will have time to catch up while you're here."

She turned her head to stare out of the door again, her gaze falling on his apartment, and said, "I suppose, Mom. He's easy to talk to, and I wouldn't mind getting to know him again." Looking back at her mom, seeing a spark of hope in her eyes, she added, "But don't read too much into that, Mom. He loves his job, and I would never want to take that away from him. But I also told him years ago it was too risky for me."

Tonya walked over and lifted her hand to cup Sophie's cheek. "Oh, my sweet girl. Life is a risk. You can't protect yourself from hurt, we all know that. But you can grab hold of life with both hands and experience the good, knowing it can get you through the bad."

She felt the sting of tears hit the back of her eyes and was grateful when her mother turned and moved over to the refrigerator, starting to take out items for dinner. "I think I'll go unpack some if you don't mind."

"Not at all, sweetie. Take your time."

She hesitated at the top of the stairs, walking slowly to Philip's room. Her parents never kept his door closed, and she had certainly seen evidence of the slow transformation over the years when she would walk by and the sunlight was streaming through the window. Right after they had been notified of Philip's death, she had sat in his room sobbing for a full day, until her parents finally assisted her up and back into her own room, tucking her exhausted body into bed. That day was etched onto her memory. Staring around his room, her vision blurry with bouts of tears. The books on the bookshelves. The posters on the wall. The worn baseball glove on his dresser top. It was not like he had been there recently, having joined the Army three years earlier, but that was where she felt his presence.

After the funeral, she never went back into his room. When she was home for a visit, she would pass by, but somehow, walking into the room that was no longer his was something she could not bring herself to do.

Why have I given this space so much power over me? No answer was forthcoming, and she hesitated with her hand on his doorframe. With a quick shake of her head and a sharp inhale, she turned, moving down the hall to her room, deciding she would rather spend her time unpacking than facing the ghosts she had no desire to face. *I'll be here for several months. Maybe, just maybe, I'll get brave.*

Considering his schedule and duties, days could go by and Callan would not see his parents. Having a Saturday evening off, his mom had texted earlier to see if he would like to eat dinner with them. He showed at their back door, moved through, and set a six-pack of beer on their kitchen counter.

"Sorry I didn't bring any food, but I figured yours would be better anyway, Mom. At least I brought some beer for Dad."

She laughed and wiped her hands on the dish towel before walking over and giving him a hug. His dad walked into the room, shook his hand, and immediately went for one of the beers. As his dad popped the top on the can, he wandered to the back door and looked out.

"It looks like Sophie's car is across the way," Thomas said, still staring outside.

"Oh, really? I thought Tonya said she wasn't gonna get here until tomorrow," his mom added, pulling the roast from the oven. "Callan, honey, can you get the silverware, and we'll be ready to eat in just a minute?"

He walked over and grabbed the silverware from the drawer and headed to the table. "Sophie did come in today. She got here about the same time that I got home, so I helped her take her luggage in. We had coffee and chatted for a little while."

The room became silent, and he looked up from

placing the spoons on the table to see his parents staring at him. "What?"

His parents shared a glance between themselves before looking back at him. His mom finally said, "You two were so close before Philip died, but I know she's been very distant since then. I had hoped that perhaps you two might have a chance to...um...I suppose saying the words *hook up* doesn't exactly give the right connotation. But I had hoped you could renew some kind of relationship while she was here. I guess that's already happened."

Shaking his head, he said, "Mom, don't get your hopes up. We just happened to pull in at the same time, and there was no way I was going to allow her to lug her suitcases up to her room by herself. We did have a few minutes to chat, but I'm not sure she's ready for anything here in Baytown."

Barbara's face fell, and she shook her head slowly. "That poor girl. I know Tonya and David have worried about her so much. When you boys joined the military, I know you all wanted to leave Baytown to see the world. This little town just seemed too small. In some ways, I guess Sophie feels the same. As much as she loves her parents, it was always so hard for her to deal with Philip's death here. I think when she moved to Richmond, it was easier to become immersed in her new life."

"Well, I get the feeling that that new life may not have been all she hoped it would be," he said. "She wasn't terribly forthcoming, but I definitely think that this new job, working for The Dunes, came at a really good time."

His mother brought the steamed vegetables over and set them on the table, and the three of them sat down. He dove into the food, murmuring his appreciation. "I should've invited Jarrod and José over, but then you would've had to have made twice the food just for those two."

She laughed and said, "Honey, you can invite your friends over anytime you want."

His dad had been quiet but then spoke up. "Son, I have no idea what your feelings toward Sophie are now. I know at one time you hoped things might evolve into a permanent relationship. But if you do still care for her, I'm going to tell you to go for it. I think maybe she just needs a reminder that Baytown could be everything she needs it to be. Embracing the fact that it holds a lot of memories of her brother while celebrating the fact that it holds a lot of people who still love her."

Callan nodded slowly, pondering what his dad had said. A man of few words, when Thomas did speak, it was always worth listening to. Finishing the meal, he helped his mom clean the kitchen before giving them hugs goodbye. Walking through the yard, he went up the stairs and into his own apartment. Flipping on the TV to a sports channel, he settled onto his sofa. With a light now on in Sophie's room across the way, he could not help but occasionally look over, his mind filled with her. This time, however, it also filled with Philip, wondering what his friend would have wanted him to do.

Sophie parked in the driveway, her breath catching in her throat as she stared ahead. Situated on the Bay with nothing but a sand dune covered in seagrass, the massive house stood before her. White with butter-yellow shutters. Three stories and a separate three-car garage with a bonus room above. Professionally land-scaped, the grass was green, and the shrubs were perfectly pruned.

Hearing her name called, she jerked out of her perusal and followed Carlotta up the steps to the front door. Carlotta Ventura had jet black hair, hanging sleek in a shoulder-length bob. Her olive complexion was perfectly made up, and while her pants and blouse appeared to fit the business casual, Sophie could tell they were expensive. Short-heeled boots completed her outfit. Sophie recognized that Carlotta wanted to dress to impress the possible buyers of property at The Dunes Resort as well as the upcoming magazine exposure.

She looked down at her own outfit, something she

would have worn at her job with the Holsten Design Company, but knew that starting tomorrow, jeans and a nice shirt would be her daily outfit while working. That was fine with her...one of the perks of working on a house where she would not be seeing potential clients every day.

Following Carlotta, she entered into a wide foyer, immediately struck with light pine flooring that extended as far as she could see. A brick fireplace with matching red brick tile on the hearth sat at one end of the long living room, flanked by two tall windows.

All of the ten-foot walls were still painted white, and Carlotta quickly said, "We want you to view this as a blank canvas. Any changes will have to be approved by us, but you may certainly work from your color palette."

To the right was a formal dining room, same white walls and pine flooring, a chandelier already hanging from the center. She pulled out her phone and began taking multiple pictures of all of the walls and space.

"You can change the chandelier as you see fit once your design takes place," Carlotta said, continuing through the room.

Following, Sophie was led into the massive kitchen with white walls, white cabinets, black marble counter-tops, and white tile backsplash. Sleek. Elegant. More snapshots were taken.

They continued the tour through the family room, butler's pantry, laundry room, and up the stairs to the large bedrooms, each with their own bathroom, and the massive master suite that filled the entire back of the second floor, facing the bay.

There was a bonus room on the third floor with its own deck overlooking the water as well. Making their way back downstairs, the two women stood in the foyer, and Carlotta turned to Sophie. "So, what do you think?"

Excitement had been pouring through her veins since she first had been offered the job, but seeing the house and knowing what she could do with that, her joy bubbled forth.

"I cannot tell you how excited I am," she said, hoping her voice was more professional than giddy. "I have no doubt that we can work together, and my ideas will create an exceptional home for you to be able to feature for the magazine." She turned around slowly, her gaze taking in all of the features and said, "I can't wait to get started."

Carlotta clapped her hands and said, "Wonderful! Let's go to The Dunes Restaurant and I'll buy you lunch to celebrate. We'll stop at the guard gate on the way out to get your permit pass so that you can come and go." She dug into her purse and pulled out a key ring with several keys hanging on it. "This is for you. Keys to this house, the garage, and the bonus room over the garage which I haven't even shown you yet."

They walked back to their cars, and within a moment pulled into the parking lot that housed The Dunes Restaurant, the golf pro shop, and the golf cart rental shop.

Sophie was surprised when they sat at a large, round table with six chairs overlooking the golf course.

Carlotta answered her unasked question, saying,

"We're going to be joined by some of the others here at The Dunes Resort."

As soon as the words left Carlotta's mouth, Sophie noticed a tall man walking toward them. He looked familiar, but she could not remember his name. His dark hair was neatly trimmed, and like Carlotta, he was dressed professionally with neatly-pressed khaki slacks, a white, long-sleeved dress shirt, and royal blue tie.

He made his way straight toward her, his hand extended, and said, "You must be Sophie Bayles. I'm Roger Thorpe, the general manager of The Dunes Resort."

His voice was smooth and his greeting warm. As Sophie took his hand, she remembered having seen him years before at the church her parents attended.

"It's nice to meet you, Mr. Thorpe."

Taking a seat next to her, he said easily, "Please, call me Roger." He looked over at Carlotta, and with a nod of his head greeted, "Carlotta."

Sophie's gaze jumped to Carlotta, where she noticed Carlotta's smile appeared more forced than usual, but it passed so quickly, she was not sure she had read the expression correctly. *It's not my business to get into their business. I just need to focus on a kick-ass design!*

A server brought the menus, but before she had a chance to look at it, two other people entered the restaurant and walked directly toward them. Both were wearing khaki pants—not as neatly pressed as Roger's—and green, long-sleeved golf polos with the logo *The Dunes* stitched over the left breast. The woman, her short, dark blonde hair streaked with gray, marched directly to Sophie, shaking her hand firmly.

"Nice to meet you. Sue Connor, Golf Pro," she said in a clipped voice, taking a seat next to Carlotta.

The man held her hand in a warm shake and said, "Sophie, so nice to have you with us. I'm Travis Mars, Head Golf Pro."

She smiled, taking his hand, but could see Sue bristle as soon Travis mentioned the word *head*. He took the chair on the other side of her and greeted Carlotta and Ralph.

A large woman came out from the door behind the bar, wearing a white chef's jacket, her hair cut in a short bob, the longer front tucked behind her ears. She also made her way directly to the table, taking the last seat. Looking across the table at Sophie, she dipped her chin in a short nod and said, "Nice to meet you. I'm Ann Berkley, Chef here at The Dunes. Hope you enjoy your lunch."

"I'm sure I will," Sophie said, feeling a bit overwhelmed. She quickly scanned the menu, deciding on her choice while surreptitiously looking at the others. Carlotta seemed more friendly with the women than toward the men. Ann appeared uneasy, and Sophie wondered if she was more at home in the kitchen than in the dining room.

Roger and Travis, seated on either side of her, made small talk with each other, leaving her awkwardly overlooked in the middle.

Grateful when their drinks and several baskets of

rolls were delivered, she felt more at ease when everyone was busy serving themselves.

"It's my understanding that you're from here," Sue said, looking directly at her.

Having just taken a bite of bread, she chewed and swallowed quickly before replying, "Yes. I was born and raised here in Baytown. My parents still live here... Tonya and David Bayles."

"I've met your dad," Travis said. "He's not a member, but I've known him to play a round or two of golf."

The Dunes Resort sold golf memberships that were extremely expensive, and most of the townspeople that she knew did not belong. But anyone could pay to play golf, and the restaurant was open to everyone. She glanced at Travis but did not sense any censure from him, as though her family were less because they did not belong.

On her other side, Roger spoke up. "I knew your parents back in the day. We went to the same church."

Swinging her gaze to him, she was about to reply that she remembered him when Carlotta made a strangling noise, something between a cough and a snort. Roger shot Carlotta a narrow-eyed glare, and Sophie retreated back to her buttered roll.

Finally, the food arrived, and she found it delicious, able to bring a smile to Ann's face with her compliment. Soon after the meal ended, Sue left, saying her goodbyes and explaining that she had a lesson to teach.

Ann retreated back to the kitchen, and Travis, after shaking her hand warmly again, said that he needed to get to the Pro Shop.

Instead of being comforted with fewer people at the table, she was left with Carlotta and Roger, their irritation...*or dislike*...for each other now obvious.

"We are very excited about the Southern Living article that will showcase the entire resort but also focus on the house that you'll be decorating," Roger said, smiling at her.

"I'm thrilled to work on this project with you," Sophie replied. "Carlotta has shown me the house, I've taken pictures, and I'm ready to get started."

They continued to chat for several minutes, discussing budget and ideas. She soon relaxed, feeling as though she were in her element. Roger listened enthusiastically to her ideas, making a few suggestions, which she found excellent. He glanced at his watch and scooted back his chair to stand. "I hate to leave such delightful company, but I have a meeting to attend to. I'm sure we'll see quite a bit of each other."

Left alone with Carlotta, she stood as the other woman did, noticing the pinched expression on her face. Walking out of the building, Carlotta said, "Don't let his smooth exterior fool you, my dear. He can be a real charmer when he wants to be." Staring at Sophie, she said, "But he seems taken with you. Perhaps that will make him easier to deal with."

Not knowing how to respond, she climbed into her car and gazed around at the beautiful landscaping as she drove off The Dunes Resort back to town. *Well, that was interesting!* Glad that most of her time would be spent alone in the large, beautiful house, she waved goodbye to Carlotta as she turned on the road toward her home.

13

Callan stood on the dock of the Baytown Harbor watching the Virginia Marine Police handcuff the two men they had just taken off the boat. Both the Coast Guard and the VMP had been called for suspected oyster poachers at one of the many oyster beds in the Bay.

The two officers, Terrence and Bob, marched the men they had arrested to their vehicle, leaving Callan and Ryan to secure the boat while Jarrod piloted the Coast Guard boat back to their dock.

Assisting Ryan with the bagging and tagging of the contraband as well as taking pictures for the police file, the two men chatted easily amongst themselves.

"I talked to your dad for a bit at the last American Legion meeting," Ryan said. "He mentioned that your latest tour of duty is almost up."

Checking the photographs he had taken, he looked over. In many ways, VMP Chief Coates reminded him a great deal of CG Chief Monroe. Both Ryan and Jeff were stocky, well-built men, a little gray at the temples, dedicated, and very intelligent. "Yeah, I need to finalize what I want to do." He was not sure why he gave that last comment to Ryan, but then, it was hardly a secret that he enjoyed being back in his hometown.

"You thinking about re-upping? Got any idea where you might be sent?"

Chuckling, he replied, "Yes and no, in that order."

Bending over to bag more material before placing the evidence tag on it, Ryan laughed as well. "I did two tours in the Navy, then came home to the Eastern Shore. For me, home was the Maryland Eastern Shore. My old man had been a fisherman...fuckin' hard life, but he was good at it. Died early though, not long after he retired. My older brother took up the business, and my mom lives with him and his wife, still in Maryland. When I came back from the Navy, I knew being a fisherman was just not in my blood but being on the water was."

"Yeah, I hear you. Growing up, I knew quite a few people whose parents were in the fishing business, but that wasn't what I wanted. My dad did a tour with the Coast Guard when he was younger and then got out, working for the county at the courthouse in Easton. My mom was a school secretary."

Ryan eyed him, a smile playing about his lips, and asked, "Bet you couldn't wait to get outta here."

Holding the man's gaze with a smile of his own, he said, "You know from our AL meetings that me and all my friends who graduated from high school about the same time joined up, just like you. At that time,

Baytown was too fuckin' small and not enough job opportunities for someone with just a high school diploma. The concrete factory, farm jobs, and fishing were about the only things around."

Bending over to tag a few more bags of evidence, Ryan asked, "If you don't mind me being nosy, what about now?"

Casting his gaze over the Baytown Harbor, as familiar to him as his own home, he sighed. "I was lucky to get the assignment here. Probably got it because as tiny as this Coast Guard station is, nobody really puts in for it." Chuckling, he said, "Let's face it...Baytown is hardly a metropolis with a lot of things to do. For most of the single people here, it's pretty boring. But for me, coming back home to be with my family and my friends who returned has been the best thing for me."

Ryan placed the evidence bags into a plastic container and snapped on the lid. Standing, he turned and faced Callan.

Continuing, Callan said, "I've already let Chief Monroe know that I'm thinking about not re-upping. I don't have long to make up my mind, though. I'd really like to stay in Baytown but need to consider everything."

Nodding, Ryan hefted up the plastic container and the two men walked over to the VMP pickup truck. "I'm gonna take this in, and Terrance will come back and get the boat."

Sticking out his hand toward Callan, Ryan said, "I don't want to make your decision more difficult, but I just want to say that if you ever want a job with the

Marine Police here on the Eastern Shore, I'll reiterate that you have a place. I've got one of my older officers getting ready to retire, and you'd be first on my list for his replacement. I don't want to piss off Jeff if he's trying to get you to reenlist in the Coast Guard, but I figure he knows your heart's still in Baytown."

He watched as Ryan climbed into the pickup truck and drove off, standing in the same spot with his mind in a whirl. Many of the duties of the Coast Guard were mirrored and shared by the Virginia Marine Police, but until recently, he had never thought about changing jobs. He leaned his head back, allowing the sun to fill him with warmth despite the chilly wind that was blowing off the Bay. His lips began curving in a slow smile as the idea of staying in Baytown took hold, now with a more concrete possibility.

Deciding to grab takeout for dinner he drove the couple of blocks and parked outside Stuart's Pharmacy and Diner. As soon as he walked in, he saw a mass of long blond curls hanging over the back of one of the plastic booths. Heading straight over, he observed the table full of papers, cloth swatches, and files. He smiled down and greeted, "Hey, Sophie."

Her head jerked up, and as her eyes moved to his, she smiled widely in return. "Hi, Callan. What are you doing here?"

"I finished my day and came in to get takeout for dinner." He looked down at the table and only saw a soda but no food. "Have you already ordered?"

"There was no one using this booth, so I decided to take a look at my notes while having something to drink. My mom is going to the auxiliary officers' meeting tonight, and Dad is playing poker with the other dads at our house. Once I get inside The Dunes house tomorrow, I can set up one of the rooms as an office, which will be good because I don't really have a place at my parents' house to do that."

"How about we get some food to go and take it back to my place? There's plenty of space for you to spread out because I never use my table. We can eat at the counter, and then you can get some work done if you want."

He watched her face carefully, seeing the wheels turn behind her intelligent eyes. Finally, she nodded, and he felt the weight lift off his chest.

"A couple of burgers and fries okay with you?"

She nodded again, this time her smile wide. He walked over to the counter, ordered two cheeseburgers to go, one without onions, then moved back to sit at the booth while she collected her belongings.

Her eyes were wide as they landed on him, and she asked, "No onions? You remember?"

Chuckling, he said, "Oh, yeah, Sophie." Sobering, he added, "I remember lots of things."

She sucked in her lips, no response coming. The server brought out the Styrofoam boxes in a plastic bag, and Callan paid for their meals while Sophie was still digging in her purse for her wallet.

"I got it," he said, stilling her hands.

Her face scrunched adorably, and for a moment he was reminded of the same look she would give as a child when Philip said something that confused her.

Not about to mention that to her, he just said, "I invited you, so it's my treat."

She stood and collected her satchels, and they walked out of the diner together, his hand resting lightly on the back of her coat. She looked up toward him and smiled but said nothing.

After he saw her to her car, he said, "See you there." She offered a little wave before backing out of her parking space.

Tossing the bag into the front passenger seat, he climbed inside his truck. Thrilled that she had agreed to have dinner with him, even if it was burgers in his little apartment, he followed her.

On the short five-minute drive to her parents' house, she tried to still the butterflies in her stomach. *I'm going to Callan's. Am I crazy?* Arriving there before she had a chance to answer that question, she parked at the back of her parents' lot. Alighting from her car, she smiled as Callan drove in right behind her, parking on the other side of the alley next to his parents' garage. Just before she closed her car door, he shouted, "Bring your things over. You can show me what you're working on."

Nodding her agreement, she reached into the passenger side and grabbed her portfolio and satchel. Walking across the alley, she moved straight toward him, her gaze raking over his handsome body showcased in his uniform.

"This way to my castle in the sky," he quipped, eliciting a giggle from her.

She walked up the stairs to the small landing at his door, waiting until he unlocked it. He swung the door open and motioned for her to enter. He was right behind her and reached his long arm to her side, flipping on the light. The room was large and open, a decent size living room on the left and small dining room and U-shaped kitchen on the right. There was not a hall, but an open door on the back wall exposed the bedroom, and she assumed the bathroom was through there as well.

The walls were painted a soft grey, and the dark blue sofa and dark grey chair in the living room gave the space a masculine, clean feel. The kitchen cabinets were painted white, and the countertops were grey. The floors were hardwood, and in the middle of the living room was a rug with a geometric pattern of gray, black, and blue.

He set the plastic bag on the counter. "You can put your things on the kitchen table if you want. I'll be right back," he said and disappeared through the door. A few minutes later he returned dressed in jeans, a long-sleeved t-shirt, and socked feet.

He walked to the refrigerator and called over his shoulder, "What would you like to drink? I've got beer, water, or orange juice." Turning to look at her, he said, "Sorry. That's not really much of a selection, is it?"

She laughed and said, "A beer is fine, thank you." She moved over to the counter and pulled the Styrofoam boxes out of the plastic bag. Glancing up, she saw that he was taking two plates from the dryer rack in the sink. "Unless you want to get fancy, we can just eat straight out of the boxes. That way you don't have any plates to wash."

Setting the two beers on the counter, he shook his head, grinning. "A woman after my own heart," he said. "Are the burgers still warm, or do I need to nuke 'em?"

"I think we're good," she said, peering into the boxes. "Oh, do you have any ketchup?"

He nodded and turned back to the refrigerator to get it, setting it between the two boxes. Walking around the counter, he hopped up on the stool next to her, his leg pressed alongside hers.

She felt the jolt of electricity and wondered if he felt it as well. He did not move his leg, and she loved the intimacy of having him close. She thought of the past and remembered she always felt that same electricity when they touched.

For the next several minutes they said very little, both enjoying the burgers and fries. Finishing, he wiped his hands on a paper towel and said, "They're not as big as the pub burgers, but when you just want a quick meal, the diner can't be beat."

Nodding enthusiastically, Sophie agreed. "That's why I was there tonight." Leaning in conspiratorially, she said, "But don't tell Katelyn, Aiden, or Brogan!"

"Oh, worse than that," he warned. "Don't you dare tell their grandfather, Finn MacFarlane, that the diner has good burgers!"

Laughing again, she relaxed.

Tossing their Styrofoam boxes and paper towels into

the trash, he grabbed their beers and said, "Why don't we sit over on the sofa, and you can explain your designs at the coffee table. That would be more comfortable."

For the next half hour, she showed him the pictures she had taken of the inside of the house and then opened her portfolio to exhibit some of the designs she was working on.

"I'm going to ask a really dumb question," he said, staring at her drawings. "I know you're going to be filling the rooms with furniture and staging it so that it will look perfect for the magazine shoot. But what's the difference between an interior designer and an interior decorator?"

Thrilled that he was interested, she said, "A lot of people use those two titles interchangeably, but they're really not. To become an interior designer, you have to go to school for that. I went to the design school that was part of Virginia Commonwealth University's Art program. It's the art and science of understanding people's behavior to create their functional space in a building or home. Interior decorating is simply furnishing or adorning a space. Now, interior designers will also decorate, but interior decorators are not designers." Her face scrunched, and she asked, "Did that make any sense, or did I just confuse you more?"

"No, no, it didn't confuse me. Actually, you made perfect sense."

Once again, Callan was giving his full attention to her, and just like the previous evening when they had coffee, she was filled with warmth.

"In this case, I don't have the owners of the house as the clients to let me know what their functionality for the space would be. My clients are The Dunes Resort, and they have set the parameters that they want it to be a space that includes the outdoor environment."

Seeing his raised eyebrows and blank stare, she threw her head back and laughed.

He shook his head and chuckled. "So, beachy?"

"In a way, yes. But we don't want to just regurgitate the same beach themes that you can find in any rental home in Baytown."

"Okay, so none of the wooden signs that say 'What happens at the beach stays at the beach'?"

Laughing again, she said, "Exactly. My design won't be beachy cliché, but I need to bring in the color palette from the area, the textures, and the feel of the Eastern Shore and design each space cohesively."

Flopping back on the sofa, he said, "I'm too simplistic for this, Sophie, but I'm impressed as hell with you."

The warmth she had felt from earlier spread throughout her entire body, and she reached over, taking another long swig of the beer. The winter sun had set earlier, and the only thing seen outside the windows was the dark night. Standing, she was able to observe the back of her parents' house. "It looks like my mom got home."

Callan came and stood next to her, staring out into the night as well. They stayed side-by-side silently for several minutes before the whisper slipped from her lips. "Do you ever wonder...what if..." She shook her head quickly and turned to gather up her papers, hoping he had not heard her question, but her hopes were not to be realized.

He stepped over and stilled her hands by placing his much larger ones on her shoulders. "Yes, I do."

She stared up into his face, her breath shallow, her heart pounding, and her mouth slightly open but saying nothing.

14

Callan kept his eyes on Sophie's face, watching the myriad of emotions so readily visible as they passed through her eyes. Grief warred with uncertainty. Fear tangled with hope. He did not want her to pull away, deny what she was feeling, retreat into herself.

Pressing forward, he said, "It's okay to think *what if.*"

She swallowed audibly and admitted, "It's been ten years, and I still hurt when think about him." Her head moved back and forth slowly as she added, "But I don't really talk about him."

It was on the tip of his tongue to ask her why, but he did not want to break the spell of honest emotion by prodding for fear she would shut down. He kept his hands on her shoulders, fighting the urge to draw her nearer to him while lightly moving his fingers in an effort to help her relax.

"I... I know my parents, whose grief was unbearable, have learned to bear it."

She sucked in her lips, dropping her gaze to his

chest, and he wondered if she was going to pull away from him.

Instead, she continued, "I think...I was afraid to get to a point of acceptance."

Her gaze jumped back to his, as though seeking what his response would be. He held himself steady, hoping that she could see his understanding of anything she was feeling. He slowly slid one hand up, curling his fingers around the back of her neck while his thumb gently caressed the line of her delicate jaw. "I think all those feelings you had, Sophie, are the same that a lot of us had."

Her breath was still shallow as she asked, "Callan, he was your best friend. How did you deal?"

Terrified of breaking the spell, he nonetheless stepped back and pulled her with him, slowly lowering them to the soft cushions of the sofa. Keeping her close, he breathed easier as she acquiesced. He angled his body so that he was slightly facing her, his right arm around her shoulders near the back of the sofa and his left hand holding both of hers tightly in her lap. Sucking in a deep breath, he let it out slowly, gathering his thoughts. His stomach clenched in nervousness, wanting to be honest with her, and yet afraid she might not be receptive to what he was going to say.

Finally, clearing his throat, he said, "It was hard after graduation when we all went our separate ways. I knew that he had found new brothers-in-arms in the Army, just as I had found new companions in the Coast Guard. That didn't diminish our friendship, but time and distance kept us from being as close as we were growing up."

She continued to hold his gaze, and he detected no censure in her eyes, so he continued. "By the time my parents got the news to me, I barely had time to request the personal leave and make it back. It was surreal for all of us Baytown Boys to have been called back to attend his...uh..."

"Funeral," she breathed, her eyes wide but dry.

Nodding, he said, "Yeah." Sucking in another fortifying breath, he said, "I guess it didn't really seem real. It was almost like we were all going through the motions, but it wasn't really Philip that we were burying. I knew that for you and your parents...and for Katelyn, it felt very real."

"When did it hit you?"

"When I saw your face. When I saw your grief." He watched as her head tilted ever so slightly to the side, a question written plainly on her face. "I wanted to comfort you, and when I held you, it felt very real to me."

Her voice, still whispering but now raspy with emotion, said, "And I pushed you away. God, I'm so sorry—"

Shaking his head, he said, "Get that out of your mind, Sophie. You had to do anything and everything you could to keep yourself going." She did not reply, and he continued, "You asked me when it hit me, but I have to confess that after the funeral, when I went back to my station, it still felt very unreal. It felt as though I would get an email from him sometime telling me what was going on. Eventually, the rest of us came back to Baytown at different times. Brogan came home to run the Pub, and then a year later Aiden joined him. Mitch and Grant had their own law enforcement careers and made their way back a couple years later. Zac did the same thing."

"But you, Callan. You stayed in the Coast Guard."

He felt his heart squeeze as her simple statement gently prodded him to look back at the first time he re-upped. *I really didn't know what else to do. But, in my heart, I knew Philip would be disappointed in me.*

"Why would he be disappointed in you?" she asked, her brows low, and a crinkle appeared on her forehead.

Blinking, he realized he had spoken out loud. Giving his head a slight shake, he said, "I... I never really thought about it before. When my first tour was over, I had no idea what I wanted to do besides the Coast Guard, and honestly, I didn't want to come back here and not have him be here. But I should have come back to take care of you. I should never have allowed you to push me away and deal with your grief alone."

She dragged in a ragged breath and said, "Callan, Philip would never have been disappointed in you." She dropped her gaze to their hands clasped together in her lap, and added, "But I know how you felt. I couldn't stand the idea of being in Baytown without him."

She lifted her gaze up to him, and asked, "What changed? Why did you put in for the Baytown Coast Guard station?"

"When I re-upped the second time, things had

changed. The other guys had come back to Baytown. My dad had some health issues—"

Eyes wide, she rushed, "Oh, my God, I'm so sorry. I remember my mom telling me, but..." sighing, she added, "I removed myself so much from here...I haven't been a very good friend."

"Sophie, don't take that on. You've been struggling with the loss of Philip as long as the rest of us have, and it was made worse because he was your brother. Don't take on more guilt."

The heaviness seemed to lift from her face, and she said, "So that's why you came back."

He nodded, giving her hands a squeeze. "It's just that I was, well, I was ready. I wanted to be close to my parents. I wanted to be close to my childhood friends. Hell, I wanted to be close to their parents. And, I wanted to be back in Baytown. I'd been overseas, I'd done tours. I had accomplished what I set out to do, which was see more of the world than just this little town. I did it. So when the opportunity came for me to put in for this Coast Guard station, I jumped at it." Chuckling, he added, "As you can imagine, it wasn't hard to get. This isn't exactly a sought-after post."

Her lips curved into a smile before she laughed along with him. "I'm sure. When I told...uh... someone that I was coming back here for several months, they couldn't believe it."

A squeeze on her hands brought her attention back to Callan, and she lifted her gaze back to him.

"Can I ask you a question? It's personal, and you can tell me it's not my business if you want," he said.

"Callan, right now, I can't imagine anything you could ask me would be considered too personal considering what we've been talking about."

Nodding, he explained, "Yeah, but this is a little different." Exhaling a fortifying breath, he said, "I was chatting with your dad a while back, and he mentioned that they thought you were going to be getting engaged soon." He watched as her shoulders slumped, and he quickly added, "It's okay. You don't have to talk about it. I shouldn't have asked—"

"No, no, it's not that," she said, shaking her head. She was quiet for a moment, appearing to gather her thoughts, and then said, "It's really not that big of a deal. I was dating someone for a while, but eventually, it became evident that he wasn't who I thought he was. Or maybe I realized that I wasn't the person I wanted to be when I was with him."

Dark brows lowering, Callan asked, "Who did he want you to be?"

"He wasn't happy when I quit the job at the agency to start working for myself, even though he knew all the reasons."

Rearing back, his eyebrows shot upward. "I don't understand. First of all, it was your choice, your career. But second of all, why wouldn't he be happy for you to take that amazing leap?"

She barked out a laugh and said, "Amazing leap? He considered it a step in the wrong direction, a risk that I should never have undertaken." Shrugging again, she said, "Sometime, if you want to know, I'll tell you the whole story. For now, let's just say that this opportunity in Baytown came at a good time in my life."

"Sophie, I'm here. Anytime you want to talk, you'll always have a listening ear with me."

"I remember that about you," she said, her smile mixed with a little sadness. "You always were the best listener." Looking at the time on the TV, she said, "This has been lovely, Callan, but I really should get home. I need to spend a little time tonight getting some more things ready for my first full day on the job tomorrow."

He stood, and with his hand still holding onto hers, gently pulled her from the sofa. He helped her gather all her papers back into her portfolio and said, "I'll walk you down."

Laughing, she said, "I don't think I'll get lost since I'm just through the backyard."

"Let's just say I *want* to walk you to your house."

He carried her portfolio and satchel, and together they went down the steps, across the alley, and through her parents' backyard. Stopping at the door, they stood facing each other, the silent night filled with emotions swirling around them.

Everything he had learned about her during the evening had only solidified his desire to spend more time with her. The love he felt for her years ago had never really gone away considering she was still in his heart. But getting to know the adult Sophie was even better.

He sat her satchel on the back patio and moved his hands to her shoulders, pulling her close. He breathed a sigh of relief when her hands glided up to his waist, her fingers gripping his shirt. Their eyes never left each other's, and he broke the silence when he said, "I want to see you. I don't want to make things difficult for you, but if you feel the same, I'd like us to spend as much time together as we can for as long as we have here."

Her lips curved ever so slightly in a smile as she nodded slowly. "I thought this would be hard," she said, her voice barely above a whisper. "I thought reconnecting would open wounds, but I really enjoyed tonight. It's the first time I can remember talking about Philip where I didn't feel gutted afterwards." She tilted her head slightly to the side and said, "I wonder what that means?"

He pulled her tighter, hoping to offer her his comfort and warmth. "It simply means that you can remember Philip fondly, with great love in your heart. Acceptance of grief does not diminish the love you and he shared."

She pulled her lips between her teeth, continuing to nod. Lifting up on her tiptoes, she kissed the corner of his mouth before lowering back to her heels. Turning, she picked up her satchel and moved to the back door, whispering, "Good night, Callan."

Just before she disappeared to the door, he called out, "Can I see you tomorrow?"

Her smile widened, and she nodded. "I'd love that."

He walked back across her backyard, as always memories of them as children racing around in his mind. He jogged up the stairs to his apartment and let himself in, the space feeling less lonely now that he could add memories of the grown-up Sophie having spent time there.

Several hours later, lying in bed, he looked at the last picture taken of him and Philip before they left for boot camps. *You would've always wanted me to take care of her, Philip. When she pushed me away, I let her. But now, I'm gonna see what happens. No matter what, Philip, I'll take care of her.*

"Hey, Sophie," her mother greeted, looking up as Sophie walked into the family room. "Did I hear Callan's voice outside?"

Nodding, she replied, "Yeah, he and I ran into each other at the diner. We decided to get our burgers to go and had them over at his apartment." The words had barely left her mouth when her mom gave a little happy squeal, earning a lifted eyebrow from her dad.

"Tonya," he warned, "go easy."

Shifting her gaze from her dad to her mom, Sophie saw her mother shrug.

"You know I've always had a soft spot for Callan, and one day hoped that...well, let's just say that I'm glad you reconnected with him."

"Did you have a good time?" her dad asked.

She plopped into the chair facing the sofa, and he turned the sound down on the television. Nodding, she said, "Yeah, I did. It was...well, it was the first time that I've talked to anyone about... Philip, except for you two and Katelyn. It just wasn't something I felt like I could do, but I'd forgotten how easy it was to talk to Callan."

Her mother opened her mouth to speak, but her father slid his hand over to Tonya's leg and gave a little squeeze, effectively quieting her.

"I think that's real nice, sweetheart," he said.

She knew her mom was itching to ask her more but was so grateful for her dad's interference. Her parents sought grief counseling after Philip's death, and she had attended a couple of group sessions at the University's counseling center but felt like she just came away sadder, so she quit going.

Standing, she offered a little smile and said, "I'm going to head on up now. I've got some work to do before I turn in, so I'll be prepared for my first day tomorrow." She walked over, hugging her parents tightly.

Her mom patted her back and whispered, "I'm glad you had a good evening."

"Me too," she said before heading up the stairs. Hearing the television volume increase, she hesitated at the top of the stairs, making sure her parents were still downstairs. Walking to Philip's door, she stopped and stepped to the threshold.

The light was turned off, but moonlight was shining through the window. She stepped slightly into the room, her breath halting in her lungs, unsure what she expected to feel. But right then, it just felt like Philip's room from many years ago.

Swallowing deeply, she turned and placed her

fingers on the light switch, hesitating for a moment before flipping it on. The overhead light only had two bulbs in it, casting a soft illumination about the room. The twin size bed that Philip had pushed into the corner to give him more floor space was gone, and in its place was a double bed, covered with a new blue comforter. His nightstand was now in the corner, a small reading lamp and a framed picture the only items resting on it.

Even from where she stood, she could see that it was the last family picture they had taken, the same one she had in her own apartment. She let her breath out slowly, surprised that she was not falling apart. Shifting her gaze to the opposite wall, she saw his closet door closed but had no desire to open it at this time. Whatever secrets it contained or whatever her parents had gone through, she did not want to know.

The bookshelf that had displayed his books and many trophies was no longer against the wall, but the dresser held a couple of his awards. She also decided that she had no desire to open the drawers now and see them empty.

The room looked similar to anyone's guest room, with a few mementos of Philip, her parents' way of moving forward while still holding on to some sweet memories.

No tears. No gasps. No falling into the floor in a puddle of grief. *What have I been so afraid of?* Even as the question moved through her mind, she knew the answer resided in one word...*time*. A sign on the wall of the counseling center at the University had proclaimed,

Grief has no timetable. Everyone moves along the journey at their own pace.

Suddenly exhausted, she backed out of the room, flipping off the light, and moved directly into her bedroom. Foregoing all thoughts of getting some work done, she got ready for bed and climbed under the covers. Turning to her side, she looked out the window and could see a light on in Callan's apartment across the yards. A strange sense of peace filled her for the first time in years. And with that peace came a sense of strength.

15

A cold wind was whipping across the bow of their boat as Callan and Sharon consulted with the Marine Police in the vessel next to them. A fishing boat had called in an alert that a huge sea turtle was ensnared in a fishing net.

Ryan and his officer, Terrence Slidell, were attempting to haul the fishing net closer so they could identify the breed of the turtle and how best to get it free with the least possible injury to the animal.

Callan leaned over the side of his boat to assist as Jarrod steered as close to the fishing vessel as he could. Sharon called out that the Virginia Aquarium's Stranding Response Team's boat was en route. Dressed for the cold weather, Callan still struggled against the wind.

Looking over at Ryan on the VMP boat, he yelled, "How big is this turtle? It weighs a ton!"

Sharon, standing nearby, said, "If it's a loggerhead, it

could be up to 300 pounds. Damn, it really should be further south this time of year."

He twisted his head back to look at her and said, "Do you think we can get the fishermen to winch up the net a little bit further without endangering the turtle?"

She radioed the fishermen, and within a minute the net was lifted a few more feet, just enough for him to be able to see that it was, indeed, a loggerhead.

"The Response Stranding Team is here," she called out, and Callan glanced to the side to see another boat coming in.

The leader from the Aquarium conversed with Ryan for a few minutes and then relayed the instructions to Callan. He continued to haul up his side of the net as one of the Stranding Team members crossed over to his boat.

"Hey, I'm Julie," the team member introduced. "If we can get it closer, I can evaluate it, and hopefully, we can set it free uninjured."

"I'm equipped to get into the water if needed," he said. Finally, the turtle's head broke the surface, and he called out to the others. The fishing boat pulled up the slack in the net, allowing more of the turtle to be seen.

"A loggerhead," Julie confirmed. As Callan and Terrence worked to keep the turtle stable, Julie measured the length and width, estimating its weight and age. "Okay, you can cut it loose," she said.

As Ryan continued to hold the net steady from his vessel, Callan began carefully cutting the ropes that were around the turtle's neck and fore-flippers while Terrence cut around the hind-flippers. After just a few minutes the turtle slipped away from the net, moving back under the water. It stayed near the surface for a few minutes as it made its way beyond the boats before they lost sight of it as it went deeper under the water.

Giving the fishermen the signal, they finished hauling in the net. Callan knew that Ryan would be getting the statement from the fishing captain, and he stood, walking away from the edge of the vessel.

Sharon and Julie were conversing, and he asked, "So, how big do you think it was?"

"It was just over 40 inches in length, and I would say close to 250 to 300 pounds," Julie said, shaking her head. "I'm surprised it's still here and not south to at least to North or South Carolina. Hopefully, it'll head back out of the Bay and end up down there."

Sharon and Julie continued to share information before Julie crossed back over to the Virginia Aquarium boat, waving goodbye.

Walking to Jarrod, who was steering the RB-M back to the harbor, Callan grinned. "I gotta tell you, I had no idea if that turtle would be alive or not. It's a fuckin' good feeling to have rescued it."

The idea crossed his mind that he wanted to share the experience with Sophie but hated to call her at work. They had both been busy for the past several days but had found time to text occasionally and chat in the evenings. Even as a teenager, he had found it easy to talk to her and was not surprised to find that as an adult, it was the same.

Checking his watch, he decided to send her a text. **Are you up for dinner tonight?**

He had no idea when she might be able to respond, but was thrilled when she texted, **Absolutely**.

Now grinning widely, he stood on the bow of the boat, barely feeling the bite of the winter wind.

Over the past four days, Sophie had not only decided on the color palette for each of the downstairs rooms but made sure to tie it together with an overall vision. Carlotta had given her permission to move forward in any direction she wanted as long as it fell within the budget she had been given in the proposal that had been agreed upon.

Wanting to add color and textural elements of the Chesapeake Bay into the décor, she decided to take a golf cart ride around the area to look at the foliage. The sun was shining, but she knew it was a windy day and wrapped a scarf around her neck before putting on her coat. Making sure she had her phone with her, she pulled on her gloves and moved into the garage, where a golf cart for her use was parked.

The wind was brisk, but she felt a sudden freedom as she drove down the lane and turned onto one of the golf cart paths. During the warmer months, she would not be allowed to have a golf cart on the course, or even the course paths, in deference to the golfers who paid a premium price for the beauty around them. But there were no golfers today, and she was excited to look around.

Winter gave off a completely different color vibe

than the other three seasons, but with her imagination and some research, she would be able to discern what items would be best for the interior of the home.

Pruned rose bushes were all around, but she preferred looking for what was naturally growing, not specifically planted by a landscaper. Stately pine trees filled the area, and the dark, rough bark caught her attention. Pinecones littered the ground, and she determined to come back early the next week with some bags so that she could gather some.

Red chokeberry with its dark green, glossy leaves still had the orange-red berries. Winterberry shrubs had lost their green but were filled with bright red berries. Deciding that she wanted to capture some of the berry colors, she pulled out her phone and snapped more pictures. A flash of purple captured her attention, and she drove to the side of the path and parked. Walking between some shrubs, she discovered mulberry bushes, their purple berry clusters brilliant against the dark green leaves.

Closer to the shore, she found beach grass, brushy bluestem, and upright sedge. Excited over her finds, she circled around to the side of the resort that was away from the beach. Continuing on the path that led to one of the many Bay inlets, tall reeds captured her attention.

Cattails! A memory of she and her grandmother snipping cattails to place in tall vases came to mind. In the winter the stalks were brown, but many of the plants still had their tall tuffs. She now changed her mind as to what kind of bag she would need to bring with her on her next trip, wanting one large enough to hold the snipped cattails that she planned on gathering.

As the path meandered along the golf course near some woods, she caught sight of woodpeckers, cardinals, blue jays, and the occasional vulture flying overhead. Continuing near the Bay, seagulls, geese, ducks, and terns were all along the water.

Snapping pictures as she occasionally stopped, design ideas began to flow along with the excitement the creative process brought. By now, she was quite chilly in spite of her warm clothes when a strong breeze hit her, and she headed back to the large house.

Scrolling through her photographs, she decided on warm brown as her anchor color, with teal, orange, and yellow as the accents, bringing in the colors of the sea, land, and sunset. Sitting down at the counter in the kitchen, she sketched out several designs and begin working on her computer. Her stomach growled, drawing her attention to the time. Calling it a day, she packed up her portfolios, wondering where Callan and she would have dinner.

With a light step, she locked up the house and moved to her car. Sending him a text letting him know that she was heading home, she drove away, her back window illuminated with the sunset.

"It's been years since I've been here," Sophie said, gazing around at the inside of the Sunset Restaurant. "In fact, it went by a different name when it first opened."

Nodding, Callan said, "It was bought about five years ago by a New York businessman. I wasn't here at the time, but my parents told me that there was a question as to whether or not he would keep the restaurant open. I think everyone was glad when it did reopen, even with a name change and a different menu."

They were sitting in a back, corner table, and while the sun had already set, they were able to see lights reflecting on the water as well as the lights on the ships anchored in the Bay.

Callan stared at her profile as she gazed out the window. The Bayles family members were all blond in such contrast to his dark-haired family. He remembered Philip's hair being almost white-blond when they were very little, slowly changing over to a darker color but still thick and curly. As a child, Sophie's hair had been an unruly riot of yellow curls. He found it strangely comforting that while styled, she still had the mass of curls hanging down her back.

"Philip brought me here."

He startled at her words, her voice so soft that he wondered if she realized she had spoken aloud. Deciding not to question her, he was pleased when she turned her head toward him, a wistful smile on her lips.

"It was the night before I turned fifteen. He was a senior and said I should have a grown-up night. So he dressed in a suit, and I put on a dress, and he brought me here. I can even remember what we ate. He had a steak, and I had shrimp. We got virgin cocktails, and I thought it was so much fun pretending to be such big deals when we were just little town kids."

Her hand was resting on the crisp, white tablecloth, and he reached over to enclose it in his much larger one. Giving it a little squeeze, he said, "I knew Philip as well as I knew myself. Taking you out that night for your birthday meant just as much to him as it did to you."

Her lips curved slightly, and she added, "This was something else that I had forgotten. When he toasted my birthday, he said that when we grew up, he'd always take me out for my birthday." A little sigh escaped, and she said, "What would I have done differently if I'd known that was never going to happen?"

He observed her carefully, but she remained clear-eyed, so he said, "I think it's better that we didn't know. That meant that every moment we had with him was spent doing fun things in a normal way." Rubbing his thumb over her knuckles, he continued, "Sometimes I think about him and what he'd be like now. When the AL members are coaching the kids, I can almost imagine him in the outfield, laughing and joking with them."

"I've never been to one of those games, but it's not hard for me to imagine him doing exactly as you say. I find myself thinking about what he would've thought about my life. You know, my apartment in Richmond, my job change." Rolling her eyes, she added, "God, if he knew what I'd gone through, he would have been so mad."

Brows slamming down, he asked, "Mad? Are you referring to what happened with that dickhead ex-boyfriend of yours?"

Laughing, she said, "Well, him too. But I was thinking about my former job."

Their salads arrived, and for a few minutes he allowed her a chance to eat, but the questions burned inside of him. Finally, she pushed her plate to the side, and he jumped in. "Will you tell me what happened?"

She held his gaze for a few seconds, then nodded with an air of resignation. "It's really a tale as old as time. I had a male coworker who was harassing me. Nothing physical, but a lot of sexual innuendos coming my way. It started slow, and no matter how much I protested, it continued. "

His voice low, he growled, "You've got to be shitting me."

Shrugging, she shook her head. "Nope. I tried talking to my boyfriend, who just kept telling me to put up with it. He said boys will be boys, and as long as the man had not actually touched me, then I had no real complaint."

Rearing back, Callan felt the heat of anger flush through his body. The server came by to pick up their salad plates and ask if they needed their drinks refilled but backed away quickly when Callan turned his angry gaze toward him.

"Callan," Sophie whispered, placing her hand on his arm. "Don't scare the server."

His gaze jerked back to hers, and he said, "Sophie, this is no laughing matter."

She patted his arm and said, "I know it's not. But it's over and done."

"You filed a complaint, right?"

"I went to the head of the company and was told by him that if I wanted to continue my career, then I did not want to rock the boat."

At that point, Callan dropped his chin, focusing on breathing. He could not remember the last time he was this angry, and his blood roared throughout his body. He felt a gentle touch on his arm and lifted his chin to see Sophie's blue-green eyes filled with worry. "I'm okay, Sophie. I just can't believe you had to go through that."

"I did file with the EEOC but also decided that it wasn't worth my time and energy to stay in the company. So, I turned in my notice and filed for my own business license. Obviously, I couldn't take any of my former clients with me, but they made a few recommendations so that I was able to have some clients right off the bat."

Her gentle touch on his arm began to have the desired effect, and he found himself calming. She sighed, and he looked at her, seeing her gaze staring back out the window.

"It's times like those that I would find myself thinking about Philip. What would he have told me to do? Would he have been upset with how I handled things?"

Leaning so that his face was close to hers, Callan said, "I can tell you exactly what he would have done. He would have confided in me, and the two of us would've showed up at your workplace, beat the shit out of your coworker, threatened your boss with a lawsuit, and then gone to your apartment and thrown out your worthless boyfriend."

He had no idea what reaction Sophie would have to his words, but she stared, speechless for a moment. Then she threw her head back and began to laugh. Long, hard, and joyfully. And the sight was fuckin' beautiful.

16

It felt so good to laugh. Sophie could not remember the last time she had laughed with such abandon. When she finally gained control of herself, wiping under her eyes to check her mascara, she focused on Callan's face. He no longer wore a scowl but a strange, at-ease expression she could not define.

"I can see you and Philip doing exactly that," she admitted, her smile still firmly on her face. Sobering slightly, she held his dark-eyed gaze and said, "Thank you."

He blinked then asked, "What are you thanking me for?"

"For one, it's been a long time since I've laughed like that," she confessed. "And you've made me think and talk about Philip in ways that haven't made me sad."

The server brought their dinners, and she could not help but compare this meal to the one she had many years ago with her brother. Callan had ordered steak, and she had ordered the shrimp. Deciding to share, she accepted some of the delicious beef on her plate while spooning some of the shrimp onto his.

They ate, their conversation no longer heavy but caught up on each other's lives. She was surprised to learn that his older sister was married, had two children, and was living in Alexandria.

"Her husband works for the government, and they seem happy. They make a trip down here about once every other month, and Mom and Dad go up to see them on opposite months. I haven't been up there yet, but I see them at holidays."

"Tell me about your job," she asked, spearing another shrimp.

He grinned widely and said, "I forgot to tell you of my exciting news today. We rescued a loggerhead sea turtle that was estimated to be close to three-hundred pounds."

Eyes wide, she quickly chewed and swallowed before exclaiming, "You're kidding! I had no idea that was something you'd do."

Nodding, he said, "It's not that common, but we assist the Virginia Aquarium when someone calls in a stranded or endangered animal. The sea turtle was caught in a fisherman's net. He did the right thing by calling it in. The Virginia Marine Police came along with us, and we were able to rescue it with the assistance of the Stranding Team from the Virginia Aquarium."

"Tell me more," she demanded softly, her eyes pinned on him.

"I never know what each day will bring. Some days

are so busy we don't get a break, and we sure as hell don't leave at the end of the shift. Other days are more routine, and we spend time taking care of some of the equipment. Our responsibility covers about 20 miles of the Atlantic coastline as well as the lower portion of the Chesapeake Bay. That also includes all the small tributaries...the little inlets around. We assist in medical rescues, search and seizure, boating assistance, screen inspecting foreign freight vessels, practice mobilization exercises. I guess the list just keeps going."

She nodded slowly and then asked, "And when you were overseas?"

He appeared to choose his words carefully, saying, "The Coast Guard can be called up by the Department of Navy, and that's what happened then. That hasn't happened in a while, and so our duties are here."

Having finished her meal, she placed her silverware onto her plate, taking a sip of wine, her eyes never leaving his face. "You love your job." It wasn't a question. She could see the evidence written on him.

He nodded slowly, then took a sip of his wine as well. "Yes...but I'm facing some big decisions."

Cocking her head to the side, she said, "Tell me."

"I've only got a couple of months to decide if I want to reenlist or leave the Coast Guard."

"But you just said you love it," she exclaimed.

Continuing, he said, "I do. I absolutely love my duties, but the Coast Guard is not the only one employing those skills. If I stay in the Coast Guard, I'll eventually have to leave Baytown, and now that I've been back here, I don't really want to do that." Laughing, he added, "I don't want to keep living over my parents' garage, but if I stayed, I would like to get my own place. I'd like to be near my parents as they get older, and I have to admit that being back around all our friends plus making new ones through the AL makes it very hard to think about leaving."

"What would you do?"

"Most likely, I would apply to be an officer with the Virginia Marine Police. They have many of the same duties that we do, but they are, obviously, Virginia and not national."

They ordered dessert, and she busied herself with the delectable chocolate lava cake and salted caramel ice cream. Her mind rolled back to the day of Philip's funeral when she pushed Callan away in an effort to safeguard her heart. *He's thinking of leaving the Guard. Does that change things between us? Should it change things?* She was no longer a grief-ridden, scared eighteen-year-old. Ten years was a long time for both of them to mature. *So maybe where we are now gives us a new chance.* Rolling the cake over her tongue, the warm chocolate slid down her throat as she swirled her spoon through the ice cream.

"Hey," his soft voice broke into her musings. "Are you slipping into a dessert coma?"

She looked up, his handsome face so close to hers. He had always been more mature than the other boys, even growing up. There was a seriousness about him, in such contrast to Philip, who loved to laugh and had an infectious sense of humor. But she had always been drawn to that side of Callan.

His brow wrinkled as he asked, "Are you okay?"

She smiled and nodded, replying, "Yeah." Pushing her dessert plate away, she said, "I'm absolutely stuffed, but this has been the nicest date I've had in a very long time. In fact, it's been the nicest date I've ever had."

Grinning widely, he agreed. "Same for me, Sophie."

As he assisted her into his truck, she held onto his arm, gaining his attention. "Callan, before we go home, I wondered if we could take a little drive. There's somewhere I'd like to go, and I'd like you to take me."

Callan was so uncertain that where they were going was the right thing to do. The date had been perfect… Sophie was gorgeous, the conversation enjoyable, and they had reconnected in a way that he never thought possible. But now?

Sophie remained quiet on the short drive, having passed the edge of town and now on a road leading to the Baytown Cemetery. As the truck turned off the road and into the cemetery, she said, "I haven't been here since the funeral."

Her words shocked him but not with judgment. Instead, his heart ached for her. He knew that visiting cemeteries was a very private, individual decision. For some, visiting the gravesite of a loved one is too painful, even years later. For others, frequent visits make them feel closer to the person who had died.

The only light available was from his headlights, and as he parked, he angled the truck so that the beam was facing Philip's headstone. He hesitated, not knowing what she wanted to do.

"Do you come here?" Her soft voice, barely above a whisper, caused him to turn his head and look at her, finding her gaze staring out the windshield.

"It used to be the first place I'd come to when I came to visit my parents. In the last couple of years, the guys and I come out here on Philip's birthday."

"That wasn't long ago," she murmured. She turned her head and stared at him, a slight smile on her face. "What do you do out here?"

"We stand quietly in a circle for a few minutes, each to our own thoughts. Then we pop the tops off our beer and offer a toast to Philip." Unable to keep the chuckle from slipping out, he grinned. "We never got to have a beer together once we were all of legal age, but I confess we shared a few when we were still in high school."

The silence in the truck had him wondering what her thoughts were about the Baytown Boys' remembrance tradition. He reached up to loosen his tie, the truck cab suddenly feeling warm in spite of the chill outside.

"I think that's perfect," she finally said.

"Really?"

Nodding, she smiled. "I think if Philip had known what was going to happen to him and could have a wish about how he would want his best friends to remember him, it would be exactly as you described."

Those words coming from Sophie filled his heart. He reached his hand across the console, clasping her cold fingers in his. "Gotta tell you, Sophie, that means the world to me to hear you say that."

Her smile faded, and she said, "It's a wonderful tradition. It makes me ashamed."

His fingers spasmed as her words stunned him. "Ashamed? Sophie, you should never be ashamed!"

She met his eyes, shaking her head slightly and said, "Callan, didn't you hear me? I haven't been here since the funeral...ten years ago."

"Sophie, if you're expecting me to think less of you, then you're wrong."

She turned her gaze back out toward the windshield, and he could no longer see what thoughts might be passing behind her eyes. Continuing, he said, "Everybody's got their own way of handling grief. Katelyn came out here all the time from what Aiden and Brogan said."

At that, her head swung back sharply toward his. She opened her mouth as though to speak, then snapped it closed.

Continuing to press, he said, "She'd come out here and sob until she was almost sick. Aiden, Brogan, or their dad would follow her out here. They'd stay in the background and then pick her up, carry her home, and her mom would sit with her until she finally went to sleep." Squeezing her fingers again, he added, "I don't know about you, Sophie, but that doesn't sound too healthy to me. That went on for several years before she finally began to start living again. At least by the time she met Gareth, she had gotten to the point of acceptance with Philip's death that she was receptive to love."

She remained silent, but he did not want her to feel guilty. "Tell me why you never came," he gently prodded.

Her voice hesitant at first, she said, "For the first couple of weeks after he died, I would go into his room. I suppose, like Katelyn, I would sob until I almost made myself sick, and my parents would have to put me back in my room. And then, one day, it was as though a switch had been flipped, and I realized he was never going to be back in that room again. So I didn't go either. I left for college soon after and threw myself into that life, never having anyone to really talk to about him. Looking back, I can see I used avoidance as a crutch." Sighing, she added, "It's one of the reasons I decided to take the job here. I did need the work, but I wasn't sure at first if I could do it. Come back here…be surrounded by everything that reminds me of Philip. I hadn't actually been back in his room in years, almost as though I was afraid to." She looked at him and said, "I went in there the other night after we talked. Talking to you about Philip was such a relief. It made me realize that I can remember him without falling apart."

"Don't you see why I don't want you to feel guilty? You didn't need to come to a cemetery to *be* with Philip…to remember him. You've kept him in your heart, and that's what works for you."

She sucked in her lips, not saying anything, but reached for her door handle. Another squeeze on her fingers indicated he wanted her to wait, and he hopped out of the driver's side and rounded the front of the truck. Assisting her down, he wrapped his arm around her and tucked her in close to his body, offering his warmth and strength.

Sophie, enveloped in Callan's embrace, stared down at the headstone that was lit by the beams from his headlights. The engraving in the marble stood out in relief.

SFC. Philip Michael Bayles
He loved his family. He served his country.
He is not forgotten.

She knelt and traced the letters with her finger. "It's actually beautiful, isn't it?"

He knelt beside her and agreed. "Yeah, it is. And the last line? He is not forgotten. It's true, Sophie. He hasn't been forgotten by your parents, although I can't imagine the pain they've gone through. He hasn't been forgotten by Katelyn, who still holds him in her heart even though she's now married and has a baby. He hasn't been forgotten by any of us, and we know that one day this cemetery will hold more of us than just him. And, sweetheart, he hasn't been forgotten by you. You've carried him in your heart and always will."

She pulled her glove off and kissed her finger before placing it over his name. Callan assisted her to stand, wrapping his arms around her once more, pulling her tightly into his chest.

She heaved a sigh and felt a weight rising from her. Leaning her head back, she stared into the face of the man she fell in love with when she was a little girl and had never truly stopped loving. She whispered, "I'm so sorry. I'm so sorry I pushed you away."

His eyes were warm on her and he said, "Don't be, Sophie. You were very young...hell, so was I. We needed to live our lives and grow up. We've had a lot of experiences in the last ten years, and I firmly believe that all of life has lessons to teach."

She lifted her arms and wrapped her hands behind his neck. "What now?"

He lowered his head, holding his lips a breath away from hers, hesitating as though seeking permission. Lifting on her toes, she closed the space and melded her lips with his. She remembered their first kiss, and as good as it was, he was a far better kisser now. She sighed against his mouth, and he slipped his tongue inside, moving it slowly against hers. It was not the kind of kiss that was a precursor to sex or one that flamed hot immediately. Instead, it was a slow burn, the kiss mimicking the meeting of two hearts.

He lifted his head, and with his fingers tangled in her curls, pressed her head against his chest. Kissing the top of her hair, he said, "You asked what now...now, it's time for us."

Sophie stood in the model home kitchen, the room she had decided to start with. She did not care if it was a cottage or a million-dollar house, she felt that the kitchen was the heart of any home. With white cabinets and white tile backsplash, she brought warmth and color into the space with pale yellow walls, glass accent lights, an oak table and chairs, and teal and cream accessories. The tall, high-back stools at the kitchen counter were also in oak.

The dishware that she had ordered was supposed to be delivered within the next couple of days, so she moved into the butler's pantry, pleased with the continued teal and cream color scheme. The dining room had also been painted pale yellow, and she was still waiting for the rug that she had ordered to go under the long, white dining room table. One wall held white built-in shelves, the back painted a shade deeper yellow.

Walking into the massive formal living room, she

inspected the dark brown textured accent wall. Deciding to leave the other three walls pale cream, she could not wait to see it once the furniture arrived. Balancing colors and textures in her pallet, it was easy for her to imagine the excitement that someone would feel when they entered that space.

With no curtains on the windows yet, the sun streamed through, and she walked over and looked toward the dunes. Deciding it was the perfect time to start collecting plants to use in décor, she grabbed her coat and purse and headed to the golf cart.

An hour later, she had sprigs of mulberry, Winterberry, Magnolia leaves, and a huge gathering of pinecones.

Desiring to go after some of the cattails that she had seen the week before, she put her bags of foliage into the seat and pulled back onto the golf cart path. The day was cold, the air crisp, but with the sun shining, her mood felt light.

Inhaling deeply, her mind wandered to the last week with Callan. Texting, talking, grabbing lunch at the diner when their schedules permitted, and late-night phone calls after hanging in his apartment. They had kissed, sometimes for what seemed like hours, but he had never pushed for more. She did not know why he was holding back, but knowing Callan the way she did, she felt certain he was taking things slow for her.

She had been in town for a month and had to admit that being back in Baytown had been good for her. She was looking forward to the evening's activities, which included a girls-only party. Since college, she had occasionally gone out with friends from work but had never had as much fun as she did when hanging with her Baytown friends.

Once again, she was struck with the beauty of The Dunes Resort. She knew in warmer weather golfers would be around in abundance, but now she felt as though she had the entire place to herself. There were certainly full-time residents that lived in the various neighborhoods, but much of the area was uninhabited and unspoiled.

Climbing from the golf cart when she reached her destination, she was glad she had brought rubber boots. Pulling off her dress boots, she slid her feet into the old muck boots she had found at her parents' house and walked toward the edge of the marshy inlet.

Stepping carefully, she bent to snip some of the tall reeds growing at the water's edge. This area was so different from the beach side, the trees and shrubs much thicker. Nearby was a section of the golf course near some wooded lots that had not been sold yet. It was one of the neighborhoods that The Dunes had not finished developing, and so it retained its natural state.

She had slung the collecting bag over her shoulder and had it almost full of cattails when something caught her eye. It appeared to be a bag, and she waded further into the water to see if she could snag it, hating the idea of pollution in the area.

Getting closer, she could see it was not plastic but appeared to be made of waterproof canvas. The water was almost to the top of her rubber boots and she did not want to go further. Leaning as far as she could reach, she managed to grab a corner, pulling it toward her.

There were no identifying marks on the bag, and she carried it as she walked back to solid ground. Once she was at the golf cart, she carefully set the bag of plants that she had slung over her shoulders to the seat and turned her attention to the canvas bag.

A strange smell rose from the bag, and she recoiled. Setting it on the ground, she stared for a moment, wondering if she should open it. Finally, deciding that she should at least look at the contents before throwing it into the garbage, she knelt next to the bag and flipped open the clip that held it together.

Pulling the flap back she peered inside at a multitude of smaller plastic Ziploc bags with melted freezer packs stuffed among them. She picked up the one on top and stared at the contents while giving her head a shake at the odor. *Crabmeat? Is that crab meat?*

Determining it was, she had no desire to open the bag and let the stench further assault her senses. *Good God, someone must have dropped this from their fishing boat! Ugh!* She let the plastic bag drop back into the canvas satchel and stood. Placing it on the back of the golf cart, not wanting it near her, she remembered seeing a trash dumpster discreetly hidden behind some tall bushes near one of the neighborhoods.

Driving there, she tossed the bag into the dumpster, glad to have gotten rid of it. Twisting around, she glanced behind her, a strange sense of being watched filling her. Seeing no one, hearing nothing, she gave her head a shake at the fanciful notion.

Climbing into the golf cart once more, she headed back to the model home, ready for her afternoon of decorating with Eastern Shore nature.

Sophie stood on the back deck of Belle's house, entranced with the beautiful two-story home that Belle's husband, Hunter, had built for her. When she had arrived, the wide front porch greeted her, and her eyes were drawn to the porch swing. The house still had a new feel to it, and while Belle had apologized at its incompleteness, Sophie thought it was enchanting.

A chilly wind blew off the Bay, and she turned, staring through the sliding glass door into the large kitchen where the other women were gathered around the island. She remembered Belle from her childhood years, always thinking her name was special since it was a Disney Princess name. Belle had certainly grown up to be a beautiful woman, curvy with long blond hair. She had a quiet smile that instantly warmed and comforted. It was not hard to imagine that she was the head nurse for a local assisted living facility.

Jillian, still as pretty as the homecoming queen she had been in high school, had adopted a fun appearance with bright clothes and her sandy blond hair pulled back in a long braid. The artwork that she displayed in the Galleria of her coffee shop showcased her eclectic taste in local art. Katelyn, the athletic one in high school, now had motherhood softening her features. Her dark hair, so like all the other MacFarlanes', was being passed on to her little boy, Finn. It was hard to imagine that she was now a private investigator, and yet Sophie always remembered that Katelyn had a strong sense of right and wrong.

She was saddened to learn of Tori's grandmother's passing, remembering fondly the many cookies they used to enjoy under the large magnolia in her backyard. But she was thrilled that Tori had inherited the Sea Glass Inn, continuing the tradition. She knew that Mitch had had a special place in his heart for Tori when they were children, and the idea that they were now married with a child just seemed right. Tori's thick auburn hair had been cut in a sleek shoulder-length bob, and as Sophie pushed her wind-blown curls back from her face, she was envious of hair that would stay in place.

The other women that were new to Baytown, obviously welcomed into the fold, were equally as nice. Ginny, a police officer in town, was quiet and very observant, but with a ready smile, she joked and laughed with the other women. It was hard at first to imagine her with Brogan, but once she saw them together, it was obvious they were a perfect fit. She had seen Ginny in town, wearing the police uniform of khaki pants, paired with a long-sleeved shirt with BPD logo, her brown hair pulled up in a regulation bun. Tonight, with her hair down and in jeans paired with a slouchy sweatshirt, she looked more at ease.

Jade, a teacher at the elementary school, had green eyes that always seemed to be smiling. A newcomer to the area, she had met and married one of the veterans that Mitch had invited to live in Baytown. Sophie had met Lia's adorable daughter earlier in the week when Aiden was entertaining her at the Pub. Emily looked so much like her mother, with long dark hair and warm brown eyes. At first, she had a hard time imagining Aiden as a father, but seeing him with Lia's daughter, it was obvious he was in love with not only the mother but the child as well.

The last woman in the group was Madelyn, one of the counselors in town. Open, friendly, and easy to talk to, Madelyn had casually mentioned to Sophie that if she ever wanted to talk, she was available. Zac had spent many nights at the Bayles' house, growing close to their family. It was not until she was an adult that she understood that Zac's father, an alcoholic, was the reason he so often escaped. Madelyn seemed to be the perfect mate for the easy-going Zac.

Philip would like them. Blinking, she wondered where that thought had come from. She glanced out to her beloved Bay and had the strangest feeling that if he was standing next to her, he would be smiling at the scene inside the house as well. Contentment passed through her at the thought, and she sighed lightly.

Another cold breeze blew across the deck, and Sophie shivered, deciding to go in. Stepping through the sliding glass door, the other women looked up and smiled.

"I was afraid you were going to freeze out there," Katelyn said, setting a bowl of potato salad on the large island that was already filling with food.

From what Katelyn had told her, they started as a

small group of old friends getting together for wedding planning when the first of them were getting married. Of course, Katelyn had also indicated that wedding planning involved copious amounts of alcohol and dancing. Jillian, Katelyn, and Tori had welcomed each new member of the Baytown Boys' women to their group, and they were just as tight-knit as always.

"Are you okay, Sophie?" Jillian asked softly.

Blurting, "I was just thinking about how much I've missed out on over the past several years. Seeing all of you here together reminds me that by avoiding Baytown, I've also lost out on time with my dearest old friends and making new ones here."

Sophie blinked as soon as the words had left her mouth, stunned that she had said them out loud. Her gaze darted about the room, only seeing understanding and warmth coming from each of the other women.

"I'm sorry," she said, her hands lifted upward as she shrugged. "This was not the right time to have said such a depressing comment."

The other women immediately began to protest, and Katelyn was the loudest. "Oh no, you don't take that back at all! This is the exact right group of people to say whatever you want to and let your feelings all hang out."

"Sophie, you've always been in our hearts, even if you weren't right here with us," Tori said. "No one has ever judged you, and we're not about to start now."

Since she had spoken aloud, the desire to keep doing so was overwhelming. "I never had anyone in college or even in the last years with my job where I had a chance to talk about Philip. At first, it was too painful, and then it simply became something that was private. Being back here, I realize that deciding to grieve all by myself might not have been the healthiest decision."

Madelyn, standing next to her, placed her hand gently on Sophie's arm. "We each handle our grief very individually. I didn't handle things very well when my estranged father died last year. And Zac certainly had not come to full grips with the death of his father either."

Katelyn, standing on the opposite side of the island, leaned forward and admitted, "Who's to say that if you had stayed here or came back often, you would've handled things any better? I was here, but it's no secret that my frequent sobbing marathons did not do much to assist me in dealing with my grief."

She and Katelyn shared a long look, their love for Philip binding them. Deciding to let it all go, she said, "I had Callan take me to the cemetery the other evening after our date. It was the first time I've been back since the funeral."

If she expected to see censure in their eyes, she was relieved to find there was none. Although the heaviness was broken when Jillian commented, "That's sort of an unusual place to go for a first date."

The silence in the room was such that she could not hear anyone breathe as their eyes widened and they stared at Jillian. Suddenly, the humor of what Jillian said struck home, and Sophie burst out laughing. "I suppose it's a testament to Callan that he took me without complaining."

Seeing that she was not going to burst into tears, the

others began to giggle as well. Jillian ran around the island and threw her arms around Sophie, pulling her in for a hug. "I did not mean to joke about something so serious. God, I'm sorry. It just slipped out."

Hugging her back, Sophie laughed. "No, Jillian, you're exactly right. It was our first date, we had a lovely dinner at The Sunset Restaurant, and then I asked him to take me to the cemetery."

As their mirth faded, they turned their attention to the food. Not waiting, they loaded their plates, stood around the kitchen island and moaned over the delicious offerings.

Madelyn asked, "I'm assuming from what you've said that going to the cemetery that night was okay?"

Nodding, she said, "Yes. After I asked him to take me, I almost panicked...wondered if I was crazy. I realized that I was holding on to fear. Fear of going into Philip's old room. Fear of going to the cemetery. I know a lot of that fear stemmed from me being so young when he died, and it just became easier to stay away than to deal with it." Shrugging, she took a sip of wine and said, "Callan has been a big help in that. He and I've talked a lot about Philip, and I've been facing my fears. I know that I still love my brother as much as I always did. I still miss him, and everything special in my life that happens, I will always think about him being there with me. But having someone to talk to about Philip has helped me move past my fears."

The others chimed in their happiness, and Madelyn admitted, "Sounds like Callan's done a good job of doing exactly what I would've done if you were in counseling. Letting you know that we each have our own grief journey and helping you face fears."

"And," Jillian added, "you get the added bonus of being able to kiss Callan, which you wouldn't get to do in counseling!"

That comment added a new round of questions about her renewed relationship with him. Blushing, she replied, "For those of you who weren't here when we were younger, Callan was my secret crush for years, but being several years behind him in school there wasn't much I could do about it. By the time he was a senior and I was a sophomore, though, he did take me to prom."

"Ooohhh, I love these kind of stories," Jade said, her eyes riveted to Sophie's.

"He was always unforgettable since he was my first kiss," she admitted.

Eyebrows lifted, Katelyn said, "I know he hasn't been your only kiss, but do you think he might be your last?"

Her brow crinkled as she pondered Katelyn's question. "I...I don't know. Life is complicated. I guess I really haven't figured that part out."

Deciding to get more comfortable, the women grabbed all the bowls of food and carried them over to the coffee table in the large den. Some sitting on comfortable chairs, others piled up in the floor, they continued to eat, drink, and talk. Now that the conversations turned to the others, she learned more about their lives and jobs.

"Oh," exclaimed Belle, placing her now-empty plate onto the table. "Do you all remember Rose? Rose

Parker? She wanted to open an ice cream shop in town but had to leave to take care of a relative?"

Sophie watched as Jillian, Katelyn, and Tori nodded, and Belle continued. "Well, she's just placed her mother in the nursing home. I wouldn't be able to tell you that due to privacy issues, but she said it was fine for me to let you know."

"Oh, is she moving back here?" Tori asked.

Katelyn jumped in, "Will she open her shop?"

Shrugging, Belle said, "I don't know about the shop, but yes, she's moving back. I get the feeling that the last few years have been hard on her."

"Well, as soon as she moves here, we need to have a welcome back party," Jillian pronounced, and the others nodded their agreement.

Sophie, sitting quietly, thought about how much she wanted to be part of that party. *But I won't be here...* A sigh slipped out, and she looked quickly down to her plate, hoping no one noticed the sadness that she felt was surely etched on her face at the thought of leaving Baytown again.

When the evening finally came to a close, Sophie hugged each of them, delighting in her newfound friends as well as the old ones.

Driving home, her thoughts were a swirl of emotions. Pulling into her spot at the back of her parents' yard, she glanced over, disappointed to see Callan's apartment dark and his truck not in sight. Walking toward the back of her parents' house, she spied them sitting in the den, curled up on the sofa together, laughing at something on the television.

She knew how devastated they had been at Philip's death. But together, they had leaned on each other and moved to a place where the grief no longer crippled them, being able to continue to enjoy life while still living in the same house and the same town. Staring at the scene in front of her, she headed inside, determined to do something she wished she had done years ago.

18

Sophie stepped into the room, and her parents swung their heads around in unison to look at her, both with smiles on their faces. Warmth spread throughout her, and she greeted them with a smile of her own.

"Hey, sweetheart," her mother said, unfolding herself from her curled up position next to her dad. "Did you have a good time with the girls?"

Nodding, she pulled off her coat and tossed it, along with her gloves, onto the kitchen stool and walked into the den, plopping into a chair. "Yeah, I did. I had a really good time. It was nice to feel like I was truly catching up with Katelyn, Jillian, and Tori. I have slight memories of Belle when we were very young, so it was fun to get to know her as an adult."

"I've so enjoyed meeting all of the new women through the Auxiliary," her mom said. "They're a wonderful group of young women."

Sophie was silent for a moment, her fingers

nervously twisting in her lap, trying to decide what she wanted to say.

Her parents shared a glance between each other before her father finally asked, "Sophie, are you okay? Is there something you want to talk about?"

For the second time that night, she blurted out her thoughts. "I went to the cemetery the other night. I got Callan to take me so I wouldn't be alone. And I went into Philip's room."

Silence filled the room, but she could see from the expression on her parents face that they understood the gravity of what she was saying. Her mother's eyes widened but no words came out. Her father simply nodded slowly, but he remained quiet as well.

Feeling as though she needed to fill the silence with words, she continued, "I haven't been back there, you know. Or maybe you don't know. But I haven't. Not all these years. So, I…um…I went. Or rather I had Callan take me. But you don't have to worry, because it was good. Well, not really good. I guess going to a cemetery is never good. But it was okay."

She sucked in her lips to stop babbling, suddenly wondering if saying it all out loud to her parents was a good idea.

Her mother's face softened as she said, "Oh, baby, I think that's wonderful."

She watched her mother's eyes fill with tears and swallowed deeply several times as her own eyes began to burn. Her father leaned forward, resting his forearms on his knees, his hands clasped in front of him, and held her gaze.

"You don't ever have to worry about talking to us about anything, Sophie," he said. "But especially about Philip. Your mother and I have wanted to assure ourselves that you were okay many times during the years, but it was evident how difficult it was for you, and so we respected your privacy." Shaking his head slowly, the lines in his brow deepened, and he said, "Maybe that wasn't the right thing to do."

Jumping up from her chair, she rushed over and sat on the coffee table directly in front of them, placing her hands on theirs. "Don't ever think that, Dad. I've finally faced a lot of the reasons that kept me away from Baytown. Mostly, I just didn't want to have the fact that he was gone in my face every single day. That might not have been the healthiest way to cope, but Callan has pointed out to me that we all grieve differently and that there was nothing wrong with my way."

"I'm so glad that Callan has been here for you," her mom said, giving her hand a squeeze.

Nodding, she silently agreed.

"Why don't you tell us what you've been thinking," her father encouraged. "You don't have to tell us anything you don't want to, but please, understand that you're not hurting us by talking about Philip."

Biting her lip, she thought for a moment and said, "I guess there's really not much of a story to tell. I suppose if he had died when I was younger, I would have learned from your example, maybe have gone to counseling here in Baytown, and would have moved through my grief journey differently."

Shaking her head, still blinking back tears, her mom

said, "I so often wished that we'd had you skip a semester of college and just stay home." She looked over at David and sighed. "But the truth of the matter was, Sophie, we were pretty much a mess, so I thought maybe college was best."

"You can't look back like that, Mom. Who's to say that if I'd stayed here longer anything would have been different? I did go to counseling a few times at the University but really didn't enjoy the group that I was in. I just wasn't at the right place in my mind at the time for it." Shrugging, she added, "I didn't have anyone to talk to, so I just threw myself into my studies and avoided Baytown as much as possible. I don't remember actually telling myself that I should not come back. It was just a subconscious feeling that if I wasn't here, I wouldn't see everyone's pain. I knew Katelyn was devastated, and I didn't want to be around that. And I couldn't imagine what it was like for you two, so avoidance became my coping mechanism."

"Sweetheart, avoidance is not always a bad thing," her dad said. "We certainly didn't go into Philip's room in those early days and do anything except sit on his bed and cry."

"When did it become okay?"

"I don't think we touched a thing in Philip's room for a full year," he said, looking toward Tonya, who nodded her agreement. "About a year and a half after Philip was killed, your mom heard that there was a need for clothing items for one of the areas that had been hit by flooding. She asked me what I thought, and I told her the time was right."

Swallowing past the lump in her throat, Sophie shifted her gaze to her mother, who reached over with her free hand and held onto her dad's, continuing the story.

"We went into Philip's room together and began going through his things. Because he was in the Army, he'd left most of his clothing here since they issued everything. We bagged up his pants, shirts, shoes that were in good shape, and tossed out the underwear. It was..." her mom struggled for a minute, brow scrunched, as though searching for the right word.

"Cathartic," her dad said, gaining her mom's nod.

"That's the word I was looking for," her mother said. "We saved a few things that had particular meaning to us, and one day, if you want to look at them or have some, they're for you as well. A couple of his Baytown Boys jerseys, his baseball glove, and his cowboy boots he loved to wear."

"The important thing for you to understand, Sophie," her father said, holding her gaze, "is that your mother's grief journey was not exactly like mine, although for the most part, we traveled it together. Yours is different, it had to be traveled in your own time. We were older. More life experiences under our belt, although nothing will ever prepare you for burying your child—"

His voice cracked, and Sophie sucked in a quick breath, no longer able to hold back the tears that rolled down her cheeks. "I should have been here with you," she said. "I know I came home for holidays and visits, but when I was here, I didn't talk about him. I didn't go to the cemetery. I didn't go into his room. I just studied, graduated, went after a good job, and began living my life, all the while with a stone hanging around my heart."

"Oh, baby, I'm so sorry," her mother gushed, giving Sophie's hand a tug, pulling her over onto the sofa where her parents settled her between them.

"Sophie, we're the ones who should be sorry. We knew you'd gone to counseling at the University, and you always seemed so well-adjusted that we made the assumption that you were dealing with everything. I kept thinking that if you needed us, you knew we were here," her dad said.

"Don't be sorry, Dad. Please. I just couldn't stand the thought of adding to your grief, and quite frankly, I don't think I could've stood being part of yours."

The three of them sat, arms around each other, quietly for several moments. The silence was not awkward, but instead, comforting.

"At the risk of ruining a beautiful moment, I have to ask," her mother said, squeezing her fingers. "Callan?"

A snort-chuckle slipped from Sophie's lips, knowing her mother was dying to ask what was happening between her and Callan. The problem was, she did not know how to put it into words. "We've been reconnecting."

"Is that what they call it nowadays?" her father asked, eliciting another snort from her.

Relieved that the heavy tension had lifted somewhat, she said, "I don't suppose it's any secret that after Philip died, I didn't want to risk my heart on anyone in the service. I had no idea how the Coast Guard was different from the other military services. I just knew that he said they were getting called up under the Department of Navy and he was going overseas. I was heading off to college, my heart was already broken, and I was determined to do everything I could to keep from feeling heartbreak again."

"And now?"

"I don't really know. I'm only supposed to be here for a couple of months, but it's been really nice to have him back in my life. I had tried talking to Tommy about Philip, how much I loved him, how much I missed him, but that didn't go so well. He seemed to understand the brother-sister relationship, but having never lost anyone in his life, he just couldn't get it."

"Good riddance," her mom pronounced firmly, huffing as she leaned back on the sofa.

Another snort. Sophie could not remember the last time she had giggled with her parents, but it felt so good. "I agree wholeheartedly!" Sucking in a deep breath and letting it out slowly, she continued, "Right now, Callan and I are just getting to know each other again. We're no longer teenagers, and the last ten years have been filled with us living our lives. But, I admit, the more I learn about the adult Callan, the closeness was easy to regain."

Her parents wisely said nothing, for which she was glad. Her relationship with Callan was something she wanted to continue exploring without feeling the need to explain. From her seat on the sofa, she watched a light flip on across the yard in Callan's apartment. Her heart leapt, and she was filled with the desire to see him.

As though her mother could peer into her mind, she said, "I think your father and I are ready to go to bed, sweetie. We'll see you tomorrow."

The three of them stood, hugging tightly, before David linked his fingers with Tonya's, and they walked toward the stairs.

Not hesitating, Sophie grabbed her coat and purse and headed out the back door. Jogging across the yard and alley, she took the stairs two at a time. Her knuckles rapped on the door, and when he opened it, her eyes were filled with him. Tall. Dark. His warm gaze made a head to toe scan and then settled back on her face, concern etched on his features. "Sophie, are you okay?"

Staring down at her face, Callan could not discern what she was feeling. Thrilled to have opened his door and found her standing on his stoop, he then took in her wild, untamed curls, flushed cheeks, and her coat still in her hand even though the night air was quite cold. Reaching out, he drew her into his apartment, shutting the door behind her.

With his hands on her shoulders and her wide aqua eyes staring up at him, he asked again, "Are you okay?"

Her mouth opened and closed a few times as though she was trying to figure out what to say. His concern was growing, and then she finally blurted, "I feel like the Grinch did near the end of the movie."

His eyes narrowed as he continued to stare at her, but before he could ask anything else, she gave her head a little shake.

"I know you think I'm crazy, but that's the only thing I can think of. That was supposed to be the reason why the Grinch couldn't feel the spirit of Christmas. His heart was two sizes too small. But then at the end, his heart grew three sizes." Squinting her eyes, she shook her head again and her shoulders slumped.

"Sophie, you're scaring me." He pulled her closer, sliding his hands from her shoulders around her back, tucking her head underneath his chin. His mind raced as he tried to figure out what he should do. *Have her sit down? Get her a drink of water? Call her parents?*

Her arms circled around his back, and she held on tightly as well, but her fingers flexed as though she could hear his thoughts. "I'm not crazy, I promise. And I'm not having a breakdown." She leaned her head back and looked up at him, her eyes clear but her brow furrowed.

"Come on, sweetheart," he said gently and led her over to his sofa. Sitting, he drew her down, almost into his lap as he kept his arms around her. "I know something's happened, but I'm not following." He watched as she sucked in her lips, her eyes dropping down, and waited.

Pulling in a deep breath, she let it out slowly before lifting her gaze back to his. "I've been facing my fears recently, something that I've needed to do but had no idea how to do it. It started when I moved back, but the floodgates have opened since I've talked with you.

Somehow, talking about Philip with you was okay. I haven't done that in, well, I can't remember the last time I spent time talking about Philip. I've held it in for so long, terrified of the pain I would feel, but you gave me a safe place."

He tucked one of her wayward curls behind her ear and nodded. "Okay, sweetheart."

That seemed to be the only encouragement she needed as the words continued to tumble forth. "With you at my side, I was able to go to the cemetery, something I've needed to do for years. I realize now that I couldn't have done it on my own. But you made that safe also. I was so afraid of going there. So afraid of feeling. So afraid of hurting. It's like I stuffed my heart in a box, thinking if I put away my memories, I was keeping myself safe."

Her words were starting to make sense, and he relaxed slightly, encouraging her to continue. He wanted her close, and she must have wanted the same thing because she shifted so that she was straddling his lap, her hands resting on his shoulders.

Continuing, she said, "Because of you, I've been able to go into his room. Sift through the good memories and not fall apart. I was able to go out with the girls tonight and not spend the entire time thinking how things would be different if Katelyn was with Philip."

"Is that what brought all this on?" he asked, thrilled that she had sought him out but still worried about her state of mind.

Her face scrunched slightly, but she shook her head. "Not necessarily, although it was one more catalyst in the right direction. It's as though I hated to see everyone in Baytown move forward, even though, quite frankly, that's what I was doing in Richmond. But being with the girls tonight, I realized that it was okay to accept the fact that life goes on for all of us, and that doesn't mean that we've forgotten him."

Her voice cracked, and he saw tears gathering in her eyes. Sliding his hand up to her cheek, he readied his thumb to wipe them away, but she blinked, holding the tears at bay.

"I came home and talked to my parents tonight."

"What did you talk about?" he prodded gently.

"Philip. I was ready to ask them about how they moved through their grief. We talked about a lot of things, and once again, I realized that talking about it did not make it worse."

Her lips curved in a soft smile as she continued to blink her watery eyes. Makeup slightly smudged. Her hair a riot of curls. And she had never looked more beautiful. Unable to stop his own grin, he asked, "The Grinch?"

She laughed, playfully slapping him on the shoulder. "That's the only description I could think of. It's like in the last week, I've given my heart permission to grow again."

Their mirth settled, and the air between them grew still. Seeing her peace, he became more aware of their physical closeness. Her weight on his lap, her warmth pressing against his groin. Her arms wrapped around the back of his neck, her fingers idly moving through his hair. Her breasts barely touching his chest. And her lips, slightly open. Her eyes pinned on his before dropping down to his mouth.

The invisible magnet pulling at both of them caused them to react at the same instant. Both tightening their arms, pressing closer together, their lips met. This was not the kiss of a tentative teenager or one between newfound friends. This kiss, with a hint of desperation, flamed between two people who had held back for too long.

19

Callan grasped her face between his hands, angling her head so that his lips had unfettered access. Her lips, soft and pliant, held a hint of the strawberry gloss she must have had on earlier. He felt her fingers digging into his shoulders, one hand sliding up to the back of his head, her nails gently scratching through his short hair.

A flash of memory from their first kiss flew through his mind, followed quickly by the thought that he still wanted to spend the rest of his life being the last person she kissed. Suddenly, his lips felt empty, and opening his eyes, he saw that she had pulled back slightly, her kiss-swollen lips barely open.

"I've wanted to kiss you like that since I was very young," she confessed, vulnerability in her eyes.

"The let's keep fulfilling this dream," he responded, one side of his lips twitching.

"Yeah," she breathed before closing the gap between them, once more sealing their lips together.

He slid his tongue into her welcoming mouth. Hers

met his, thrust for thrust, tangling in a dance, tasting and tempting, memorizing the feel and essence. She shifted slightly, and the pressure on his already hard cock increased. He had no idea if she realized she was doing it, but her body was instinctively seeking the friction it craved.

He did not want this night to be about sex, not when she had shown up on his doorstep full of emotion. She moved again, and he slid one hand down to her ass, gripping it tightly to still her.

"Uhmph," she grunted in protest, moving her hips again.

"Fuck, baby," he mumbled against her lips. "I'm trying to do the right thing, but you gotta help me out here."

She leaned back once again, her eyes intently staring into his. "I want you to do the right thing, too. I'm just not sure we have the same idea about what the right thing is."

A weight pressed down on his chest, his desire for her coiling tightly inside. His fingers flexed against her soft ass, and he fought to keep from lifting his hips into her. "I can't guess what you want, Sophie. I can't take a chance on reading you the wrong way. And I sure as hell don't want to take a chance on ruining anything between us."

She leaned closer, her lips a whisper away from his, her eyes hooded, her breath washing across his face. "There's no way you could do anything that would ruin what we have, who we are together. And there's no way you're reading my body's response to you the wrong way." She moved ever so slightly closer until her lips were barely touching his as she said, "I want to see where this goes. Explore whatever's been rekindled between us. Callan Ward, I want you to make love to me."

His fingers flexed against her ass again as his other arm wrapped around her back, banding her tightly to him. His tongue thrust deeply inside her mouth once more, and now, with all doubt removed, he sucked on her tongue, reveling in her taste.

Standing, with her still in his arms and her legs wrapped around his waist, he stepped through the door into the bedroom. Walking straight to the bed, he knelt and set her on the edge. Still kneeling on the floor between her legs, he slid his hands up to cup her cheeks once more, almost afraid that she was a dream.

Smiling as though reading his mind, she said, "I'm here. We're real."

Kissing her again, his hands slid to the bottom of her sweater, finding petal-soft skin underneath. Sliding his hands up her back, he pulled her closer to the edge of the bed so that their bodies were once again tightly pressed together as his tongue continued its exploration over her jaw and down her neck, sucking slightly on her wildly-fluttering pulse.

Grasping the bottom of the sweater, he lifted it upward over her breasts, drawing it over her head, tossing it behind him. Her breasts filled the cups of her pale blue bra, and he moved his lips from her neck down to the soft mounds. Her head leaned backward, and a soft moan left her lips as he tugged the cups down with his teeth and pulled her nipple deeply into his mouth.

Her fingernails dug into his shoulders, and the slight pain shot straight to his already aching cock. He leaned back, eyeing the front closure of her bra and grinned as she quickly flicked it open.

"Thought I'd help a guy out," she said with a wink.

Reaching back to grasp his shirt, he pulled it over his head in a deft move and tossed it behind him as well. "I'm glad," he replied, not hiding his honesty. "I sometimes wonder if bras aren't invented by people that just want to see a man try to fumble in an attempt to get to the treasure underneath."

His mirth ebbed as his gaze dropped to her breasts, and he cupped their weight with his hands, his thumbs rubbing over her hard nipples. He gently pushed her back onto the bed, and as much as he hated to leave the attention he wanted to give to her breasts, he slid his hands down to her feet, pulling off her shoes and socks before moving to the waistband of her pants.

"Lift," he ordered gently, and as she obeyed, he maneuvered her pants and panties over her hips and down her legs, tossing them to the ever-growing pile of clothes. Now, with her totally naked and him still kneeling between her thighs, she was completely open to his appreciative perusal.

"My, God, Sophie. You're beautiful." He leaned forward, kissing along her inner thighs before blowing a breath over her soft folds. He heard the sharp intake of her breath and, lifting her legs over his shoulders, sealed his mouth over sex. Her fingernails rasped against the top of his head, and for the first time since he had his short, regulation haircut, he wished it was longer, just to feel her tangle her fingers in it.

But soon all rational thought left his mind as the scent of her arousal and the taste of her on his tongue filled his senses. She began to rise underneath him, and with his hands on her hip bones, he held her in place, determined to give everything he could to her. With his tongue flicking her clit, he inserted a finger into her core, crooking it, searching for the spot that would bring her pleasure.

"Callan," her hoarse whisper called out as her fingernails dug into his scalp, her head moving back and forth on the bed.

Adding another finger, he circled his lips on her clit and sucked. Her hips jumped forward, pressing her deeper into his face as her release washed over her. He felt her legs quiver and slid his fingers out so that his mouth could lap her slit.

Her legs fell open, and he placed kisses along her thighs before moving up over her belly. Standing, he looked down at her body, resplendent as it glowed in the moonlight. Her eyes fluttered open, and her lips curved until she was smiling brightly.

Moving his hands to his own jeans, he shucked them quickly, his aching cock now finally released from its confines. It had been a while since he had been with a woman and hoped the box of condoms that he kept in his nightstand was still good. Grabbing one, he ripped the foil and rolled it on, grinning down at Sophie as she propped herself up on her elbows and stared at him.

He climbed over her body and, hooking his hands under her armpits, shifted her so that she was completely reclined on the bed. Resting his lower body on hers, he held his weight off her chest with his forearms planted on the mattress, enclosing her with his hard body.

His thumb swept over the soft apple of her cheeks, and he kissed her lightly, his tongue barely touching hers. "We only do tonight what you want to do," he said. "We can stop right now if you want. Just having you in my arms fulfills a dream I thought would never happen."

Her eyes twinkled in the moonlight as she smiled. With her hands moving up and down his muscular arms, she said, "If you try to stop now, it'll rile me, and I'll tackle you here in this bed."

He chuckled and said, "Can't rile up my woman, now can I?"

Before she had a chance to respond, he latched onto her lips again, taking and giving, offering and needing, wanting her to feel every emotion that was racing through his body. Shifting his hips as she opened her knees wider, he placed the tip of his cock at her entrance. Moving slowly to allow her body a chance to adjust, he slipped in, inch by inch, until fully seated. As her warm sex sheathed him, all other thoughts flew from his mind other than making her body his own.

Sophie gasped at the sense of fullness. It was obvious

that Callan was well endowed, as evidenced by the tight fit and friction she felt as he began moving in and out of her body. Tommy had been her first lover since she left college, and she had only had a couple of boyfriends during those years. Tommy had been well-built, his muscles from his gym membership, but the rock-solid body moving into hers was sculpted from hard work and exuded a sense of power that excited her.

His eyes staring down at her as his hips thrust were mesmerizing. It was as though he did not want to miss a moment of staring at her face. She tried to return his perusal as the coil deep inside tightened. Her hands roamed from his shoulders, over the flexing muscles in his back and ass before making their return journey toward his neck. The pinnacle was coming closer, but as her breath rasped in her lungs, she wondered if she would make it.

He shifted his hips slightly, putting a different pressure on her clit, and he growled, "Are you close, baby?"

Fighting the desire to close her eyes, she held them open, seeing the sweat beading on his forehead. Unsure of her voice, she nodded, and as her fingernails dug into his back and her legs tightened around his waist, she cried out as her body shuddered. Wave after wave of pleasure moved through her, and she was barely aware of his roar as his release hit him as well.

Her legs tightened, her heels dug into his ass, silently begging him to not leave her body. He continued to pump slowly until there was nothing left.

When he was finally able to speak, he said softly, "You've just given me everything I've ever wanted and never thought I could have. I don't want you to leave this bed. I don't want to leave your body."

Her hands tightened around his back, and she whispered, "Then don't."

He kissed the end of her nose before sliding his lips over her cheek, along her jaw, nibbling on her earlobe. "I gotta get rid of the condom, babe. Please, I'm begging you, don't leave this bed."

A slight giggle slipped from her lips, and she replied, "I don't think you have to worry about that. I'm not sure I can move."

A look of pure, male satisfaction crossed his face, and he slid out gently. Kissing her lightly, he climbed from the bed, stalked into the bathroom and dealt with the condom.

Even though her body felt boneless, she rolled over so that she could watch every step he took, admiring the view of his ass as it walked away, then admiring the whole package as it walked toward her.

With a cocky grin on his face, he climbed back onto the bed. "You see something you like, babe?"

She grinned widely, and with a nod of her head toward his nightstand said, "I hope you've got more condoms in there."

Sliding his body along hers, he wrapped his arms around her, pulling her in tightly. "Considering I just opened it, there'd better be plenty."

Lifting an eyebrow, she quipped, "Always prepared?"

"It's been a while." Before she had a chance to question him further, he volunteered, "Haven't dated anyone in a while, and I've never been too big on random hookups. Plus," he grinned, "I haven't brought anybody to this apartment. My parents give me total privacy out here, but just the thought of Mom possibly knocking on the door is a cockblocker."

She laughed, the idea of Barbara Ward popping by to bring homemade cinnamon rolls and finding Callan tangled in the sheets with a woman hilarious. Biting her lip, she said, "I suppose that's my cue to make sure I get outta here soon. I'd hate to scar your mom for life!"

His arms tightened, and he shook his head. "No way, not yet. We've still got more condoms in that box." Sliding his nose along her cheek, he whispered, "And you've got to know that if my mom ever found you in my bed, she be thrilled."

He lifted his head and peered into her eyes, and her breath halted in her throat. Her smile sobered, and reaching up, she cupped his face, saying, "Everything you have and everything you are, I like, Callan. In fact, I've liked you for as long as I can remember."

Covering her body with his, he slid his fingers to the back of her head, tangling in her curly waves, his gaze holding hers captive. "Damn, Sophie. You absolutely humble me, babe."

Whispering, she said, "I can't lie. Not to you, never to you."

20

As Jarrod handled the CG boat, Callan was on the radio getting the latest coordinates from both Jeff and Ryan. The Coast Guard and the Virginia Marine Police had responded to a call from a cargo ship anchored in the Bay awaiting permission to travel to Baltimore. A small boat was moving in circles around the ship, coming dangerously close.

"I swear, if these are drunk college students, I'm gonna...fuck, I don't know what I'm gonna do," Callan growled to José, standing near him.

Approaching the massive bulk carrier, the Yokohama, he could tell it was an approximately forty-five-thousand-ton ship, seven hundred feet in length. It was traveling under the flag of Panama and was filled with shipping containers.

And, just on cue, an older model Mastercraft boat came speeding around the back corner of the carrier. The winds and choppy water made for a dangerous situation as the boat went airborne before crashing back into a wave.

On the first pass, it appeared that while there were three or four people in the boat, only two were wearing flotation devices. The shouts coming from the boat gave evidence to their youth and possible intoxication.

"Fuckin' hell," Callan said.

Terrence maneuvered the VMP boat in pursuit, and Jarrod swung the CG vessel to the side of the cargo ship. A few minutes later the boat came into sight, and Callan ordered them to stop as José manned the guns. They had no intention of using them but needed the threat of firepower to get the miscreants' attention.

Thankfully, they slowed, and Jarrod pulled alongside them, with Ryan's boat on the other side. Now that he was closer, Callan could see that the boaters were even younger than he thought. He boarded their boat from one side as Ryan climbed aboard their vessel as well.

Checking IDs, they discovered three teenage boys and a teenage girl. She seemed genuinely terrified, as did one of the boys. The other two, alcohol-induced bravado made them cocky as well as stupid.

The girl, in tears, kept saying, "I didn't want to do this. I told him not to do this. They just kept going, they kept going faster. I didn't want to do this."

As Ryan read the driver his rights, Terrence moved them one after the other into the VMP boat, placing the driver under arrest. That seemed to sober the others, and they quickly lost their bluster.

"Shit, man. My dad's gonna fuckin' kill me," one of the boys said while the others looked on glumly.

As the Marine Police pulled away, the Coast Guard boat followed more slowly, towing the teen's boat. Glad to get away from the closeness of the cargo vessel, they first went to the Marina to turn in the boat to the VMP.

Callan made his way over to Ryan to see if he needed assistance and greeted Colt Hudson and Hunter Simmons, the Sheriff of North Heron County and one of his deputies. They had arrived to take the four teenagers into custody, transporting them to the county jail in Easton.

"I wouldn't want to be them when their parents get the call," he commented.

Ryan shook his head and said, "I'm always amazed at the stupidity of some folks who get in a boat and have no business doing so, but then, those four kids can legally drive, so they could get behind the wheel of a car and act just as irresponsibly."

Jarrod was ready to head back to the station, so Callan shook Ryan's hand and jumped back onto the CG boat.

The large house was finally quiet, but Sophie did not mind. The rooms had been a hub of activity earlier in the day as several trucks rolled into the driveway, loaded with furniture and accessories that she had ordered.

Moving from room to room, tablet in her hand, she had directed the movers with the efficiency of a drill sergeant. Making sure that corners were not bumped and stairs were not scraped, she kept an eagle-eyed vigilance on all the proceedings.

The trucks and men were now gone, leaving her with a house that was beginning to look more like a home instead of an empty, cavernous space.

The master bedroom contained a king-sized bed of warm maple, matching dresser with a tall mirror, and a chest of drawers. An upholstered bench was nestled in the bay window, coordinating pillows creating a reading nook. The rug had been delivered the previous day, and she could not wait to get the bed linens and curtains.

The other upstairs bedrooms would be finished last, not because they were not important, but because she knew Southern Living's photographer would focus on the master suite as well as the downstairs.

Walking out of the master, she took the main staircase to the first floor, her smile growing wider as she looked at the formal but comfortable blue sofa and pale-yellow chairs flanking the fireplace in the living room. The rug provided texture and contrast while still bringing out the colors. A coffee table and matching end tables pulled the sitting area together. More furniture would be delivered in a couple of days, and then she would be ready to add in her accent pieces.

The sun hit her face as it lowered in the sky over the water and came through the window. She walked over and looked out, admiring the view. Having been indoors all day, she was filled with the desire to go out and watch the sunset.

Knowing the best place to watch would be off the golf cart path in an uninhabited area of The Dunes, she wrapped up warmly, locked the doors, and hopped into the golf cart. A few minutes later she found the perfect spot, tall seagrass covering the dunes with thick shrubs behind her.

The sun seemed to drop quickly, and she watched the yellow orb slowly disappear into the horizon, its brilliance reflected in the choppy water as the wind blew briskly. The sky turned from light blue to a palette of orange, pink, and red, before deepening into purple. She snapped multiple pictures, rethinking a few of the colors she decided to put in the family room and upstairs bedrooms.

Sitting on the sand with the tall seagrass all around, she relaxed. *This was something I never did in Richmond. I never relaxed. Watch the sunset. Breathe in the air.* The appeal of Baytown slammed into her, and for the first time the idea that she did not want to leave when this job was over hit her. *Could I stay? Run my business from here?* Thoughts of her parents, her friends, and certainly Callan flew through her mind. Blowing out a deep breath, she closed her eyes and let the peaceful evening soak in.

"You see anyone?"

Sophie's eyes jerked open as the sound of a man's voice carried across the water. Peering through the tall reeds, she watched a small boat in the inlet, its motor turned off, as two men rowed past her.

"Nah. No one's ever here."

Both men were dressed in heavy coats, dark knit caps pulled down over their ears and foreheads, with gloves on their hands. Warding off the cold, their apparel also kept their features indiscernible in the shadows.

"You know what they said. Someone's been here."

Uncertainty filled her, and she was afraid of making any noise, halting her breath in her throat. The men quickly rowed by, disappearing around a slight bend. Once they were out of sight and she could no longer hear them, she scrambled to her knees and ran back to the golf cart, her body bent over in an attempt to stay hidden.

Listening carefully, she heard no sounds, but with the sun having already dropped in the sky, the deepening shadows appeared ominous. Feeling foolish, she nonetheless started the golf cart and hurried back down the cart path, not wanting to be seen by anyone.

Within ten minutes she was back at the large house where she lowered the garage door behind her and sat for a moment, her hands still on the steering wheel. Safe but feeling even more foolish, she sucked in a deep breath and walked out the side door to her car.

Driving the short distance to her home, she replayed the men's simple conversation in her mind, trying to figure out why it had made her so nervous. Many people who lived on the Eastern Shore spend time in the water on boats. *A couple of men out fishing, hurrying to get home is no big deal.* She drove through the gate, leaving The Dunes Resort behind. Turning onto the road that led into town, her mind continued to roam. *If nothing was going on, then why were they wondering if someone was around?*

By the time she had made it home, she convinced herself that the shadowed evening had given her the spooks. Pulling into the back of her parents' lot, she climbed from her car, unable to keep her gaze from drifting over to Callan's apartment.

The light was on in his living room, and she grinned when she saw him standing there, hands on his hips, a wide smile on his face as he stared down at her through the wide window. He turned and disappeared, and she knew he was heading to the door, so she quickly locked her car and jogged across the alley. By the time she made it halfway up the stairs, he met her.

Taking her hand in his, he led her the rest of the way up the stairs and into his apartment. As soon as he kicked the door closed, he backed her against it, his lips claiming hers. All thoughts of anything else flew from her mind as their tongues tangled and their hands began stripping each other.

Callan could not believe how much he missed Sophie, and it had only been two days since he had seen her. When he had gotten home, he noted that her car was not parked in its normal spot. He had fixed a simple supper, both continually checking his phone for a text and going to the window that overlooked the back of the Bayles' yard. Finally, she had pulled in and parked, and he watched with pleasure that the first thing she did when she alighted from her car was to look up at his apartment.

Now, with her in his arms, her back against his door, and his mouth on hers, all he wanted to do was cover her body with his own. His kiss was demanding, but she met him thrust for thrust. The feel of her soft tongue raking across the roof of his mouth shot straight to his cock, making it even more painful than it already was.

Her arms encircled his waist, pulling him in, and their bodies touched from chest to knees. Her hands moved back to her waist, squeezing between their bodies, and he separated just enough to give her room to get her coat unbuttoned.

Sliding it off her shoulders, it fell behind her next to the door, and he kicked it to the side. His hands now moved to the bottom of her sweater, and as his finger-tips grazed over her soft skin, he tugged it upward over her breasts until it joined the coat on the floor.

He lifted her in his arms easily, and her legs wrapped around his waist. Pressing his hips in, his swollen cock was now against her hot core, but the layers of clothes between them were still in the way. He pulled the cups of her bra downward, exposing her breasts, kissing his way from her lips down her neck to her nipples, sucking one deeply into his mouth.

Clutching the back of his neck, she slid her other hand up, her nails dragging slightly over his scalp. Every little sound she made in the back of her throat, every movement only served to make him harder.

She began clawing at the material of his T-shirt on his shoulders, and he joined her desperation in wanting the offending material off. He lifted his leg, pressing his knee against the door, effectively giving her a seat while he reached down and jerked his shirt off, trying not to elbow her in the face. Leaning back in, he recaptured her mouth with his, only this time with flesh against flesh, her breasts against his chest, and he groaned in satisfaction.

They continued to kiss, their mouths sealed as their fingers explored each other. Finally, he muttered, "What you want, babe?"

Not moving her lips from his, she replied, "You. I want all of you. I need all of you."

Lowering his leg so that her feet could touch the floor again, his hands moved to her pants, finding her hands already there. Breaking the kiss, she slid her pants down, and bending, jerked off her boots so that her pants could be kicked to the side along with the other clothes piling by the door. Her legs became tangled and he held her shoulders to keep her from toppling over. Once that was accomplished, he started the process of removing his jeans but halted as he stared at the naked beauty in front of him. She was an angelic figure, looking up at him with her wide, aqua eyes.

Still holding his gaze, her hands replaced his on his pants, hooking her thumbs in the waistband and starting to shove his jeans down, just enough so that his cock sprang free.

Groaning again, he asked, "In a hurry, baby?"

"Aren't you?" Without giving him a chance to

answer, she dropped to her knees and wrapped her hands around his girth, sliding her nails gently up the length. Grinning as he hissed, she slipped him into her mouth and began working him up and down.

Overcome with the vision and the sensations, he placed one palm flat against the door and the other hand cupped the back of her head, his fingers tangling in her thick curls. He dropped his chin and watched as she bobbed up and down, her magical mouth alternating between licking and sucking. Her hands held him steady as they grasped his ass, her fingernails digging into the tight muscles.

She continued her ministrations, and he felt his balls pull up and tighten. Not wanting to blow into her mouth, at least not this time, he reached down and grabbed her under her arms, lifting her straight up, pressing her back against the door again.

"Wrap your legs around me, babe," he ordered, and as soon as she did, his cock felt her warm sex, this time with no clothing barriers between them.

He slid one hand under her ass, fingering her slick folds, thrilled to find her ready. Holding her gaze, his mouth a whisper away from hers, he asked, "Do you want this? Can you take me?"

Her finger squeezed his shoulders as her lips curved into a smile. Jerking her head up and down, she moaned, "Yes, please. Now."

Reality trickled into the back of his mind, and he started to lower her. Seeing her pout, he groaned, "Condom."

"I'm clean," she said. "I was tested last month and haven't been with anyone."

With his lips still pressed against hers, he muttered, "Clean too. Tested recently, and it's been a long time since I've been with someone."

"Then what are you waiting for?"

Wanting to take care of his precious armful, he settled her opening on the tip of his cock, gently entering her inch by inch. Tight, warm, slick, heaven.

"Tell me if it's too much," he said, thrilled when she clutched him, moving slightly to urge him on. Once fully seated, he began thrusting, the tight friction nearly making him come immediately. Kissing her, he matched his tongue thrusts with his cock and felt her sex tightening more. Wanting to make sure she came, he slid his hand between them, fingering her swollen nub.

She cried out as her inner walls squeezed his cock, her head hitting the door she groaned out her release. He lost control and reared back as he powered through his orgasm. Thrusting over and over until every drop was emptied from his body, he continued to press her against the door in an effort for closeness as well as to keep his legs steady.

As his mind began to clear, he lowered her feet to the floor. With more clarity, he hoped he had not hurt her in his enthusiasm. Cupping her face with his hands, his gaze roved, but all he saw were clear eyes and a wide smile.

"Don't look so worried, Callan," she said, her voice soft as her hands moved up his shoulders. "I wanted that as much as you did. I needed that as much as you did."

Bending, he took her lips gently and asked, "Can you stay?" Heart light as she nodded, he pulled her in tightly, kissing the top of her head. "Let's get dressed, and I'll feed you." He hoped that she would stay for the night, and as she began sliding her clothes on, he was hit with the thought *I hope she stays forever.*

21

Rolling over in bed the next morning, Sophie stared at Callan's profile, relaxed in slumber. His dark hair was so thick that even shorn in a service haircut, her fingers itched to run through the longer strands on top. His dark stubble grew quickly, lending an air of danger to his calm persona. Lying on his side facing her, one arm wrapped around her waist and his leg tangled in hers, it was as though he claimed her even in sleep. *I could get used to this. So easily. But what happens if he reenlists and has to move away?*

Biting her lip, she forced the tangled thoughts from her mind and leaned in to place a gentle kiss on his lips. Deciding to fix breakfast, she slid from the bed and made her way into the bathroom. Staring into the mirror, she was horrified at the massive, sex-tangled hair and makeup-smeared face. Grabbing a washcloth, she scrubbed her face clean and remembered she had a small bottle of lotion in her purse.

Making her way quietly into the living room, she

dressed, dug around in her purse and moisturized her face. Dragging a brush through her curls, she pulled them up into a ponytail as best she could.

By the time he came stumbling into the kitchen, sweat pants hanging low on his hips, his chest and abs on glorious display, she was just plating the eggs, bacon, and toast.

"Good God, babe," he said, his voice still sleep-raspy. "This is the best sight I could have first thing in the morning. I could get used to this."

Holding his plate in front of him, she quipped, "The breakfast?"

He took the plate from her hand, placed it on the counter and stalked around until his body was pressed up against hers. Taking her lips in a searing kiss, he replied, "Breakfast looks good, but I was talking about you."

She laughed and said, "Eat up. I know we both have to get to work this morning." Still clutching his waist, she held his gaze, her nerves fluttering and added, "For the record, I could get used to this, too."

Determined to satisfy her curiosity, Sophie took the golf cart out in the daylight, going back to the area she had been at the previous evening. The sun was shining in the brilliant blue sky, the winter air chilly but not as cold as it had been. Earlier, using her computer, she had looked at the overhead map view of The Dunes Resort, familiarizing herself with the side that was facing the inlet. There were only a few houses that had been built right at the apex, but it appeared no other houses backed onto the waterway.

With her small purse worn across her body, she carried a large sack, still gathering some pinecones and berries as she went. In the distance, she caught sight of a small wooden pier, extending about ten feet into the water. Having not seen it on her previous sojourns, she was curious. Moving closer, she startled at the sound of her name being called.

"Sophie!"

Jerking around, she saw Roger walking toward her, his brows lowered. "What are you doing over here?"

"I'm collecting some of the greenery and berries that are on this side. I wanted to use them in decorating," she replied, glad she had brought the sack with her today so that she had an excuse for being in the area. Cocking her head to the side, she asked, "And what has you out this morning?"

She watched as he blinked several times before he replied, "I always walk over the grounds several times a week. It gives me a chance to make sure that everything is fine. You really shouldn't be over here. The vegetation is very fragile."

Uncertain how the natural shrubs and trees could be considered fragile, she nonetheless simply nodded. They stood staring at each other for a moment before he gave a quick nod and hurried on.

Deciding to take a circuitous route back to the golf cart, she wandered down a path in the direction of the small pier. Seeing someone in front of her, she startled as they turned quickly.

With surprise on her face, Sue asked, "What are you doing over here?"

Sophie began to wonder if that was going to be the question of the morning. "I was gathering some of the vegetation so that I can use it in the decorating."

Sue's eyes narrowed slightly, and her mouth worked as though she was trying to decide how to reply. "You need to be careful," Sue warned. "I always come out and check the grounds, and you want to make sure not to disturb anything on the course."

Her brow scrunched as she considered Sue's words, considering she was not standing on the golf course. "Okay," she said slowly. "I do stay off of the course, so I assumed it was okay for me to look at the foliage over here."

She watched as a grimace crossed Sue's face, but the golf pro did not say anything else. Sue simply gave a curt nod and moved along the path in the direction that Roger had gone.

Having never seen anyone wandering the woods near the edge of the inlet before, she was surprised that it seemed so well traversed this morning. Continuing closer to the small pier, she heard a stick snap behind her. Turning, she observed Travis moving into sight. His eyes darted to her face before looking over her shoulder in the direction where Sue had gone.

"What was she doing here?" he asked.

Wondering why he was asking her, she simply

replied, "I don't know. She said she checks the golf course every morning."

Hands on his hips, Travis huffed. "She knows good and well that this golf course is mine to survey. She's got the one on the other side. I don't know why she thinks she has to get into my business."

Remaining silent, she wondered if he was going to question her, but did not have to wait long.

"And you?"

Before she had a chance to give her standard answer, his gaze dropped to the pinecone still in her hand. "Oh, you're collecting." His eyes shifted around before landing back on her face. "The ones here are pretty small. If you want some really large pinecones, you should go back to the main road coming into The Dunes."

"Uh, thank you," she blurted. "Well, I guess I'll be moving along."

"Good, good."

Instead of moving away, he continued to stand there and stare at her, so she felt the need to escape. Passing him on the path, she headed toward her golf cart. Coming out of the woods, she saw Ann standing near her cart.

The head chef twisted around and stared at her, saying, "I wondered whose golf cart this was. There's normally no one over here in the early mornings."

Stepping closer, she tossed her bag into the floorboard of the golf cart and decided to challenge before she was challenged. "What are you doing out so early this morning?"

Ann bristled and answered, "I like to take a morning walk. It helps me think and gets the blood flowing before have to stay in the kitchen the rest of the day."

That appeared to be the most honest comment she had heard all morning. Nodding, she replied, "Me too. I was doing a little collecting and wanted to see the wooded side instead of just the dunes."

Ann dipped her chin and nodded toward the bag in the golf cart. "What have you got in there?"

"Just pinecones and some berries. I've been collecting for the past week, deciding to use them in some of the decorating."

"So this is your first time out here on this side of the resort?"

Running her tongue over her lips, her curiosity was building as to why everyone wanted to know what she was doing. "No, it's not the first time. I've made several visits over here at different times during the day. You never know what you'll find."

She held Ann's gaze, her stomach clenching slightly as the older woman's brows lowered, her jaw hardening. Wondering if she was going to warn her away, she was surprised when Ann just bobbed her head and turned to walk away. Breathing a sigh of relief, she startled when Ann called over her shoulder.

"Just be careful, Sophie. You never know when you might stumble into something you don't want to know anything about."

She had just made it back to the house, holding her bag full of pinecones and cuttings, and was ready to accept a new shipment of furniture when her phone rang. Seeing who was on the caller ID, she answered, "Good morning, Carlotta."

Without giving her a proper greeting, Carlotta immediately said, "You need to be very careful being in the sections of The Dunes that are uninhabited. I know there can be wild animals, and you just never know what you might come across. We certainly don't want anything to happen to you so I would advise you from now on to stay on the main paths."

"I'm curious, Carlotta, who called you so early this morning to let you know I was over there?"

"Now, Sophie, that's not really pertinent. I try to make it my business to know everything that goes on at The Dunes. So please, stay within the confines of your decorating areas."

Carlotta disconnected, and Sophie stood in the kitchen, staring at her blank phone. What had started out as mild curiosity was now flaring into suspicion. *Somebody is hiding something that they don't want me, or probably anyone, to know about.*

Wanting to talk to Callan, she knew it would have to wait. Today was Valentine's Day, and he had invited her to the AL Oyster Roast. Before she had a chance to ponder the situation further, she spied a delivery truck pulling into the driveway, and her attention was diverted back to her job.

22

Callan kept his fingers linked with Sophie's as they walked into the large reception hall next to The Sunset View Restaurant. It was the room that was often used for wedding receptions, community gatherings, and parties that required a lot of space. There was a tent outside that they passed on their way in from the parking lot that had the roasters firing, and some of the AL volunteers were bringing in platters of oysters, fried fish, and boiled crab and shrimp.

Once inside, they observed tables along the side that were loaded with side dishes and desserts that the Auxiliary members had provided.

"Oh, my gosh," Sophie exclaimed. "There's so much food!"

Chuckling, Callan said, "Yeah, but look at the crowd coming in."

They glanced around and with his height advantage found several tables pushed together on one side where most of their friends had gathered. Giving her hand a little tug, he said, "Follow me, and we'll get to the food."

Leading her to the far side, he gave nods and chin lifts to many along the way. Hearing her laugh, he looked down and saw her smiling up at him.

"Do you know everybody in town?" she asked. "I may have grown up here, but there are so many people I don't know."

"I know a lot through the AL and the ball teams that we coach. Others I've met through my job, especially the fishermen and some of their families."

Once they arrived at the tables, he watched as she moved to greet the couples that she already knew. Tori and Mitch and their little one. Jillian and Grant. Katelyn and Gareth. Ginny and Brogan. Madelyn and Zac. Lia and Aiden. Belle introduced her to her husband, Hunter, one of the deputies who worked for the county.

Her mother called from another table, and she moved toward her to greet many of the Baytown Boys' parents that she knew growing up. Mitch's parents, Ed and Nancy Evans, along with Jillian's parents, Steve and Claire Evans, enveloped her in hugs, all exclaiming how much they had missed her. Corrine and Eric MacFarlane came over next, Corrine bouncing her grandson, little Finn, in her arms.

Katelyn's grandfather, Finn, pulled her into his embrace, saying, "You were always a bright spot of sunshine when you were a little girl." Looking over at Callan, he said, "I hope you're planning on keeping her here."

Callan grinned but watched as pink blush stained her cheeks. Drawing her back into his arms, he said, "Maybe we all just need to convince her that Baytown's the place to be."

He gave a chin lift to his parents sitting next to David and Tonya, and then, taking the attention off of her, whispered, "Let's get in the food line, babe."

Once they were away from the others, he asked her, "Are you okay?"

Her lips curved softly and she replied, "Yeah. It was a little overwhelming seeing everybody all at once." Her eyes clouded over as though she were far away, and she added, "I thought it would be awkward, but it really does feel like just being home."

Her words speared straight through him, and the desire that she might want to stay beyond her job with The Dunes flickered into a small flame.

Moving through the lines at the long tables, she was amazed at how much food everyone managed to pile onto their plates. Especially Callan and his friends. She was glad the paper plates were sturdy or else she would have been afraid that they would have crashed under the weight.

"Are you getting enough?" Callan asked.

She glanced over her shoulder and up and laughed. "Not all of us eat our body weight in one sitting." Jason was across the serving line from them, and she saw that he had even more than Callan had piled up. Hunter and Brogan were the two largest men, and she lifted an eyebrow at them carrying two plates each.

While in the line, Callan introduced her to more people. His Coast Guard buddies, José and Jarrod, and his Chief, Jeff. The Sheriff of North Heron, Colt. All of the names were beginning to run together, but one thing remained the same with each person she was introduced to—they all seemed to have great respect for Callan, something which did not surprise her at all.

Making their way back to the table, they squeezed in, ready to taste the food that had been tempting them since they arrived. The microphone at the front of the room squawked, drawing everyone's attention to a small platform on the opposite end.

"I should have known we wouldn't be able to get past a community gathering without hearing from the Mayor," Callan said, drawing chuckles from those around.

Sophie twisted in her seat to watch the portly man dressed in a suit and tie, unlike all the others that were more casually attired, continue to tap on the microphone. Finally, someone in the crowd yelled, "It's on! We can hear you!"

Someone from their table said, "And it won't matter if we can't," to the laughter of everyone around.

"As Mayor of this fine town, I just wanted to thank everyone for coming out tonight and supporting the American Legion. Their tireless efforts benefiting our fine community are well known amongst all of us.

Please make sure you thank the sponsors of this event—their names are displayed by the door—and the American Legion Auxiliary who provided the delicious side dishes. I want you to know that I and the town council are working on your behalf in complete transparency and we hope to have more events like this. So enjoy your meal, and thanks again for coming out."

Turning back to the others at her table, brow lowered, Sophie asked, "What on earth was the transparency that he was talking about?"

"A few months ago, Lia uncovered a huge financial theft that involved the man who used to be the town manager," Callan explained. Nodding toward the man sitting across from them, he said, "I know you've met Lia, but here's one of the other accountants in town. This is Scott Redding."

She smiled at the handsome man before looking around the table, giving a tiny shake of her head. Catching Katelyn's questioning gaze, she mouthed *There are so many gorgeous guys in Baytown.* Katelyn nodded while laughing before turning her attention back to her baby.

As she finished her food, Sophie observed all the people sitting at the tables close to them. The original Baytown Boys. All of them now with beautiful wives or fiancées. Their parents, all friends with her parents. Callan's coworkers at the Coast Guard. Members of the American Legion. A small grin played about her lips as she thought of Philip. *He would so love this.*

She looked over at the table where her parents sat,

watching them laughing and chatting with their friends. She knew that they must look at each of the Baytown Boys, and while loving all of them as they watched them grow up and mature, had to deal with their son never getting that chance. But once again, this thought did not make her sad, just reflective. The saying *life goes on* was so very true.

Looking back at the original Baytown Boys sitting near them, it hit her that Callan was the last single one. Sliding her glance to him, the idea that he could have settled down with someone else sliced through her.

"Hey, what was that frown for?"

Blinking, she felt the heat of blush crawling up her face as she realized Callan was staring at her, his brows lowered in concern.

Giving her head a quick shake, she said, "Nothing." Seeing him continue to stare questioningly, she added, "I was just thinking about how nice it was here with everyone. I never had friends like this in Richmond."

His face gentled, and he reached over to cover her hand with his. "This is why I don't want to reenlist in the Coast Guard," he admitted. "Baytown is home. It's always been home, but with you here again, it's even better."

Before she could smile, he bent toward her, his lips meeting hers in a soft kiss. He leaned back and winked, seeming to not notice everyone at the table staring at them. Her cheeks heated once again, but as she glanced around, she noticed the wide smiles of all of their friends. Sucking in her lips, she ducked her head and continued to eat, grateful when the conversations started around them again. *Well, it seems like no one has a problem with us being together.*

Looking across the crowded room, she noticed Roger and Travis standing together, their heads bent toward each other, deep in conversation. Off to the side, slightly behind them, was Sue, whose narrowed gaze was pinned directly to the two men. Carlotta was sitting at the Mayor's table, chatting with both him and his wife. She had seen Ann standing outside near one of the roasters and wondered if she was just working for the evening and not enjoying the dinner.

Her thoughts slid to the events from the morning, and she turned to Callan and asked, "Do you ever go back into the inlets that are behind The Dunes Resort?"

Her question seemed to catch him off guard as his forehead crinkled in thought. "Inlets?"

"Yeah, the ones that go behind the residential area that isn't developed yet and the golf course. I don't really know how else to describe them, but they're on the back side of the golf courses and residences."

Shaking his head, he said, "I don't think I've ever been back there. Why?"

Before she had a chance to respond, a shout of laughter from the other end of the table rang out, and their attention was diverted. Callan stood and grabbed her empty plate along with his and kissed the top of her head, saying, "I'll get rid of these and grab some dessert."

Jason slid over into Callan's now-empty chair, and she looked at him questioningly. He was handsome with his long hair, beard, and tats, and she wondered why he was single.

"This probably isn't the most appropriate time, but I just wanted to tell you how happy you've made Callan. I might not be one of the original guys, but he and I have gotten to know each other over the last couple years. I've got a lot of respect for him, and, well, I'm glad for him that you're here."

Her heart warmed, but at the same time, his words made her nervous. She had no idea what she was going to do when her time at The Dunes Resort was up, and he had not fully decided about his plans.

As though Jason could sense her unease, he hastened to add, "Hey, this wasn't supposed to make you feel weird. I know it's early days now. I guess I just wanted to let you know that I've never seen him so happy."

Her heart just a tad lighter, she smiled and nodded. "Thanks, that means a lot."

Callan returned, shooting Jason a pretend glare as he placed a plate full of homemade pies, cobbler, and cake down in front of Sophie.

She gasped, saying, "Oh, my God, Callan! What do you expect me to do with all this food?"

He kissed the top of her head again as he slid into his seat, now vacated by Jason. "I expect you to share it with me."

She noted that he did not bring a separate plate for him and pushed the plate back between them. "Then I hope you're still hungry because all I can do is taste each of these."

Laughing, he dove in, and together, they quickly made the food go away. As the event came to a close and the Mayor made another speech, calling up the officers of the AL to receive the proceeds check from the benefit, people began to stand and slowly make their way out the door. Sophie once again found herself engulfed in more hugs by all their friends and family. All welcoming. All warm. All giving her the feeling that Baytown was, and always would be, home.

23

Several hours later, lying in bed with their arms and legs wrapped around each other, Callan was idly stroking Sophie's curls away from her face. Her slow, even breathing indicated she was almost asleep, but as his sated body relaxed his mind, he suddenly thought of the question she had asked earlier, and his curiosity had him give her a slight shake.

"Sophie, babe. Why did you ask me about the inlets near The Dunes Resort?" She stirred slightly, her eyes blinking open, an adorable crinkle between her brows.

"Oh, um…I was just wondering, that's all. There have been a few strange things that have happened over there that just made me wonder what they were used for."

His interest piqued, he shifted back slightly so that he could see her face in the moonlight. "What kind of strange things?"

"I've gone over to that side of the golf course a couple of times. It's behind some woods where there are lots to be sold for homes, but they haven't sold yet, so it's super private." Yawning widely, she added, "I went back there to just look at some of the plants that I might want to decorate with. You know, like pinecones, evergreens, berries." She closed her eyes, snuggling against him.

"And?" he prodded.

Blinking again, she sighed. "One day, at the water's edge when I was looking for cattails, I came across a canvas bag, I pulled it out of the water and looked inside—"

His body jerked as he bit out, "Jesus, Sophie. You have no idea what could have been in there. You find something like that, you bring it to someone else to look into."

Her eyes fully open now, she said, "Why on earth would I do that? I just thought there might be some ID inside in case I could return it to whoever lost it. But the only thing that was in it was bags of crab meat."

"Crab meat?" He sat up in bed and twisted around to turn on the nightstand lamp. Looking back at her, he repeated, "Crab meat?"

Sitting up as well, she shoved her mane of hair off her face and huffed. "Seriously, Callan? I admit when I first saw plastic bags in there, I thought that maybe I'd stumbled across some drug find—"

"Jesus." He dragged his hand over his face, shaking his head slightly.

"Yeah, it was pretty stinky. There were some of those freezer packs in there as well, but they were completely thawed, so the whole thing was super icky."

"What did you do with it?"

"There's a dumpster near the condos, so I took it there on my way back to the house and threw it away." Cocking her head to the side, she asked him, "Why?"

Sighing, he said, "I don't know. Curious, I guess. I don't like things that don't make sense, like a puzzle that needs to be solved."

"I just figured that somebody had gone crabbing, and one of their bags must've fallen over the boat."

"That still doesn't make sense." He reached his hand out to flip off the light when she spoke again.

"I wouldn't have really thought anything about it if it hadn't been for the men I saw on the boat the other night."

Turning slowly, his dark eyes pinned her to the bed as he asked, "What men? What boat? And what the fuck do you mean by the other *night*?"

"I don't really mean night," she backtracked, her arms crossing her body defensively. "I just mean right after sunset."

"Sophie, get to the men and the boat."

"Jeez, Callan," she grumbled. "I'd gone back out to see the sunset through the woods instead of just across the Bay. It was peaceful. I sat in the middle of some tall grass and just watched the sun in the sky through the trees. I closed my eyes for a few minutes because I just felt...good." She leaned forward and placed her hand on his arm as though begging him to understand. "I haven't had that kind of peace in so long, and I realized I was desperate for it."

He sighed and nodded, encouraging her to continue.

"I was startled when I heard a voice and opened my eyes to see a small, flat-bottomed boat being rowed into the inlet. They couldn't see me because I was sitting down and hidden by the seagrass. I also couldn't really see them because they were bundled up against the cold weather. Big coats, caps pulled over their ears, gloves, plus, it was just after sunset."

He thought for a moment, then said, "There are lots of reasons why someone might be back there if they were out fishing. As far as I know, there are no residential properties that back onto that inlet. Well, at least not ones where people are living. I'll take a look and see what I can find."

"I went back the next morning to see if I could find anything but—" Her words halted as he cursed under his breath, and she said, "Do you want me to tell my story or not? If so, stop getting pissy."

His ire shot up a notch, and he barked, "I'm not getting pissy. I'm getting irritated when my girlfriend tells me she's doing things that could be dangerous."

Her eyes widened and her mouth dropped open. "Girlfriend?"

The word *girlfriend* had just slipped out so naturally he had not given it a second thought. Sighing, he looked at her shocked face but was pleased to see that she did not appear upset, merely curious. Her bottom lip was pulled through her teeth, and her aqua eyes never left his face. She was staring intently, and he needed to explain.

Reaching over, he took her hands and held them between his own. "I can't lie to you, Sophie. The word girlfriend just came out, and I know I should apologize that I haven't actually asked, but it seems like that's the word that fits. I know we both have a lot going on in our professional lives, but reconnecting with you has given me a new purpose, a new focus. I don't want to be with anyone else, and I hope you don't either."

The pounding of his heart eased as her lips curved into a smile. She whispered, "Girlfriend," as though trying out the word. If her smile was any indication, she was happy with the title.

Still sitting on the bed, facing each other, they leaned forward, sealing their unspoken vow with a soft kiss. Muttering against her lips, he said, "As much as I would like to keep doing this, I want to get back to what happened after you saw the men."

Narrowing her eyes, she said, "That's not very romantic."

He cocked his eyebrow, and she nodded, rolling her eyes. "Okay, okay. The next morning, I went back to see if I could find the small wooden pier that I had noticed the day before. But suddenly that area was Grand Central Station. Roger Thorpe, the general manager, showed up and warned me that I really shouldn't be there. Then Travis Mars and Sue Connor, the golf pros, showed up separately and said the same thing. I ran into Ann Berkeley, the chef at The Dunes Resort Restaurant, and she said she was just out walking. But by then I thought it was a strange occurrence that everybody was in a section that nobody was really supposed to be in. By the time I got back to the house, my phone was ringing and Carlotta Ventura, the realtor, said she had heard I was there and wanted to warn me away as well."

Continuing to hold her hand, he rubbed his thumb over her soft knuckles, but his mind was racing with possibilities. Shaking his head slowly, he lifted his gaze to her, finding her quiet, giving him space to think. "I don't know, babe. Could be nothing. Probably is nothing. But I confess it sounds suspicious enough that I'd like to do a little checking. We're in charge of securing the waterways around here, so I'll talk to my Chief, Jeff, and go out with Jarrod or José to take a look around."

"I feel kind of foolish, Callan. I mean it seemed so suspicious at the time, but as I just said the words aloud to you," she shrugged, "it doesn't really make a lot of sense. I've already figured out that golf pros are super particular about the courses, although since I don't play golf, it seems like you have a lot of people walking on them all the time anyway. I get Roger was being finicky, because as the general manager, I know he's in charge of everything and probably figured I was whacking away at his plants. And the men on the boat? Probably just out fishing."

Nodding, Callan agreed. "You might be right, but I'd feel a lot better going out and checking. But you need to avoid that area. Just in case there's something going on over there, I don't want you in the middle of it."

"I've now got deliveries coming in every day, so I'm busy taking care of the house. I have another couple weeks to get it finished, and then I'll start working on the condo design. Believe me, I don't want to have everyone at The Dunes fussing at me!"

They slid back under the covers, and he flipped off the light on the nightstand. Tangling together once more, his mind continued to race as he felt her succumb to sleep. It was another hour before he was able to follow her, the odd events replaying in his mind.

24

Jeff had listened to Callan explain what Sophie reported, nodding as he took notes. "She said there was a wooden pier back there?"

Nodding, Callan said, "Yes, sir. She said it was very small and only extended about ten feet from the land."

"I know that Roger Thorpe had requested that The Dunes Resort be allowed to have a dock for resort members who wanted to launch kayaks into the inlet. But the last I heard, that was going to be closer to the Bay and not back where you say Sophie was. Also, I know that project had not been approved yet by The Dunes' management."

"If there's nothing else on my duty roster today, I was hoping to take one of the RB-S and patrol back there to take a look for myself."

Jeff had stood and walked over to a map on the wall that showed all the waterways in the area around Baytown that fell under their protection. Shaking his head slightly, he turned around and said, "I agree, it's worth looking into." He sat back down and added, "I'll call Ryan and ask if the VMP have come across anything."

"Thank you, sir. Is it okay if I take Jarrod?"

"Yes. While you're out, go ahead and explore the rest of the inlet and some of the others around, and make that your patrol today. There are several smaller inlets that feed into Logan's Pond, and we want to be thorough."

Leaving his office, he grabbed Jarrod on the way out of the building and they headed down to the dock. Moving out in the small boat, they pulled out of the harbor, making their way south to the end of the Baytown property, which also happened to be the area of The Dunes Resort. Curving around the small peninsula, they began moving northeast into the inlet. Following the shoreline into Logan's Pond, they maneuvered their vessel all the way to the end, not seeing a wooden dock.

On the east side were several properties, mostly owned by local farmers with an occasional house in sight. On the west was wooded property owned by The Dunes Resort, and from his knowledge of the area, he knew that they were home lots divided for sale but had not been developed yet.

Moving back out of the inlet, Jarrod called, "You want to take the smaller one that curves by the golf course?"

Nodding his affirmation, Jarrod steered them toward the north, moving them into a smaller inlet that was surrounded on both sides by land owned by The

Dunes Resort. Either side was bordered by trees, shrubs, and thick undergrowth that divided the golf course from the water. Looking ahead, he spied a small structure tucked behind a partially fallen tree.

Signaling to Jarrod, he kept his eye on the target, watching as a small wooden dock came into clearer view. Jarrod slowed the boat, and they drifted closer until they stopped. Callan took pictures before testing the stability of the structure by stepping over onto it. Walking to the end, he looked at some footprints in the mud at the shore's edge, but when he followed them, they disappeared into the grass. The area was not visible from the golf cart path, so anyone using it would have to know about its location.

"Got anything?" Jarrod called.

Nodding, he said, "Fairly recent footprints. They disappear into the woods. Only thing on the other side is the golf cart path and course."

"You think this is where Sophie was?"

"It's gotta be," he said, his gaze still surveying the area.

"This time of year there are few golfers, so it'd be easy for someone to come out here unseen. Drop something off...pick something up."

"We're thinking the same thing," he said, climbing back on the boat. "It's just too weird that as remote as this is she would have run into so many people converging at this place in the dead of winter. But what they were doing and why, I've got no fuckin' clue."

They continued to patrol for another hour before

heading back to the station, where Callan reported to Jeff.

"I talked to Ryan, but the VMP haven't been investigating anything in that area," Jeff said. "We can put it on our rotational patrol, perhaps even at night."

"Thanks, Chief. With your permission, I'd like to involve Mitch Evans as well. Since the resort lies in the town boundaries, I'd like the Police Chief to know as well."

"Good," Jeff acknowledged.

"Why did she stick her hand down in something she couldn't identify?" Mitch asked. "Jesus, that sounds like something Jillian would do."

Callan was at the Baytown Police Station talking to Mitch and some of his officers. Grant, Lance, and Ginny were at the table. He knew that even though Jillian was Grant's wife, she was Mitch's cousin, and he was exactly right.

"She said it smelled funny—"

"Which would be another reason not to stick her hand down in a bag," Grant quipped.

"I know, I know," Callan agreed. "But when she saw the plastic bags filled with something unidentifiable, she was curious. Once she had it out, she could tell it was crab meat."

"That's just weird," Ginny said, her nose wrinkling.

"Poaching?" Lance asked, but as the words left his mouth, he was already shaking his head.

"To get that much crab meat, you'd have to cook them, get the meat, and bag it up. She said there were melted ice packs in there as well, so whoever had them planned on transporting them."

"I honestly don't know," Mitch admitted. "So far, there's been no crime, but I don't like puzzles that don't have answers."

"That's exactly what I said," Callan said. "Jeff is having us continue to patrol the area, so maybe we can find something and solve the mystery of the crabs at the same time."

"What about The Dunes Resort manager? Would he know about the dock on the back side of the golf course?"

"Since he was one of the people who were out there the morning Sophie went back, I'd rather not mention it to him. If someone is using it to bring something in, I don't want to give him warning," Mitch said.

Placing his hands on the table to lift himself up, Callan thanked the group. "I'm heading out. I'll let you know if we find anything."

With goodbyes said, he headed out of the Police Station and walked down the street to Jason's auto shop.

Jason had met Zac when they were in the Navy, and not having a supportive hometown to return to, Zac had invited him to move to Baytown. A gifted mechanic, he was also a licensed tattoo artist, having created many of the tattoos that their friends sported.

Callan walked past the small storefront that Jason used in the evenings and weekends to do his tattoo work and into the office of the mechanic's garage. Jason was just coming from the back, wiping his hands on a rag before shoving it into his pocket. Long hair, often streaming around his shoulders, was pulled up in a man bun for safety around the car engines. As soon as his eyes hit Callan's, Jason grinned widely.

"Hell, man. Been a while since you've come around the shop." Jason nodded toward an empty chair in the office, and Callan took him up on the silent invitation to sit. Both settling in, Jason asked, "What's up?"

"Just thought I'd stop in for a few minutes. I was over at the Police Station reporting a few strange things that Sophie had seen, but that may be all it is...just something strange."

Jason's face immediately showed concern as his eyes narrowed, and he tilted his head to the side. "Is she okay?"

Nodding his assurance, he said, "Yeah, yeah. She was over at The Dunes, out in the woods on the east side near one of the inlets of Logan's Pond. Of course, she had to go over there when it was almost dark. And then got spooked when some men in a boat came by. She thought they might be going to a little wooden dock that's back there."

Shaking his head slightly, Jason commented, "Hate to point out the obvious, Callan, but this is a fishing community. I'm not sure I would count that as being strange."

"I know. I guess it was just that the whole thing gave her a creepy feeling. There actually isn't supposed to be a dock over there, so I did go to check it out. It's been used recently, so someone's going back there. The day before, she found a bag that had plastic baggies of crab-meat in it. It was already ruined, and she said it smelled bad so she threw it away."

Jason leaned back in his chair, his eyebrows now lifted toward his head, and said, "Okay, you're right. That doesn't make any sense."

Lifting his shoulders in a shrug, he said, "At first I wondered if maybe there was some kind of illegal activity going on, but Mitch hasn't heard of anything. My Chief has me putting that area now on our patrol, both day and night, so we'll keep an eye on it." He leaned back in his chair as well, his eyes taking in the small office. He knew that the original owners had divided the area so that there would be a separate business next door, and Jason had purchased both of them. "How's your tattoo business going?"

"Not too bad. It's busier in the warmer months when we have more tourists come through. But considering it's the only tattoo shop in the county, I get a decent business. At least enough to keep it open Thursday and Friday evenings as well as weekends. It doesn't bring a ton of money, but I enjoy the artistry."

"Fuck, Jason, that means you're working all the time."

"What the hell else am I going to do? All you guys have fallen in love, gotten married, and are making babies."

Throwing his hands up in mock defense, he said, "I'm not that far gone yet."

"Not yet," Jason quipped. His face warmed, and he added, "I gotta tell you, Callan, I'm real glad for you. I

247

told that to Sophie the other evening. When I came to Baytown at Zac's invitation, I couldn't believe there was such a group of really good guys. Good people. Good friends. Fuck, just good. And you're one of the best, so if anyone deserves to get the girl they've always pined for, it'd be you."

A witty retort died on his lips as Callan realized Jason's words were absolutely true. *I got the girl I'd always pined for.* A grin slid across his face as he nodded. "It feels good. Thanks."

Standing, he turned back to Jason, and asked, "Whatever happened to that woman that was hoping to open an ice cream shop here in Baytown and got pissed when you bought the property she was looking at? I know she was friends with Jillian and Katelyn and that whole gang, but then she just disappeared, and I never heard anything else about her. The only reason I thought of her now is because at one time she wanted to open her shop where your tattoo place went in, right next door."

Jason's lips turned down in a frown, and he rubbed his chin. "Rose. Her name was Rose Parker. Honest to God, I didn't know she wanted the place next door, but I'd already had my offer in to the real estate agent. It seems that she came along the day after, but the contract had already been signed and money put down. I've got no doubt that pompous Mayor Banks would've much preferred to have had an ice cream shop than my tattoo shop."

"She could have gone for another place. Hell, Baytown's got quite a few empty storefronts. If she was that thin-skinned, I'm not sure she would make a very good businesswoman."

Jason rushed, "No, no, I don't think it was that. I think the timing just wasn't right. I heard Jillian say that Rose had to leave town to go take care of a family member that was ill."

"Then it's just as well you got the building."

Shrugging, Jason shoved his hands in his pockets and said "I felt bad for her. I just got the feeling that life was kind of handing her one difficulty after another."

Staring at his friend carefully, Callan remarked, "Seems like you remember her really well."

Glaring, Jason said, "Nah. She was pretty and seemed real nice when she wasn't pissed at me for getting the contract first. She kind of reminded me of a little kitten. All soft and cute but watch out for those claws."

Throwing his head back in laughter, he shook Jason's hand before walking out, calling over his shoulder, "Yeah, sounds like you're the one with a soft spot!"

25

Several days later, Sophie plastered a smile on her face as she sat at a table in The Dunes Restaurant, wishing she were with her friends instead of Roger, Travis, Sue, and Carlotta. The only one not present was Ann, but she knew the chef was in the back preparing their meal.

Carlotta and Roger were talking about the upcoming spring photo shoot with Southern Living Magazine.

"I was over at the house the other day, and I'm so impressed," Roger enthused, his smile wide. "I know I was concerned about the decor being too *beachy*, but you have incorporated the colors brilliantly. The pinecone, evergreen, and berry wreaths are stunning. And the cattails! How you managed to make something that could be cheesy into classy...well, my hat's off to you."

Warming under his praise, she felt her tension lift. It was obvious that Sue and Travis were bored with the conversation, but then Roger turned the conversation to the golf courses, wanting them in peak condition for the spring.

Glad to no longer be the center of attention, she turned to Carlotta, who had been busily tapping on her smartphone. Finally setting the device down on the table, the realtor turned to her and asked, "Are you ready for the condo design?"

"Yes...in fact, I was over there this morning. The space is beautiful but so much smaller than the house, so it won't take long." Pulling out her iPad, she opened the designs she had created, including the colors. "I want to use paler colors since I want to create the idea of maximum space."

Flipping through the screens, Carlotta's face relaxed into a smile. "These are beautiful, Sophie. I think it will photograph well." Her phone buzzed again, and Carlotta's attention moved back to the screen as she tapped out another reply. A grimace crossed her face before casting Sophie an apologetic gaze, saying, "A real estate agent is never off duty."

"I can see that," she laughed.

"Yes, but work at what?" Sue quipped, her left eyebrow lifted.

"My work is important," Carlotta fired back. "I'm securing the future of this resort. Your golf memberships only go so far...my home sales bring in the big money."

Everyone's attention was diverted when Ann and two servers brought out their food. Sophie dove in, once more ready to get back to work and away from the undercurrent that seemed to be darting around the table.

Ann sat down heavily at the table to join them, and soon she and Roger were in a debate over the expansion plans for the restaurant.

"So, how much longer do you have here?"

Turning to the side, she realized Travis was speaking to her. Swallowing her bite, she said, "I'll be finished in about another six weeks. I'll spend the next few weeks working on the condo, then I'll make sure everything is perfect at the house."

"Are you planning on sticking around town?"

His question sounded pointed, but she was uncertain if there was a hidden meaning behind the words.

"Well, my plans are fluid at this point," she answered. Taking a sip of iced tea to wash down the bite of food that seemed to stick in her throat, she pushed her chair back and announced, "Thank you for the lunch, everyone. Ann, it was delicious as always."

Hurrying out to the lobby, she darted into the ladies' room. After she finished, her hand was on the door to push it open, and she heard dim voices, as though the speakers were close but not close enough for her to distinguish who was speaking.

"I don't trust her."

"She'll be gone soon."

"What can she know? And, if she does, what will she do?"

"Hopefully, nothing."

The voices carried down the hall, and she made her escape. Hurrying toward her car, she noticed the row of golf carts lined up along the sidewalk. Assuming they were in for maintenance since there were few golfers out today, her eye was caught by a canvas bag lying in the floorboard of one of them. *It looks like the one I found.*

She walked over, attempting to appear casual, wanting to discern who the bag belonged to without drawing undue attention to herself. Glancing around, she saw no one and was almost to the bag when her phone rang.

Grabbing it quickly, she looked at the caller ID, recognizing one of the businesses she ordered from. Finding that they were at the house, ready to deliver the last of the patio furniture, she knew she needed to leave.

Just then Travis walked out of a side door, and slung over his shoulder was a canvas bag like the one in the golf cart. He walked toward the carts, and she ducked down behind her car and watched. He moved to a different cart and tossed his bag to the seat before driving off. Starting her car, she backed out of the parking and began to leave, her mind swirling with confusion.

"Hey, Callan," Tanisha called out as he walked into the station. "Chief is looking for you. He said for you to go to the conference room as soon as you got here."

With a chin lift acknowledgment, he turned and walked back down the hall. The conference room door next to Jeff's office was closed, and he knocked on the doorframe first.

"Come on in," Jeff replied.

Stepping through, he was surprised at the gathering inside. Eyes darting around, he recognized Mitch, Colt, and Ryan forming a law enforcement gathering. There were three other people in attendance, two men and a woman, all wearing jackets with NOAA insignia.

The National Oceanic Atmospheric Administration had a presence in the Bay for science-based management and conservation of fisheries, marine mammals, endangered species, and their habitats. Curious, he moved into the room and sat down, turning his attention to Jeff. His Chief, never one to mince words, got to business immediately.

"Callan, you'd be hearing about this investigation soon because we've been asked to assist. You're in here today because of possible information that you may have become aware of."

Looking around the room again, he observed the serious expressions and wondered what information Jeff could be referring to. Shifting slightly in his seat, he looked back to his boss.

"We've got local law enforcement here, as you can obviously tell, with the Baytown Police, North Heron Sheriff, and the Virginia Marine Police. We also have Brady Dobson, Chuck Roberts, and Vicki Smith, investigators from the NOAA. I'll turn this over to Chuck."

Callan looked at the man who began to speak, his square jaw cleanly shaven and his gray hair military short. Stocky in build, he had piercing blue eyes that bespoke intelligence.

"We've been investigating the Chambers Seafood Company that is based out of Manteague, Virginia.

What started with a complaint from a consumer made its way to Sheriff Hudson, and he turned it over to us. With an inside informer, we've spent months building a case against the company. As you may know, seafood fraud is very lucrative. The United States is the second largest importer of seafood in the world, and the fraud in that business brings in between one to two billion dollars a year."

Callan had been aware of the NOAA investigations into seafood fraud, the Chesapeake Bay being one of the areas they focused on but had no idea it was as widespread or lucrative as Chuck was indicating. Giving his full attention to the investigator, he nodded for him to continue.

"Most people go to a restaurant and order seafood that's advertised on the menu, having no idea if that's what they're really eating or not. But the fish could've been illegally imported, with high levels of mercury, or from endangered species, or from illegal fishing practices." Giving a rueful chuckle, he added, "Of course, sometimes when we open shipping containers with seafood, we never know what we'll get. Drugs and guns have even been found buried inside the packages of seafood. The goddamn criminals will sell the drugs and guns, and then sell the seafood that's been sitting around that ship for months. People eat at a restaurant, maybe get sick, and have no idea why or what their bodies are being exposed to.

"The legal importation of seafood is obviously fine, but a company in the United States who is importing may not know where it's coming from. It's estimated that over twenty percent of the Indonesian crab imported came from illegal fishing practices. On top of that, all the criminal has to do in shipment is replace the labels indicating 'Product of Indonesia' with labels declaring 'Product of Maryland', therefore gaining a higher price. For one shipment alone, the importer could get an extra half a million dollars. And believe me, they do not want to be caught. The fines and jail sentences are huge."

Callan was amazed at the information coming forth, but as soon as the word crab had been mentioned his thoughts jumped to Sophie. *Jesus, what did she stumble into?*

Chuck continued, "We have enough evidence to go after Chambers Seafood as knowingly obtaining illegal seafood, but we're looking to find the supplier. We tested some of their crab and found that it contained DNA from crab that came from outside U.S. waters. We brought Sheriff Hudson—Colt—back into our investigation since Chambers Seafood is in the County of North Heron. We've been keeping an eye on the waterways, using Ryan and the VMP, but have not been able to discover where it's coming from. You brought forward some information that made its way back to Colt, therefore to us."

Chuck pinned Callan with a hard stare and said, "I'd like to hear what your girlfriend discovered."

For a second, the word *girlfriend* spoken by someone else reverberated through his mind. He knew he had surprised her the other day when he used that term, but somehow hearing it from someone else made it seem more real. As quickly as that thought came, he jerked slightly, bringing himself back to the matter at hand.

Describing what she told him she found and where, he continued with his part of an initial investigation. "So, while I did find the small wooden dock that does not look like it has been there for very long and footprints right off the dock, there was nothing else that I could see."

"What she found was raw crab?" Vicki asked, her eyes wide in incredulity. She looked over at Chuck and Brady, saying, "That makes this even more horrendous. That could indicate that the crab had never been pasteurized before transporting."

Callan's mind began to race with the possibilities of the investigation and how it might involve Sophie. Looking at Chuck, he asked, "Are you thinking that what she found came off of a ship in the bay?"

"The Lim family crime organization in Thailand is known for their seafood fraud, but in Asia, they appear to be greatly protected. The crime families have huge influence over the government and are able to maintain their freedom. Our job has been to find the proof we needed to shut them down as far as importation here. We were not sure how they were getting the tainted seafood to Chambers, but with what Ms. Bayles discovered, we now think that it may be transported in a variety of ways, including being brought from the ships and taken to inlets where it is picked up by a person or persons who will then transport it to Chambers. Our inside informant has given us what we need to crack down on what is coming by cans through the large cargo ships. We've boarded them, obtained evidence, but there is still some coming in in smaller quantities."

Clarifying, he said, "So, we've possibly got someone getting illegal crab off of some of the ships, bringing it into the Logan's Pond Inlet near The Dunes Resort, where someone has built a small dock, and picking it up to make a delivery."

"That's what we think," Chuck agreed. "We had no idea where it might be coming into until our contacts with the local law enforcement gave us the information about Ms. Bayles. Obviously, she had no idea what she found and therefore threw it away. It's interesting that she told you about the people she ran into in that area the next day. It's also interesting that they all seem to want her to stay away."

Eyes shifting to Jeff, he asked, "Do you want us to patrol at night?"

"NOAA has authority in this case, but that's the reason we're all meeting here today. We all want to be cognizant of what's going on and how best to capture the ones responsible. Chambers is in Colt's jurisdiction, so he will be monitoring the comings and goings there as best he can. The Dunes Resort is in Mitch's jurisdiction, but we don't want to tip off anyone who might work or live there that we are watching. Our and Ryan's officers have jurisdiction over the waterways around here and will be best suited to watch." Jeff added, "I'm also assigning you and Jarrod to go with the NOAA this afternoon when they board a transport ship in the Bay. You'll be joined by the CG out of Portsmouth."

A thrill of excitement moved through Callan, excited

to have the opportunity to work with the NOAA investigators and fellow CG for a bust of an international crime organization.

Mitch, having been silent up to now, looked at Callan and asked, "Is Sophie staying out of this? Has she been back to that area out of curiosity?"

Shaking his head, he replied, "No, she's been busy with the designs and was irritated that she'd been warned away but has no need to go back. At least, that's what she's assured me."

As the meeting continued and the officers began divvying the duties, he was glad that she was busy. *As long as she's not near that dock, she should be safe.*

26

One of the difficulties the Coast Guard has in approaching a suspected watercraft, whether it was a small boat or a massive container ship, is the open water. Unlike law enforcement on land, the element of surprise is rare, making the job more difficult for the Coast Guard and easier for the criminals to get rid of evidence.

Boarding ships for routine checks often gave the CG a chance to have the element of surprise on their side when they began searching. The ship they approached was sailing under a Liberian flag but came from Thailand.

Taking orders from the Portsmouth CG officer in charge, they moved with the others, weapons drawn, as they searched in the areas below deck. Most of the NOAA investigators went to the containers that were labeled for imported seafood and began random testing. Listening to the radio in his ear, Callan knew that they had found repackaged tins and a stack of labels, 'Produced in Maryland', nearby. He could also hear that the captain of the cargo ship, first claiming to only speak Chinese, was now speaking English and proclaiming he knew nothing about the relabeling of produce, even though the work was being done on his ship.

Entering the ship's large galley, Callan, Jarrod, and the others found what they were looking for. Off to one side, huge pots on massive stoves held crabs being boiled. Almost 20 Asian workers were standing at tables, the cooked crabs piled up in front of them. With practiced and deft movements, they each would crack them, dig out the crabmeat and toss it into large buckets. In a room right off the galley, more workers took the cooked crab meat and packed it into tins before sending them down a chute that would seal them with the lid. More labels with 'Produced in Maryland' were in boxes, waiting to be attached to the tins.

In his career, he had seen the elaborate means for transporting drugs and guns, but this was his first view of the intricate and yet so simple set up for seafood fraud.

As soon as the workers saw the CG approaching with their automatic weapons, a flurry of scrambling ensued. With a few barked orders from a CG member who spoke their language, the workers quickly settled, their hands flying into the air.

They were handcuffed and taken to a waiting area while some of the CG began gathering evidence. Bagging up some of the crab while Jarrod took photographs, Callan looked over his shoulder as Brady and Vicki came in.

She seemed almost gleeful as she exclaimed, "Finally. Getting one of the big players in this industry is huge. In the grand scheme, it might be a drop in the bucket, but every one of these guys we can shut down helps protect the food industry in the United States."

Callan asked, "Can you tie this into Chambers Seafood?"

"We'll do DNA testing on it, but from what I understand, there's someone that's been arrested that's giving us information on where they distributed."

Brady looked at the operation that had been going on in the galley and shook his head. "The relabeling of packaged crab is bad enough, but this crab isn't pasteurized so whoever's been getting this is really endangering people's lives, especially if there are high levels of mercury in it."

Brady and Vicki moved closer to the table and looked at some of the evidence bags Callan had laid to the side. "If this is what Sophie found, then whoever is picking it up and delivering it to Chambers has to know what they're doing is wrong. Now, if they can just be caught."

His jaw hardened as his dark eyes settled on them. "We'll get them."

The condo was so much easier to decorate because of its much smaller size. Sophie had spent the afternoon receiving the furniture that was delivered, making sure it was in the right room. With all the furniture in place, she would be able to spend part of the next several days placing the décor. The curtains were hung, dark green with black and yellow accents, showcasing the walls that she left eggshell white. Tall, potted, fake palm trees that appeared real were worth the extravagant price when they were placed in either corner of the living room. The sofa in a soft yellow and two chairs in pale green gave the room an elegant appeal.

Deciding that for the rest of the week she would spend her mornings in the condo with the last of the decorating, her afternoons would be spent at the large house where she could watch the winter sun set. Checking her watch, she smiled, deciding to head back to the house. It only took her five minutes to drive from the condos to the area of The Dunes where the show house was located. Walking in from the garage, she had become so familiar with every nuance of every room that it almost felt like her own. *Well, my own if I could afford a two-million-dollar house!*

Walking into the living room, she opened the blinds and stared out onto the Bay. She had received a text from Callan telling her that he would be late, and as she viewed the large cargo ships and fishing vessels in the distance, she wondered if he was out on the water. Her mind turned over the details that she knew about his job, and acceptance moved through her. She had been so despondent after Philip's death that the idea of being with anyone who had a dangerous job was an unacceptable risk. Having suffered such heartache, she wanted to guard her heart at all costs. But her mother was right…life is full of risks.

He had mentioned not reenlisting in the Coast Guard, instead taking a job with the Virginia Marine Police. Sucking in a deep breath, she let it out slowly, her heart full. *He could do any career he wanted, and my love would still be the same.*

The realization made her almost giddy, and she could not wait to tell him. Seeing the sky began to turn the magnificent colors, she wrapped her scarf tighter and pulled on her gloves, determined to watch the sunset from the beach. Locking the door behind her, she looped her purse over her shoulders and crossed the short distance through the seagrass and over the sand dune.

The wind had a bite to it, but for the latter part of February, it was not too bad. She pulled her cap down over her ears and walked along the white, sandy beach. Stopping a short way from the house, she watched as the sun continued to lower in the sky.

A loud shot rang out, and the sand near her feet flew up. Jumping, she turned around quickly, wondering what she had heard and seen. Another shot rang out, and this time it came closer to her. Realization dawned, and she dropped to her knees, scrambling and crawling toward the dune.

Shit! Shit! Shit! Someone's shooting! Pressing back into the sand dune as far as she could, she hoped she was hidden by the tall grass. Her breath coming in pants, she pulled her phone from her purse with shaking fingers. Dialing 911, she cried, "Someone's shooting out on the beach!"

The emergency dispatcher calmly asked for her identification and location.

"I'm Sophie Bayles, and I'm on the beach at The Dunes Resort. I'm in the Plantation section of the resort, just on the beach below the large house on the point."

Answering the dispatcher's questions as best she could, her eyes continued to dart around, but she saw no one and heard no other shots.

"Can you get safely to the house?"

"I don't know. I don't want to move."

The dispatcher assured her that the Baytown Police were on their way. She continued to listen to the dispatcher's calm voice and answer her questions, the adrenaline now making her entire body shake. It seemed like forever, but she finally heard the sirens. It took another moment, but hearing her name called out by Mitch, she threw her phone back into her purse and screamed out his name.

Mitch ran over, and she rushed into his arms. He held her closely, murmuring, "You're okay. We've got you now, Sophie."

Working to steady her breathing, she gulped in air.

"Hey, Squirt. You doin' okay?"

She turned at the sound of Grant's voice, her lips curving slightly at the nickname Philip had given her, not having heard it in a long time. Strange how comforting that nickname sounded now. "Yeah." Jerking her head up and down, she repeated, "Yeah."

Lance stalked over and gave her a head to toe assessing look, offering a chin lift before turning to

Mitch and saying, "We don't see anyone here. There are no footprints on the sand besides Sophie's, so they weren't on the beach."

Mitch had steadied her with his hands on her shoulders and leaned down so that his face was close to hers. "Tell us exactly what happened."

Running a shaking hand into her hair to pull her loosened, windblown curls out of her face, she said, "I was just walking along, enjoying the sunset." She turned slightly and pointed out toward the beach. "I had made it to right over there when I heard a shot. Almost instantly a puff of sand shot up near my feet." Her brow furrowed as she shook her head. "I didn't know what was. I've heard gunshots before, but truthfully, it's been years ago. My brain just couldn't process what was happening fast enough, so I stood there. Then I heard another shot, and the sand right next to my feet puffed up again. That's when it finally dawned on me that someone was shooting at me!"

She observed Mitch give a curt nod to Grant and Lance, sending them out to the beach to where she had pointed. "I want you to stay here with Ginny. Okay?"

Once more, she agreed with jerky motions of her head and sucked in another ragged breath. She watched as Mitch joined Grant and Lance then jolted as Ginny moved over and touched her arm.

"Sophie, can you think of anything else that you saw? Had you seen someone else on the beach earlier? Did you hear anything on the water? Did you see any boats go by? As you walked along, did you hear anything unusual?"

She turned and looked at Ginny, admiring the pretty woman's calming touch and soft voice. In the middle of the craziness of what had happened, her heart was suddenly filled with happiness, knowing that Brogan had found love with Ginny. Blurting, "Does it bother Brogan that you're a police officer?"

Ginny blinked at the sudden change of topic, but instead of insisting that Sophie stick to the subject at hand, she smiled and replied, "He struggled at first. He's a man that likes to be in charge. Not necessarily in charge of me, but he likes to be in control of situations. Of course, most of the time he's not around when I'm doing my job. But the few times that he was, he struggled."

"He seems fine with it now." Her voice sounded strange to her own ears as she talked about Brogan and Ginny right after she had been shot at, but she was curious.

Ginny's smile widened, and she agreed. "He wants me to be safe. He doesn't want me to get hurt. But he knows that I'm good at my job, and I won't take unnecessary chances. So," she shrugged, "he's glad that I have a job I love."

Nodding slowly, Sophie's lips twitched nervously into a small smile. Reaching out, she clasped Ginny's hand and said, "I'm glad. I'm glad you have a job that you love and are so good at. And I'm glad that you have Brogan. He's a good man. He deserves a good woman."

Hearing Lance calling out on the beach, her own situation slammed back into her, and she jerked. "Good grief, you asked me questions, and I started talking about you and Brogan."

"It's okay," Ginny replied, her smile still in place on her pretty face. "You're dealing with the shock. And sometimes talking about something mundane helps with that."

Grateful for Ginny's understanding, she said, "You asked me if I saw anything or heard anything. I didn't. In fact, the thought crossed my mind that out here it was as though I was the only person in the world. I didn't hear anyone else, I didn't see anyone else, there were no noises at all. I didn't hear the gulls calling. There were some geese that flew from behind me overhead, but other than their honking, I heard nothing."

She and Ginny looked up as Mitch and Lance approached, Mitch holding up a plastic bag. She was uncertain what she was looking at, but he explained, "We found two bullets in the sand near where your footprints had stopped."

Shoulders slumping, her knees suddenly felt very weak. Ginny slipped her arm around her waist, giving her the steadiness needed to lock her knees in place. "I know this sounds stupid, but I'm really glad you found those. I mean, I know what I heard and what I saw, but it's all so unbelievable. I was actually beginning to wonder if I had imagined the entire crazy incident, so as scary as it is that you found those, it means that I haven't lost my mind."

Shaking his head, his jaw tight, Mitch said, "You definitely didn't imagine it, Sophie."

"She heard no birds other than some geese that flew

from right behind her, Chief," Ginny said, repeating to Mitch what Sophie had said.

Their gazes shot to the dunes behind them, and Mitch gave a chin lift to Lance, pointing in the direction of the dunes. "See if it looks like someone was up there. The geese may have flown away from someone up there."

Sophie asked, "But why was somebody shooting? I know sometimes they let hunters on the resort to shoot geese or deer, but I haven't heard anything about that happening now. And there was no warning given out at all."

She observed Mitch, Grant, and Ginny all sharing a look but had no idea what it meant. Before she could ask, she heard shouting from behind them, and as they all turned their heads in unison, she saw Roger and Travis coming toward them.

Roger's face was red, and he began to shout as he approached. "What on earth is going on out here? I hear sirens, and I show up finding the police walking around, possibly stepping on delicate plants and seagrass!"

By the time Roger reached their group, he was still red-faced but now breathing heavily. His eyes raked through them before landing on Sophie. Now addressing her specifically, he said, "What is going on? What have you done?"

"Me? I haven't done anything!"

Before anyone else could speak, Travis joined them. Addressing Mitch, he said, "What's going on?"

Roger huffed and said, "That's what I've been asking."

Sophie opened her mouth to reply again, but Ginny gave her arm a slight squeeze, and when she looked over at her, Ginny shook her head. She remained quiet, gratefully allowing Mitch to answer the question, the slow dawning of realization finally hitting. *Someone was shooting and could have hit me!*

27

Watching Mitch in fascination, Sophie was impressed with not only him but also Grant. Both so professional and completely in charge, she could not help but think how proud Philip would be of them. Grant, the cute high school guy that all the girls wanted to be with, now happily married and a dedicated policeman. Mitch, the serious athlete, now fulfilling the role of Police Chief with an air of calm intelligence.

So focused on those thoughts, she almost missed what Mitch had asked Roger and Travis, but seeing their shocked faces brought her back.

"What do you mean, where were we?" Roger sputtered.

"The question is very obvious," Mitch replied. "Where were you in the last hour?"

"I was in my office at The Dunes Resort Sports Center."

Mitch's gaze swung to Travis, and the golf pro answered, "I was on the course. I always take a turn around the course on my golf cart in the evening before leaving."

"Did you hear anything or see anything suspicious?"

Roger's ire began to deflate, and his gaze moved between Mitch and Sophie. Shaking his head slowly, he said, "No. Nothing strange at all. What's going on?"

Before answering Roger's question, he looked at Travis. "You were out on the course. Did you see or hear anything?"

"No. There was no one out. I didn't see anyone or hear anything."

"There's not supposed to be any controlled hunting at this time—"

Roger cut in, "Absolutely not. That's not allowed!"

"And yet someone shot at Ms. Bayles." Mitch had barely gotten the words out before both Roger and Travis gasped, their eyes wide.

"Oh, my God! Are you hurt?" Roger asked, his focus now on Sophie.

Shaking her head, she said, "No. I wasn't hit."

"Thank God for that," Travis said. "This will be a nightmare if this gets out. We've got a tournament coming up in two weeks, and the last thing we want is for people to think that there is shooting on the course!"

Sophie gasped, and Travis turned to her, his features softening slightly. "Sophie, I'm not trying to be insensitive over what you thought happened, but The Dunes needs the money that these golf tournaments bring in. We can't have people canceling out of an irrational fear."

Before she had a chance to respond in indignation, Mitch held up his hand, the evidence bag with two slugs in it and said, "There's nothing irrational about it. Sophie was shot at." Turning to stare at Travis again, he said, "And yet you claim to not have heard anything."

Roger and Travis stared at the bag, their eyes growing impossibly wider. Roger's hand hit his chest as he proclaimed, "Oh, my God! This is insane!" Looking at Sophie, he asked, "Are you okay?"

"No, I'm not okay. Being shot at while enjoying the sunset was not what I expected to have happen!"

Travis was shaking his head, his fist on his hips, saying, "I didn't hear anything. This is madness. Why on earth would somebody be out here shooting? We have very set weeks that someone can come out here to shoot geese, and it's always advertised. Everyone in this area knows that you can't hunt here outside of those weeks." He twisted his body, appearing to look up and down the beach, before turning behind him and looking at the dunes. Facing the others again, he said, "It must have come from the water. Someone must've been shooting at waterfowl from a boat on the water. That's the only thing that makes sense!"

Mitch did not reply but instead said, "I'll let you give your statements to Lance." He nodded toward Lance, who escorted the two men back over the dunes.

Once they were out of earshot, Sophie looked at Mitch and said, "There wasn't a boat, of that I'm sure. I wasn't just staring at the sunset, I was looking out over the Bay. To be honest, I was thinking of Callan and how much he loves being on the water. So my gaze was going back and forth over the whole area, not just toward the setting sun. There were no fishing boats, no canoes, no one kayaking. The only thing I could see on the water was in the middle of the Bay...some of the large cargo ships, and of course, they're so far away you can barely see them."

Mitch handed the evidence bag to Grant before turning back to Sophie, his eyes still hard. "I believe you, Sophie. The angle that the ammunition hit the sand indicates that the shooter was over the dunes." He nodded his head toward the dunes in the opposite direction from where Lance had escorted Roger and Travis.

A bank of tall seagrass covered the dunes, and it was not hard to imagine how easy it would be for someone to hide there. Plus, just behind the dunes was a stand of trees, making it easy for someone to fire a weapon and then run into hiding. If they knew the area well, they could quickly disappear on foot or golf cart to get somewhere safe in the time that it took for her to make her call and the police to arrive.

Swallowing deeply, she forced herself to breathe. "So someone wasn't just firing a gun, but they were firing it at me? Someone was trying to kill me?"

"Not unless they were a fuckin' bad shot," Grant said, earning a quick glare from Mitch.

"I don't understand," she said, looking between them.

"Sophie, right now we don't know anything other than what we've found," Mitch said. "What Grant is alluding to is that at this distance someone would have to be either a bad shot if they were hoping to hit you, or all they wanted to do was scare you."

"Scare me? Jesus, all I'm doing is designing some property here. It's not like I'm investigating some major crime!"

"We're going to take a look at everything," Mitch promised. "Ginny, why don't you take her back to get her car and drive her back to her house."

Staring out onto the darkening sky, she said, "I don't even know what to tell Callan."

"I know he's out on a mission right now," Mitch said. "I've already let his Chief know, so Callan will be finding out soon. We'll let him know we're taking you to your parents' house."

"Oh, Lordy, my parents," she moaned.

Ginny wrapped an arm around her and said, "Don't worry about it. When I take you home, I'll talk to them and explain it."

Thankful to have her friends' assistance, she nodded and allowed herself to be led away from the beach.

Shot at? Fuckin' hell, shot at? Trying not to wreck his truck, Callan kicked up gravel from his tires as he sped out of the station's parking lot. The automatic gate swung open, and he stomped on the accelerator, fish-tailing the backend until his tires could grab asphalt.

They had come in from their productive raid, all of them feeling the adrenaline high from knowing they were closer to busting an international seafood fraud ring. As soon as he stepped into the station, Jeff grabbed him by the shoulders and barked, "I need you to stay cool, but I got a call from Mitch. Someone took a couple of shots at Sophie when she was on the beach at The Dunes."

Before he could process what the Chief had told him, Jeff continued, "She's fine. Wasn't hit. She called 911, and the BPD got her. They're investigating, and one of them took her to her parents' house."

He started running down the hall, shouts of *'Good luck'*, and *'Let us know what we can do'*, coming from the others.

It only took five minutes to drive from the station to her house, but each second seem to crawl slowly. Mind racing, he could not imagine how scared she must have been. *Why were hunters out now?* As soon as Mitch found out who was shooting near the private beach, he hoped he had a few minutes alone with them before the police took control.

Jerking into the alley, he came to a screeching stop outside his parents' garage. Jumping down from the cab of his truck, his feet pounded the ground as he ran toward the Bayles' back door.

Someone must have already heard him because the door was thrown open by the time he got there. Seeing his dad at the Bayles' kitchen door did not surprise him, considering the two families were so close.

"Son, she's okay. She's in the living room with the others. I've been on the lookout for you."

His father's firm hand on his shoulder helped him catch his breath and settle his anxiety slightly before he stalked down the hall to the living room. Not wanting to scare Sophie with his anger, he tried to tamp it down, but the instant their eyes landed on each other, it ramped back up again. Her aqua eyes were large with shadows underneath against her pale face.

She jumped from the sofa and ran toward him, leaping into his arms just as he opened them wide to catch her.

"I'm okay, I'm okay, I'm okay," she repeated, her face buried in his neck.

With one hand tangled in her mass of curls and the other banded tightly around her waist, he held her body close to his, breathing in her sweet scent.

He closed his eyes tightly, memorizing the feel of her in his arms and the acceptance that she was right where he wanted her to be. He had no idea how much time had passed before he finally opened his eyes, and peering over her shoulder, observed her parents, his parents, and Ginny in the room quietly chatting, giving them a moment of privacy.

He settled Sophie's feet back on the floor but kept her body tightly pressed to his. Eyes pinned to Ginny, he asked, "What happened?"

Sophie shifted his arms and looked up at him. "I can talk, Callan."

He dropped a kiss to her forehead and muttered, "I know, baby. I just don't want you to have to relive anything right now." She must have understood his need to hear facts without her fear because she remained quiet, simply nodding against his chest.

Ginny stood and walked closer. "I haven't heard anything further from Mitch, but what I can tell you is that Sophie reported two shots that landed near her feet when she was on the beach. We were able to find both bullets exactly where she indicated they would be. I can also tell you that from early indications, the shooter was in the tall grass on the dunes behind her."

His investigative mind quickly began sifting through what Ginny was telling him, as well as what she was not. *At that close range, no hunter would've mistaken her for a bird or a deer. Someone with weapons experience would have been able to have hit her at that range unless they wanted to frighten her, or they were a terrible shot.* He gave a curt nod to Ginny, and just as she moved away, a commotion sounded at the front door.

Hearing the clambering going on outside, he closed his eyes and sighed. *Oh, Jesus, here comes the brigade.*

Within a moment, the Bayles' living room was filled with Katelyn, Gareth carrying little Finn, Aiden and Lia, Tori, Jillian, Belle, Jade, Madelyn and Zac, and Brogan, who immediately moved straight to Ginny.

While the women pulled Sophie from his arms, plying her with questions and clucking over her, he noticed Brogan and Ginny off to the side having what appeared to be a quiet argument. A quick glance around the room showed that Aiden was tuned in to his brother and sister-in-law as well.

"You don't go into the middle of an investigation in this condition," Brogan growled, his voice fierce but his arms wrapped protectively around Ginny.

The room became very quiet, everyone's eyes moving from Sophie over to the couple in the corner. Ginny blushed before casting a sharp-eyed gaze up at

Brogan. "Sorry. I'm on light-duty but was close to the resort when the call came in."

Sophie and the other women rushed to Ginny, immediately assuring themselves she was fine. Brogan made his way to the men, shaking his head. He looked at Callan and said, "Sorry, man. Not trying to dump one more thing onto this already crazy shooting at Sophie, but I nearly had a shit fit when I found out that Ginny had headed right into the middle of that investigation, not knowing if the shooter was still out there."

Clasping his friend's hand in his, Callan said, "No problem, Brogan. I know you don't want to take a chance on her and the baby."

Shifting the conversation back to him, Brogan asked, "What do we know?"

"Not much, other than she was shot at twice while she was on the beach, and the shooter was in the tall grass on the dunes."

A hand on his arm had him turn and observe his mother standing close by. "Callan, honey, your dad and I are going to order pizza and subs for everyone. Is that okay?"

Aiden immediately said, "Mrs. Ward, let me do it. I can have one of the servers from the Pub bring enough food to feed everybody."

It did not take long for the bizarre incidence of the day to morph into a supportive gathering of family and friends.

Callan tried not to hover, but the desire to keep Sophie in his arms was overwhelming. He took pleasure noticing that every time she moved away from him to talk to someone, after a few minutes her head would turn, and her eyes would search the room until they landed on him. He would smile, and that seemed to be all she needed to relax the tension in her shoulders and go back to her conversation.

After the food was eaten, the gathering began to dissipate, Katelyn and Gareth, Aiden and Lia, Madelyn and Zac, and Belle leaving together, after hugs and promises to let them know any news that they heard. His parents also went back to their house after good-byes to David and Tonya and pulling Sophie into a deep hug.

Standing next to Sophie, he could hear his mother whisper, "Stay safe, sweetheart. Now that we've got you back, we don't want anything to happen to you."

Shaking his father's hand, he watched them walk out the back door and through the yard toward their house.

When he walked back into the living room, he observed Tori, Jade, and Jillian saying goodbye as well.

Jillian said, "We were staying, hoping our husbands would drop by with more information, but of course, with an active investigation, I should've known better."

Sophie thanked Ginny for staying with her after the shooting, receiving her promise that Mitch would be in touch to let her know what they found.

"I know this sounds silly," Sophie said, "but I need to be back there tomorrow for work. I'm nearing the end of the designs, but everything has to be perfect before the photo shoot with Southern Living."

"Why don't you sleep late tomorrow morning and

take it easy. I'll let Mitch know that you've got to go back, but I want someone with you."

"That'll be me," Callan stated emphatically.

Sophie twisted her head around and looked up at him, saying, "Honey, I appreciate that. But you've got a job to do. I know whatever you were doing today was big, so you can't tell me that you don't have things you need to do."

Kissing the top of her head, he whispered, "I'll talk to my Chief. We'll figure it out."

"Tell you what, Callan," Ginny said. "You go into work tomorrow, talk to your Chief, and I'll be with Sophie until you have a chance to get there."

He knew her solution was best, but it galled him to not be able to be the one to offer full protection to the woman he loved. Feeling her soft curls against his jaw as she stayed tucked in close to him, the words reverberated through his mind. *The woman I love.* In the midst of the craziness of the day, that thought made his heart sing.

28

The moonlight shone through the window, illuminating the couple in bed. Soft curves and hard planes. Light blond curls and ebony black.

Sophie held Callan's intense gaze, reveling in the emotion pouring from his eyes, wanting to assure him that she was fine. Her fingers gripped his shoulders as she straddled his hips, slowly moving up and down on his cock, the feel of his body connected to hers sending shivers throughout. She felt everything intensely. His large hands spanning her ass and hips. His fingers gripping into her soft flesh. His knees bent, the hairs on his thighs rubbing against her back. His jaw tight, but whether with need or concern she could not tell. The muscles underneath her hands bunched and corded with their movements.

Without preamble, he surged upward and over, flipping her to her back without ever losing their connection. She started to complain, having desired to bring him pleasure, but one look at his face and she knew he needed to take back some control. Considering the way his hips drove into hers, his cock filling her, no complaint came forth. Instead, her fingers clung to his shoulders even tighter with the pleasure that was sent throughout her body.

His hands now cupped her face, his fingers tangling in her hair as he held his chest barely over hers with his body propped up on his forearms. Over and over he thrust, first slowly and then with more intensity, until all thoughts flew from her mind other than the connection of their bodies.

He shifted slightly, sliding his left hand from her face, down her chest, his thumb and forefinger tweaking her nipple before continuing its path over her belly to the prize he sought. Rubbing circles over her swollen clit, he pinched it lightly. She cried out, no longer able to keep her eyes on him but instead shutting them tightly as her body shook when the orgasm washed over her. Muscles tingling, limbs quivering, she felt wave after wave of pleasure move through her.

Her legs tightened around his thighs, and she slid her hands down his muscular back to his firm ass, gripping it tightly as he followed her with his own release. Her eyes now stayed on him, and she watched the muscles in his neck tighten and his face redden as he groaned aloud.

They lay for a moment, her body covered with his, both drawing in ragged breaths as their heartbeats pounded. The feel of his heavy weight on her was comforting, and she wondered if it was possible to sleep in that position. She felt his body shift off, and she groaned at the loss.

"Gotta take care of you, babe," he said. Rolling off the bed, he stood and stalked toward the bathroom, calling over his shoulder, "Stay just like that. I want dessert, so don't move."

His last words caused a grin to slide over her face, knowing he was not finished with her. She shifted to her side so that she could watch him walk loose-limbed and confident back to the bed. She admired the play of muscles as he moved. His body was lean and sinewy, not bulky. He exuded pure strength, and she loved how she felt both protected and admired by him.

He placed one knee on the bed and swung around so that he was straddling her ankles. His wide smile gleamed white in the moonlight as he slid his hands under her knees and lifted them up and apart, her feet now planted in front of him.

Biting her lip, she closed her eyes for just a second, anticipation running through her body. He did not make her wait as he carefully wiped her with a warm, wet washcloth. Tossing it to the nightstand, he dropped his head to her tummy, circling her belly button with kisses before moving over her mound. He licked her slit, his tongue delving inside her sex, and her fingers dove into the thick hair on top of his head.

Her inner muscles began to coil again, and she could not believe she had another orgasm in her after having felt so sated just a few minutes earlier. She raised up on her elbows, desiring to hold his gaze as he peered up at her from between her thighs. Uncertain if she had ever seen anything so sexy in her life, she was sure she had never felt so good.

His mouth moved up until it latched onto her clit, sucking until she was writhing on the bed underneath his ministrations. She flopped back onto the mattress, her fingers now digging into the sheets that she clutched. With one last hard suck, her coiled body sprung loose and she cried out her pleasure.

He continued to suckle as the sensations crashed over her, only slowing as her body began to come down off its high.

Barely aware of the bed moving, she opened her eyes enough to see him crawling over her, licking his moist lips, until he was directly above her. His warm gaze was soft, his eyes roving over her face.

"I love you, Sophie. I've known for a while. The feelings I've had for you since we were children have never gone away, but I didn't know how to tell you. I don't want to scare you, but—"

"I love you, too," she rushed, interrupting him.

Neither spoke for a few seconds, his brow furrowing slightly. "Really? You don't have to say that."

She reached up and cupped his stubbled jaw, her thumb running over his lips. "I'm not just saying it because you said it first. I'm saying it because I realized today that I've always loved you. With everything that happened, I haven't had a chance to tell you. I fell in love with you when I was a little girl and you let me tag you so that I wouldn't always be *it*."

A slow smile curved his lips, and he asked, "You remember that?"

Nodding, she said, "Oh, Callan. I'm not lying when I tell you I've been in love with you that long." She thought about how she rejected him years earlier, and her heart ached at that memory.

"Hey, what's wrong? You went from telling me you loved me to having such a sad look on your face."

"I'm sorry I hurt you years ago. I was just—"

He stilled her words with a quick shake of his head, but she begged, "Please, let me tell you." Gaining his slow nod, she continued. "I did love you then, and I know that love is supposed to conquer all. But I was too young. Too naïve. And losing Philip, I was too frightened. Looking back, I don't think I ever stopped loving you, but I forced myself to walk away, thinking I was guarding my heart. But all I really did was hurt us both."

"Sophie, I think what you did was the smartest thing you could have done. I loved you then, I've loved you since we were children. Losing Philip also messed with my mind, causing me to doubt and question everything I'd been so sure of. I had no idea what I was doing with my future, so as to you guarding your heart, you also guarded mine."

The silence moved between them, easy and gentle, and he kissed her lightly. Lifting his head, he said, "We need to talk about where we go from here."

Not giving him a chance to speak further, she rushed, "There was something else I realized earlier today. I want to be with you, Callan. I can use my skills from almost anywhere, working from home. So if you want to stay in the Coast Guard, that's fine with me. I'll go where you go. If you re-up and get transferred somewhere else, I'll go, too. We can always come back to Baytown for vacations to see friends and family. And if something happens and you get deployed overseas, then I'll keep your home ready for your return."

"You'd do that for me?" he asked, his gaze warm upon her face.

She smiled and nodded. "I do anything for you because I now know that my heart will always belong to you."

He lowered his head, claiming her lips once more, only this time she felt the intensity he was pouring into her. Her arms circled around his back, pulling him tightly, once more loving the feel of his weight on her.

She felt cool replace heat as he lifted his head, and she murmured in discontent.

"There's something I need to tell you, too, Sophie. I had already made up my mind that being stationed here in Baytown not only gave me excellent Guard experience, but reconnecting with family and friends has completely changed what I want in life. I'm no longer the eighteen-year-old who wanted to leave a small town and see the world. I now know that everything I've ever wanted is right here in this small town. Until you came back, it was missing the most important thing. And now that we're together, it has everything I want. But there is the question about where you want to be. If you want to go back to your career in Richmond, I can be part of the Virginia Marine Police that's based near the James River. "

Shaking her head, she said, "No. I don't want that. I've already had my landlord ask about my apartment.

He has others interested in renting it. I want to stay here with you and our family and friends."

His grin wider, he said, "Then I'll let my Chief know, and I'll put in an application for the VMP here on the Eastern Shore."

A giggle burst forth from her, and she asked, "So, this is it? You and me? Staying here?"

Laughing, he nodded. "Yeah, babe. This is it. You and me. Right here." Sobering after a moment, he added, "You don't need to protect yourself any longer. From now on, I'll guard your heart."

29

The beauty of the morning had morphed into not-quite-so-beautiful when Mitch called Callan while they were eating breakfast and wanted both of them to come to the station. Now, forty-five minutes later, they were ensconced in the BPD conference room, the entire gathering rather squished. A round table sat in the middle of the room, surrounded by metal chairs which were all filled, with a few others standing to the side.

She had recognized most of the participants and was introduced to those she did not know. Ginny, Grant, and Lance were there as well as a Baytown officer she had not met before, Burt Tober. Colt and Hunter from the North Heron Sheriff's Department, along with Ryan Coates from the Marine Police and Callan's Chief, Jeff Monroe.

Feeling like a bug under glass, Mitch had asked her to explain everything that she had found the day she discovered the wooden pier and the events from the previous day's shooting. Repeating her story for what seemed like the millionth time, she did as she was asked, glad for Callan's comforting hand holding hers.

"Sophie, we're going to bring you up-to-date on an ongoing investigation that we think you may have inadvertently stumbled onto," Mitch said. "The reason we have so many people here today is that part of this investigation takes place in Baytown which falls under our police jurisdiction. Sheriff Colt Hudson is working on another aspect of the investigation that takes place in North Heron County. And since part of it takes place on the water, the Coast Guard and the Virginia Marine Police are involved as well."

She sucked in her lips, her mind following everything that Mitch was saying but incredulous that there was such a far-reaching investigation. The whole situation was surreal, and if it was not for Callan's fingers rubbing gently over her knuckles, she could have convinced herself that she was still asleep and experiencing a weird dream—the kind that when you wake up you wonder what you ate the night before.

Mitch, still looking at her, had grown quiet, and she realized a response was needed. Nodding quickly, she said, "Okay. I understand."

Colt spoke next, saying, "We've been investigating a seafood company that's in the northern part of our county and have involved the Marine Police as well as the NOAA. In simplest terms, this seafood company has been making a huge profit by buying inferior, illegally caught crab from Asia and mixing it with their own Maryland crab. They package it as a product of Maryland and sell it at the higher prices. The NOAA fights against illegal fishing, illegal catches coming into the United States, and the improper use and sale of seafood here as well."

She watched the large man shrug his shoulders and add, "I'll be honest, I didn't know it was such a big business. But from what I've learned, seafood fraud is a multibillion-dollar industry that feeds into many of the Asian organized crime syndicates as well as lining the pockets of some in the States. While the seafood company in North Heron may be small potatoes to the overall organization, what they're doing is illegal as well as potentially harmful to customers, and we plan on taking them down."

She nodded her understanding and swung her gaze to the next person who began to speak. Ryan continued the explanation. "I didn't know how all this was tied in together until you had talked to Callan and the Coast Guard did some reconnaissance. Plus, there was a major bust on one of the Taiwanese freighters in the Bay yesterday. Now, we're pulling it all together and have a better picture of what was happening. We just don't quite know who all the players are, and that's what we're hoping to find out."

Feeling the eyes of everyone on her, she attempted to quell the nerves twisting her stomach. "I'm not sure how else I can help," she said. "The bag that I found was quite disgusting, and as soon as I realized it had spoiled crab inside, I couldn't wait to throw it away. But I didn't see anyone or hear anyone, and didn't see any identification on the canvas bag at all."

"You said you ran into several people a day or so

later," Callan reminded. "People that worked at The Dunes Resort, and all seemed miffed that you were there."

Nodding, she said, "That's right, but I don't know that that was an uncommon thing to have happen. Roger Thorpe, the general manager, has always been pleasant, but he cares very much about the overall appearance of The Dunes Resort. He's overseen the planting and care of the gardens, golf courses, and neighborhoods. When he saw me with cattails and pinecones and some evergreen sprigs, I thought he was going to have a fit. Of course, Travis and Sue, the golf pros, also have to go around and check on the golf courses every day. I think they do that first thing in the morning and in the evening after the last players have gone."

Looking around the room at the intense expressions focused on her, she said, her voice shaky, "I'm still not sure what it is you're looking for."

"We know that a lot of the illegally-caught and illegally-transported crab comes in on large cargo ships that anchor in the Bay as they await permission to travel to Baltimore. What we recently found out and actually caught in the act yesterday is that they will cook some of the crab, get the meat, and package it in tins that they label as 'Product of Maryland'. Part of their operation is that they will bury those tins in the middle of a lot of their other legal goods, and once they dock they can sell those to a number of middlemen who then sell them to restaurant owners who think they're buying the real thing," Mitch explained.

Jeff nodded to Callan, and she twisted her head to look up at him. Callan took over the explanation, saying, "What we also found yesterday was that they were taking some of the crabmeat and packing it in bags along with ice packs similar to what you described. Under some intense questioning, we were able to determine that they get it off the freighter at night, and someone brings it into a remote area to pass it on to the next person in the chain. This is actually what's getting to the seafood company in our area. They're buying it directly from the source, cutting out the middleman, saving even more money. Then, selling it fraudulently at a much higher price, they're making a killing."

Shaking her head slowly, her eyes stayed on Callan. "You do know this all sounds crazy, right?" As soon as the words came out of her mouth, her gaze darted around the table, glad to see that the others did not appear angry, but instead seeing their lips quirked into smiles. "I'm sorry. I shouldn't have said that aloud. It's just that I've never been involved in a small crime, much less something on this scale." Inhaling deeply, she said, "International fraud? Right here in this area? And by someone I may have met?"

Looking back at Callan, she said, "Honey, I realize that by finding that bag and then throwing it away, I've handled and gotten rid of evidence. But surely, whoever dropped it there or was supposed to pick it up, didn't and has to know that I don't know anything!"

"Babe," he said, his voice soft as he squeezed her hand again. "Somebody thinks you might know something. Otherwise, why did they take a shot at you?"

Callan watched as she opened and closed her mouth several times, but no words came out. Finally snapping her mouth shut, she scrunched her nose and shook her head as though in pain.

"Sophie, babe, you don't need to worry about this."

She added a furrowed brow to her ever-changing expression and asked, "How can I not worry?"

Mitch said, "We needed to talk to you, Sophie, so that we could understand exactly what happened from your perspective, from what you did to what you saw and heard. All I can tell you right now is that this is a current investigation, and we're all working on it. We're making progress, but we're having to work backward. We have the big picture, and we now have the big players. What we still have not identified is who is getting onto the resort and picking up the bags of crab to take to the seafood company. But that's not your concern."

Colt took over, saying, "What we need is for you to do absolutely nothing. We don't want you talking to anyone about anything that you've heard here. We know that when you go to work today, some of the people from The Dunes Resort will probably be questioning you. Say nothing to them. Act like you gave a statement to the police about the shooting and that's all you know."

Nodding slowly, she said, "Okay. I can do that, no problem."

Breathing a little easier now that she seemed to understand what they needed, Callan added, "We also need you to stay in your designated area. From what you've told me, that means the big house or the condo you're working on. I know that you might have to go to the restaurant or offices, but we don't want you anywhere other than those buildings. No more walking on the beach, and definitely no more going around the golf course or near the inlet."

He gave her hand a squeeze and she held his gaze. "I promise, Callan. I have no desire to get shot at again and absolutely no desire to get in the middle of your investigation."

He heard a collective sigh of relief from everyone in the room, and he said, "I'll walk you out to your car, babe. Keep your phone with you and call if you see or hear anything suspicious at all. My guess, with you just continuing to work, you won't know anything."

He pushed his chair back and held her hand to assist her up. The others in the room thanked her, and she offered a short nod. Escorting her out to her car, he enveloped her into his embrace, breathing in the sweet scent of her shampoo. "Is it crazy that in the middle of all of this mess, all I can think about is the way you smell and how I want that on my pillow every day?"

She giggled-snorted in relief, and he loved the sound of her mirth.

Leaning her head back, she looked up at him and smiled. "I don't think that's crazy at all, because all I can think about now is you and me. Us. Together."

Bending, he took her lips in a searing kiss, unheeding of their location. Hearing sounds from behind them, they broke apart as someone came out of the police station. Watching the blush cross her adorable face, he kissed her lightly and said, "Stay out of trouble."

Watching her drive away, his smile slowly left his face, and he headed back into the station so that the group could continue to plan their trap.

The on-site security employee stopped her just as Sophie was about to drive onto The Dunes Resort. Rolling down her window, she called out, "Do you need me?"

The smiling woman nodded as she walked over to Sophie's car. "Good morning, ma'am. Ms. Ventura said she had tried to call you, but your phone must have been turned off. She wanted me to let you know that she'd like you to come to her office as soon as you get here today."

Because her phone had been blowing up with messages from friends checking on her, Callan had turned the sound down. Plastering a smile on her face, she nodded and thanked the woman. Just as she was about to roll her window up, she asked, "I was wondering if everyone gets stopped coming and going out of The Dunes if they don't have a residence or employee sticker on their car."

"Oh, yes ma'am. We keep a log of everyone coming and going. Those who come to play golf. Those who come in to eat at the restaurant. They're the only ones who are allowed to be on the resort, other than residents and employees. But of course, there are also tradesmen and delivery men all the time. The Dunes Restaurant gets deliveries every day, of course."

Thanking her, she rolled her window up and headed toward the resort's offices near the restaurant and pro shop. Entering the building, she could already hear the raised voices coming from Carlotta's office. Sighing, she hesitated before going in, listening to the conversation.

"It has to be a random hunter. Who else could it possibly be?" Roger groused.

Carlotta was heard next, saying, "All I know is that I want this kept out of the media. I'm calling Sophie in as soon as she gets here to let her know that I don't want her talking to anyone. The last thing we need is for this to get out and have Southern Living Magazine cancel the photo shoot!"

"That's rather callous, isn't it?" Ann asked.

"Well, it's not like she got hit by the stray bullet," Carlotta said in return.

Deciding not to put off the inevitable, Sophie knocked before pushing open the door. Forcing her lips to curve into what she hoped was a smile, she said, "Hello, everyone. I'm sorry I'm a little late, and I do apologize for having turned off my phone."

"Not at all, not at all!" Carlotta gushed, hurrying over on her high heels to grasp Sophie's hands. Squeezing them almost painfully, Carlotta continued, "We just wanted to see how you were. We were all so, so worried."

A soft snort came from behind, and while Sophie did not turn around, she was sure it came from Ann. She did catch Carlotta's narrowed-eye glare shot toward someone behind her, but it was quickly replaced by her smile again.

Leading Sophie over to a chair, she said, "We just wanted to assure ourselves that you were fine and that this unfortunate incident was not going to interfere with the work you were doing for us."

"I was certainly shaken yesterday, but I'm fine and ready to finish everything so that we'll be ready for the photo shoot in two weeks."

A huge sigh of relief audibly left Carlotta's lungs as she plopped into a nearby chair. "Oh, my dear, I'm so pleased to hear you say that."

Roger, coming around from the side, patted Sophie's shoulder and said, "Carlotta speaks for all of us when she says that we are very pleased that you are uninjured and can continue to work. Of course, we would like to avoid any negative publicity. I hope that it doesn't sound too callous for us to ask that the incident be kept as quiet as possible."

Holding his gaze, she said, "I haven't spoken to any media about what happened, but surely you realize that it is a police investigation."

Roger's brow lowered as he appeared to consider her words carefully. Travis and Sue, neither having spoken so far, gave each other a long look, but she was unable to attach any meaning to it. Ann stood suddenly and pronounced, "I have a restaurant to run." She cast a look over her shoulder as she was walking toward the door and said, "Glad you weren't hurt." With that, she left the room.

Travis stood, shaking his head, and said, "The last thing we need is the police swarming all over the golf course. I warned Chief Evans yesterday that I didn't want his officers stomping all over the greens."

He stalked out of the room as well, and Sophie had to hide her grin at the idea of Travis thinking that he was going to tell Mitch how to do his job.

Sue walked over, and with a curt nod toward Sophie said, "Seems like you keep managing to be where you shouldn't be. Hopefully, now you'll stay in the main house or the condo and finish your job." Having said her piece, she walked out of the room, leaving Sophie with just Carlotta and Roger.

Looking back at those two, she stood and said, "If there's nothing else, I'm going to get back to work. I'm going to start out at the condo and make sure that it's ready. I'll spend the afternoon at the main house if you need me."

Stepping out of Carlotta's office, she walked down the carpeted stairs but halted before turning the corner, hearing voices once again. Tired of eavesdropping on conversations, she could not deny that the fear from yesterday had not left her. Still cautious, she hovered near the bottom step, listening to two females. She thought it was Sue and Ann but could not be sure.

"I'd be careful if I were you. You seem rather blasé about the whole thing."

"And you seem rather jacked up about it. I wonder which of us looks more guilty?"

The voices faded away, and Sophie leaned back against the wall, her hand clutching the banister for support. Inhaling deeply through her nose, she let it out slowly, willing her nerves to steady.

As she moved around the corner, she heard Roger and Travis' voices coming from an alcove near the men's room.

"It's getting too hot here," Travis said.

Roger replied, "Just hang on. Once the hype is over, we can keep doing what we were doing, and no one will be the wiser. It's been working for us, and it'll keep working for us."

"You'd better be right. There's a lot riding on this."

"Are you threatening to leave?"

"No…no, I don't want to. I'm too involved." A heavy sigh was heard. "But I'm tired of hiding all the time."

Backing away from the corner, Sophie headed out a side door. Hurrying to the parking lot, she climbed into her car and backed out of the space. As she drove down the road she glanced into her rearview mirror, seeing Travis standing near a golf cart, his eyes pinned on the back of her car.

3 0

Callan watched the proceedings with great interest. Having been part of cooperative missions between multiple agencies numerous times, he was used to these types of meetings, but having his friends take the leadership roles was different.

The inside informant at Chambers Seafood had given the formation to Colt that there was a small-time fisherman from the tiny town of Manteague, so their group now included Wyatt Newman, its Police Chief.

Essentially, they had all the pieces of the puzzle with the one exception of who was receiving the illegal crab meat from the fisherman, dropping it off at The Dunes, and transporting it to Chambers.

"What a complicated puzzle this is to unravel," Grant complained. "It seems to me that the easiest crime to commit is one where very few people know about it, have their hands in it, and therefore are less likely to get caught."

Mitch replied, "It's no different than running drugs

or guns that come into our country. There are multiple people involved all along the way. Everyone's got a stake in the pipeline continuing, and everyone only knows their part. The people working on the ship have no idea what they're doing or why they're doing it. They're just told to cook crab. The next person is just told where to deliver it, without know who's picking it up."

"The Manteague fisherman was an old friend of Chambers, who fell onto bad luck and needed money. Again, he did as he was asked, got paid decently, and never met up with the next person in the chain," Wyatt added.

"So why add in someone else to the mix?" Callan asked. "Wouldn't it have been easier for the fisherman to just take it directly to Chambers and not risk another drop-off? And why The Dunes Resort? There are hundreds of little inlets that he could have taken it to."

"My guess is that The Dunes Resort golf courses, which are isolated and empty at night, provided a certain security. No one was going to be around, so he didn't have to worry about being seen," Mitch said. "If he'd unloaded any of the illegal crab at an actual dock or harbor, he could have been seen."

Shaking his head, Callan surmised, "If he hadn't dropped that one bag and the pickup person not notice it, they could still be getting away with it."

"Crazy as it seems, Sophie stumbling onto it is what's allowing us to break open this case right now," Colt said.

Callan looked across the room, receiving rueful expressions from Grant, Ginny, and Ryan. With a slight chin lift for their acknowledgment of his girlfriend being a necessary catalyst in the case, he turned his attention back to Mitch. "Okay, what's the plan?" he asked.

"Tom Sanderson, the fisherman from my neck of the woods," Wyatt began, "has agreed to assist us, and we'll approach the DA for a lesser sentence based on his cooperation. He's told us of the next drop-off, which is supposed to be tonight. He'll take the bags we give him and do everything he was supposed to have done as though he was delivering the real items."

Colt said, "I'll have some officers watching Chambers Seafood in case something goes wrong on your end and the person slips past the net Mitch is setting up. That way, if nothing else, we can get them when they make the delivery to Chambers." Shooting Mitch a grin, Colt added, "Not that you're going to miss them, man."

The group chuckled before Ryan took over the explanation. "The VMP will be in boats stationed around the inlet. We'll monitor when Tom goes in and make sure he's with us when he comes out. We'll also note anyone else who happens to go in and out by boat."

Jeff said, "I'll have my team further out in the water, also monitoring anyone else who might try to get in or out. We'll coordinate with the VMP to make sure the water area is covered."

Callan turned his attention to Mitch, waiting to see what the BPD would be doing.

"We'll work in conjunction with Colt's deputies to assure that we have enough manpower on the ground. Right now, Ginny, still assigned to light duty and promising to obey that policy, has agreed to coordinate between the various agencies that are going to be involved this evening. Burt, Lance, Grant, and I, along with several of Colt's deputies, will be on the ground near the small dock where the drop-off is to take place, as well as stationed at the entrance to The Dunes."

Callan understood the magnitude of such an inter-agency mission but wondered where Jeff was going to assign him. Being out on the water had always been where he wanted to be, but now he chafed at the idea that he would not be closer to the action, wanting to see the arrest of the person who had shot at Sophie. So lost in thought, he almost missed Jeff addressing him, until Jeff called out his name a second time.

"Yes, sir," he said hastily.

"You're off duty tonight," Jeff announced.

Blinking, he repeated, "Off duty?"

"You weren't on the schedule to work tonight anyway," Jeff said. "While I would never question your professionalism, I don't see any reason to call you in for tonight."

He held his Chief's gaze for a moment, under-standing what Jeff was telling him. His boss knew that he would want to be closer to the action. Fighting back a grateful grin, he simply offered a chin lift and said, "I appreciate that, sir."

Mitch turned to him and said, "Since you're going to be off duty tonight, maybe you'd like to hang out with Ginny?"

The sun was hanging in the early evening sky, but Sophie was still at the design house. Callan was working late, her parents were at a town council meeting, and she was at loose ends. Wandering through the massive, now-beautifully decorated house, she smiled as she moved from room to room. All the furniture was in place. All the pictures had been hung. Decorative dishes filled the glass-front cabinets in the kitchen. The floors were polished, and the rugs gave the rooms warmth. The linens on the beds and in the bathrooms pulled together the colors of her pallet.

On either side of the fireplace were tall vases filled with dried cattails, seagrass, and pine branches at the base of the arrangements. On the dining room table was a wide centerpiece created from sprigs of rhododendron surrounded by a base of pinecones. Small touches of the Eastern shore's nature were evident in each room.

The house was huge and elegant, a design that she was immensely proud of, but not home. Her small apartment in Richmond came to mind, but it was not home either. Not anymore. As the certainty of that realization settled firmly in her mind, she placed calling the landlord on her list of things to do the next day to let him know she would not be returning.

"So, I'm moving back to Baytown?" She asked the question aloud even though she was speaking to herself. She often found that hearing her own thoughts made it easier for her to untangle the ones that did not make sense. Having said it aloud, she waited to see her own reaction.

A slow smile spread across her face at the thought of calling Baytown home again. Her design business was already being run out of her apartment, therefore it would be easy to run it from Baytown. Her brow furrowed slightly as she thought about the travel involved when she was setting up a design in someone's home.

"But lots of people travel in their work." Hearing those words aloud, she considered the population just across the Chesapeake Bay. The Hampton Roads area was comprised of Virginia Beach, Norfolk, Chesapeake, Newport News, Hampton, Portsmouth, and Suffolk, with a total population of close to two million people. "Just in this area alone, I wouldn't have to travel far."

Now, with those words ringing in her ears, her smile widened. The thought of her and Callan staying together, building a home near their family and friends filled her heart. "And if he should take a job with the Marine Police? Can I handle the risk of his dangerous job?" She waited for a moment to see her reaction to those words, but only peace settled around her. "Ginny and Brogan. Tori and Mitch. Jillian and Grant. They make it work." Smiling, she acknowledged, "And so can I."

Clapping her hands, she twirled around in the massive living room, her heart lighter than it had been in years. Wishing she could talk to Callan, she knew that he was working late.

A knock on the front door startled her, and unable to keep the glee from filling her at the thought that he may have gotten off work early, she ran through the foyer and threw open the front door.

She blinked in surprise, seeing Ann standing on the front stoop of the house. She glanced around, checking to see if anyone else was with her, but it appeared Ann was alone. "Ann? Uh…hi."

Still wearing her chef's coat, Ann tucked her hair behind her ears and said, "Hi." She smiled, or at least Sophie thought it was a smile, considering it looked more like a grimace.

Uncertain why Ann was there, she asked, "Is everything okay? Is there something I can do for you?"

Shifting her weight from foot to foot, Ann gave off the appearance of being nervous. "Not really. I was just walking around and saw all the lights on here. When I saw your car, I figured you were inside."

Still uncertain as to the reason for Ann's impromptu visit, she cocked her head to the side and asked, "Um… did you want to come in and look around?"

Still shifting on her feet, Ann nodded. "Sure. If it's not a problem."

Opening the door wider, Sophie stepped back, and with a sweeping gesture of her arm invited the other woman in. "It's no problem at all. The design and decorating are ready for the magazine shoot. I was actually wandering from room to room, checking on everything. I'd love to show it to you."

For the next thirty minutes, she escorted Ann throughout the rooms in the house, happy for the appreciative murmurs that came from her. Ending in the kitchen, she could not help but grin as Ann's hands trailed reverently over the chef's grade stove, double ovens, and stainless sub-zero refrigerator.

"Looks real nice," Ann said. "I don't know anything about house design other than kitchens, but I can tell this is beautiful."

Warming to her rather closed-mouth visitor, Sophie replied, "Thank you. I'm glad to see that the house, especially the kitchen, meets your approval. I consider that high praise indeed."

Jerking her head around, Ann suddenly asked, "Would you like to have dinner? The evening service is just getting ready to get started at the restaurant." Shrugging, she said, "I know I should already be there, but the prep work was done, and I felt like I needed a little fresh air. Unless you've got other plans, you could try our special for tonight, on the house."

She opened and closed her mouth a couple of times, stunned at the invitation that was as impromptu as Ann's visit. With no other plans for the evening, she nodded, the idea of a chef-inspired dinner sounding wonderful. "Sure, I'd love to. Let me grab my coat and purse." Suddenly thinking back to something Ann said when she first arrived, she asked, "Did you say you were out walking this evening?"

Shoving her hands into her pockets, Ann nodded. "Yeah. Helps me think." Shrugging, she added, "I don't usually do it right before the supper service, but for some reason tonight, I just felt the need to get out of the kitchen for a bit."

Certainly understanding the desire for enjoying the

sunset and the evening on the shore, she said, "We can take my car."

They piled into Sophie's car, but as she turned the ignition, only a rumbling sound could be heard. Trying several times, she sighed heavily. "I can't believe it's not starting. I know it's an old car, and I really should have had Jason take a look at it, but it was working fine when I came here today."

Seemingly nonplussed, Ann asked, "Is the resort's golf cart in the garage? It's only a little chilly tonight, so we could use that."

"I guess we'll have to. My parents will be back from their church meeting in another hour or so, and I can call them to come pick me up." Hitting the fob for the garage door, they moved toward the golf cart.

"Do you mind if I drive?" Ann asked. "We can take the wandering path to get back to the restaurant. There are a couple of great places to see the sunset."

Shrugging, she handed Ann the golf cart key and climbed into the passenger seat. As they headed down the road, she said, "Thank you for inviting me. A nice meal is exactly what I need tonight."

Ann said nothing, but continued to drive, a smile playing about her lips.

"I grew up on the Eastern shore."

Sophie had been staring at the sun beginning to set through the trees when Ann's words struck her. Surprised at the personal information forthcoming from someone who had been rather taciturn, she looked over at Ann and said, "I didn't know that."

"No reason why you should. We were just across the state line, in Maryland. My dad was a fisherman. He had crab pots, and he and my brother would go out every single day. He never made much. Growing up, I didn't realize how poor we were. Now, working at The Dunes Resort, I'm amazed at how much the real estate costs around here. Some of these people pay more per month for their house then my parents paid in a whole year."

A strange unease slid through Sophie, uncertain of its meaning. Ann was just making conversation, and yet it seemed so very personal. Uncertain if Ann was attempting friendship or just talking to pass the time, she tried to think of something to say.

"Um...my family used to go to Maryland each summer for a sea glass event. It seemed like there were hundreds of booths filled with sea glass art. I was always enthralled, but then we'd head over to the food tables where the scent of frying fish, roasting oysters, and crabs covered in Old Bay seasoning filled the air."

Ann nodded, saying, "I bet we were probably there, too. My dad always liked to show off his Maryland crabs at any of the local events."

"Does your father still fish?"

A rueful snort erupted from Ann, and she replied, "Fishing is a hard life. Long before anyone ever talked about sunscreen, my dad was out on a boat twelve hours a day, sometimes with no cap on. He ended up with skin cancer, died a few years back. My brother went into the business, but he just didn't have the heart for it. He ended up working for one of the fish companies in the area."

The unease that she felt began to blossom into full-blown nervousness. *Maryland crab. Father was a fisherman. Growing up poor. Brother working for a fish company.* Her throat dry, she forced a swallow, her hands clasped around her purse in her lap. Glancing around, she realized while Ann had been talking, they had driven further away from the direction of The Dunes Restaurant.

"Uh..." she croaked, then cleared her throat. Trying again, she said, "Don't you need to get to the restaurant? You said it was almost time for the dinner service." Offering a strangled laugh, she added, "I'm really looking forward to trying your meal."

Ann's foot pressed harder on the golf cart accelerator, speeding them along the path. "We'll get there. My assistant chef has everything well in hand. I just wanted to let you see the sunset from here."

Ann jerked the golf cart off the path, careening up an incline on the course. Sophie did not play golf but knew that Travis would be upset if a golf cart was driven over the greens. The image of Travis and Sue having apoplectic fits if they could see them now filled her mind. Before she had a chance to protest, Ann lifted her hand and pointed in the distance.

"See? Look over there."

She followed the direction Ann was indicating and for a few seconds forgot that she had been suspicious. The view from the top of the green allowed her to see beyond the trees to where the sun was setting over the water in the distance. Ann was right, the view was spectacular. Dragging her gaze away from the splendor, she turned and observed Ann still staring ahead.

"I know Travis would have a conniption if he saw me up here with the golf cart. I tend to walk up here when I'm by myself, but figured we were in a hurry to get back to the restaurant. I've never played golf. Could never see the point of chasing around a little ball over all these acres. If you want to enjoy it, then just walk or drive around, not whacking a ball."

Thoroughly confused, Sophie ventured to speak. "So, are we going back to the restaurant now?"

Ann turned to look at her and smiled. "Where else would we go?"

Without another word, Ann pressed on the accelerator again and headed down the hill, Sophie's unease returning in full force.

Callan and Ginny sat inside of her small SUV, Mitch having decided they needed to be in an unmarked vehicle in case someone saw them. Near the drop-off point, they had gotten there before sunset, backing into the woods so that they would not be seen.

She maintained radio communication with Mitch and Colt while Callan was in constant contact with Jeff and Ryan.

Looking over at him, Ginny said, "Burt reports that there are quite a few cars coming into The Dunes Resort's gates, some residents, and some who are going to the restaurant for dinner."

"Jeff has outfitted Tom with the fake bags and says he has moved into the inlet. Ryan has him in his sights. Once he makes the drop-off, he'll go back to Jeff who'll turn him in to the State Police."

Squinting in the distance, he saw faint headlights. "Golf cart," he said.

"Mitch, a golf cart is passing nearby on the path heading toward the dock," Ginny radioed. The golf cart turned short of where they were parked. "Could you identify the driver?" she asked Callan.

Shaking his head, he said, "No. The light's too dim, and with them in a big coat and a hat pulled down over their face, I can't tell." He knew that Mitch, Grant, and

Lance were in the woods near the dock and would be able to catch whoever was coming.

"Shit!" Ginny cursed.

Callan swung his head around and looked in the direction she was staring. Another set of dim headlights were coming from the other direction, also from a golf cart. Barely able to make out the occupants, he sat in stunned shock when Ann and Sophie whizzed by. Jolting, he growled, "What the fuck?"

Ginny, already on the radio, alerted Mitch to the second cart heading in their direction. Callan's hand was on the door handle when Ginny caught his arm.

"Callan, hang on. Whatever's happening, she'll be safer with Mitch—"

A shot rang out, halting Ginny's words while reverberating straight through Callan's heart.

They were heading in the direction of the restaurant, but Sophie recognized the area of the golf course they were nearing. It was where she had been gathering reeds when she first found the bag of spoiled crabmeat that she now assumed came from illegal sources. Shifting her gaze to the side, she could not tell if Ann showed any signs of knowing that area other than just as a way to get to the restaurant from her sunset view on the golf course.

Clutching her purse in her hands, her awareness heightened, she breathed a little easier when it did not appear that Ann was slowing.

A crack rang out through the night, and just like before, it took Sophie a second to identify the sound as a gunshot.

"Fuck!" Ann shouted, jerking on the steering wheel, causing the golf cart to career off the path and into some shrubs.

Instinct taking over, Sophie jumped out of her seat, scrambling through the bushes while crouching low. Another shot rang out, and she heard someone close by grunt loudly. Heart pounding, she looked over her shoulder and saw Ann lying on the ground. Pushing her way back through the low-growing shrubs, she made her way to Ann's side, blood oozing from a wound in her right shoulder.

"Oh, Jesus. Oh, Jesus," she repeated, ripping off her scarf and holding it tightly against the wound. Another shot rang nearby, followed by the sound of others in the brush and authoritative voices calling out.

"Get to safety," Ann grunted, her face a mask of pain.

"I'm not leaving you," she said, bending low over Ann's body, hoping to protect both of them.

"Sophie! Sophie!"

Jerking her head around at the sound of Callan's voice, she called out, "Callan! Be careful!" Seeing him push through the brush, she felt faint with relief.

He dropped down to his knees next to her, saying, "Baby, are you okay? Are you hit?"

Shaking her head, she said, "No. It's Ann. Ann got hit."

He lifted the scarf and called out, "Mitch! Get an ambulance!"

As Callan took over applying pressure to Ann's wound, Sophie flopped back on her heels, her heart still pounding as floodlights filled the area, illuminating the scene. Blinking at the sudden light in the darkness, she watched in stunned awe as Grant and Lance walked over, a hunched figure between them. Grant carried the bag Tom had left on the shore, and Lance was placing a gun in an evidence bag.

As the figure came into the light, she stared, disbelieving, as Sue's bitter face appeared, her eyes narrowed in anger. Staring at Sophie, she barked, "You! You were always at the wrong place at the wrong time!"

"Sue?" Her gaze jumped from Sue to Mitch, down to Callan, and then back again. Finally landing again on Mitch, she said, "It was her?" Looking back at the angry woman in handcuffs, she asked, "But why?"

"I hate this place."

Staring dumbly at her, Sophie cocked her head to the side, not understanding. Staying silent, she held Sue's gaze.

"I hate this resort that's in the middle of fucking nowhere. Jesus, I was once at a premier course in upstate New York. Before that, one in Beverly Hills. But every time I get replaced with a man. I took the job here," shaking her head in derision, she spat out, "and I've got more experience and talent than Travis, and yet he's the Head Pro. Head Pro! Can you believe I'm under him?"

Glancing down at Callan still kneeling next to Ginny as they both worked on Ann, she could see by his lowered brow that he was as confused as she. Turning back, she sucked in her lips as she stared at Sue, overcome with shivers after the adrenaline rush.

Just then, Zac arrived with the ambulance, and they quickly and efficiently loaded Ann into the back. Callan turned and immediately wrapped Sophie in his embrace, his lips resting on the top of her head as he murmured, "Jesus, Sophie. I was afraid it was you that had gotten hit."

Shaking her head against his chest, her arms wrapped about his waist, she said, "I'm fine, sweetheart. I'm fine. I have no clue what's going on, but I'm fine."

They both turned and watched as Mitch, Grant, and Lance escorted Sue to their police vehicle and drove away. Ginny reported to Jeff, Ryan, and Colt that they had apprehended the person responsible for delivering the illegal seafood.

They climbed into Ginny's SUV and went back to the police station. With Callan's arm still wrapped around her, they walked into the reception area where they waited to see what Mitch needed from them.

Within half an hour, Mitch called them back to take her statement. With Callan at her side, she retold the events of the evening, from Ann showing up, to her car not starting, to being concerned that Ann might be the person they were looking for. Finally, ending with the shooting, she gratefully rested her weight against Callan's chest as he pulled her closer.

Looking at Mitch, she said, "Ann talked of her family. Her father had been a crab fisherman before he died, and her brother now works for a seafood company."

Mitch did not appear surprised, but she was when he stated, "Ann's brother was the informant at Chambers Seafood. He contacted Colt when he discovered some of the crab they were selling was not Maryland crab."

Eyes wide, she said, "I wonder if Ann knew."

Mitch shook his head and admitted, "I don't know. We'll talk to her tomorrow. Zac said that the bullet went straight through her upper arm, so she should have a full recovery."

"But Sue? I still don't understand."

"From what she's said so far," Mitch said, "she inwardly seethed for the last couple of years at working for The Dunes under Travis and being out here on the shore. She resented her life here. She met Chambers at a benefit golf tournament and went out a few times with him. He was looking for someone to pick up the illegal crab, and with her working at The Dunes, near a place that was perfect for a drop-off, he offered her enough money that she would easily be able to find a new place to live that she considered better."

Shaking her head slowly from side to side in disbelief, she asked, "She became a pawn in his elaborate scheme—"

"No," Callan interrupted, his voice harsh. "She was a willing accomplice, knowing exactly what she was doing and didn't mind shooting someone to protect herself."

Looking up at him, she said, "You didn't let me finish. I was going to say that she started as a pawn but then became desperate and greedy. Believe me, I haven't forgotten that she shot at me and ended up shooting Ann."

Mitch spoke up and said, "We've got everything we need from you tonight, so you two need to go home and get some rest. I'm going to have to meet tomorrow with The Dunes Resort management to give them what information I can before this hits the news. Would you like to be there?" Gaining Sophie's enthusiastic nod, he said, "Then I suggest you guys meet us tomorrow morning at ten o'clock."

Looking up at Callan, she said, "Are you done for the night? Because if you are, I so want you to take me home."

Kissing the top of her head again, he said, "There's nowhere else I'd rather be than home with you."

3 2

Once again, Callan lay awake in bed all night with Sophie in his arms. His mind replayed the scene of her and Ann moving past in the golf cart heading directly toward danger and the sound of a gunshot, followed by a scream.

As the early morning light began to filter through the blinds, her features came more into focus. The wild mass of blond curls. Her pale complexion. Her gorgeous eyes were hidden behind her closed lids, but her thick lashes lay against her cheeks as she slept. He knew exhaustion had finally pulled her under last night and was so glad that she had found sleep.

His arms tightened around her involuntarily, and he watched as her eyelids fluttered open. He wondered if she would be fearful when she woke, but as soon as her eyes landed on him, a beautiful smile brightened her face.

She reached her hand up to cup his jaw, her fingers

trailing light patterns over his stubbled cheeks. "Good morning," she said, her voice soft and light.

Even saying the words 'good morning' back to her was not enough, so he leaned down and took her lips. They were soft and pliable under his, and he relished the taste and feel of her. Finally lifting his head, he grinned as he mumbled, "'Mornin', beautiful."

As the early morning fog lifted from her eyes, her face became serious, and she said, "Before everything got crazy last night, there was something I wanted to talk to you about."

He began to brace for whatever she wanted to tell him when a loud knock on the door reverberated through the small apartment. Both startled, their gazes shot to each other, and they shook their heads at the same time, indicating neither knew who it would be.

Climbing from the bed, he pulled on his jeans and padded out through the living room to his door. Throwing it open, he was forced backward as his parents and Sophie's parents rushed into the room.

"Where's Sophie? My daughter gets shot at last night, and I have to find out about it from the gossip mill early this morning," Tonya all but shouts.

Catching a sympathetic look from his father, he hoped to hold them off until Sophie could get dressed. He heaved a sigh of relief when she entered the room wearing jeans and one of his T-shirts. Attempting to pull her unruly curls into a semblance of a ponytail, she said, "Mom. You can't come barging in here without letting me know!"

"Well, excuse me for being worried," Tonya huffed, walking over and pulling Sophie into a warm hug.

"I'll get some coffee going," Barbara said, smiling up at Callan. Both his parents moved into the small kitchen, his dad pulling down mugs and his mom getting the coffee started.

Leading her parents over to the sofa, she made sure they were settled before she turned back to Callan. Her lips curved into an apologetic, one-sided smile, and he grinned back. Taking her hand, he sat down in one of his chairs, pulling her into his lap.

"I know you're going to give me the line 'it's an ongoing investigation', but what can you tell us?" David asked.

Callan nodded, giving Sophie permission to tell them whatever she wanted. She shook her head and said, "Callan, why don't you start? You know more about the investigation than I do."

He waited until his parents brought over the coffee mugs for everyone, and he watched as Sophie leaned forward to fix his just the way he liked. As strange as it was for their parents to be in his apartment in the early morning, the comfortable, warm feeling he felt oozed through his whole body. He wanted this. He wanted her. Beyond a shadow of a doubt, he knew he had made the right decision to not re-up in the Coast Guard but instead stay with the Virginia Marine Police. If he could spend every Saturday morning waking up to her and then sharing coffee with their parents, his life would be complete.

"Callan?"

He jerked, seeing Sophie hold out the cup to him, and realized his thoughts had taken him away from the subject at hand. "Sorry," he mumbled, relieving her of the hot mug. Taking a fortifying sip, he knew the caffeine would be needed to get him through the day since he had slept very little.

"The North Heron Sheriff's department received a tip from someone who worked at Chambers Seafood Company that told them they suspected illegal crab coming from somewhere other than Maryland was being repackaged and sold at a much more expensive price. That's how Colt first became involved. As the investigation continued, they unraveled Chambers' elaborate scheme. In the Coast Guard, we know that a lot of illegal guns, drugs, fish, and other goods make their way into our country from cargo ships from around the world. We catch a lot, but more slips by."

"Is that how you became involved?" his mom asked.

"Not right away. Colt didn't bring in the Coast Guard or the VMP until he discovered that Chambers was using an old fisherman out of Manteague harbor. The guy would go out at night, collect bags of illegal crab and drop them off at a location that was out of the way and yet easy for the pickup person to get to. Then he could go back to Manteague, and if anyone suspected him, there was nothing coming into the harbor on his boat. There's a small inlet that runs near the golf course at The Dunes Resort that's not near anyone. That became the drop-off point."

He watched the four parents' eyebrows lift to their

hairlines in surprise, all crying out almost in unison, "The Dunes Resort?"

Sophie piped up and said, "As strange as that sounds, it makes sense. That section is not populated by any houses and is very wooded. You can drive by on a golf cart nearby and never see anything. You don't even know that an inlet is there unless you happen to be going through the woods, which, of course, is how I found it."

Callan continued, "Since that's in Baytown's jurisdiction, Mitch got involved. Yesterday morning, the Coast Guard raided a Thailand cargo ship in the Bay. We found their operation of repacking crab from tins labeled 'Produced in China' to tins with the labels 'Produced in Maryland'. But what was more concerning was that they were also boiling crabs, had a ton of workers digging out the crabmeat and packing it in bags with ice around it. That was some of what Chambers was getting his hands on...unpasteurized crab and passing it off as pasteurized, Maryland crab."

Shaking her head, Tonya said, "That's crazy! That many people involved in that kind of scheme! I don't understand!"

Sophie's father turned and put his arm around his wife, giving a squeeze. "Big money, sweetheart. That's the motivation."

Nodding, Callan agreed. "Fishing fraud is a multibillion-dollar a year industry," he said, drawing gasps from the others. "Chambers was paying very little for the crab, repackaging it, and turning around and selling it at a very high cost. He had the old fisherman that was working for him, but he needed someone at The Dunes who would retrieve it from the drop-off point and get it to him. Someone that no one would suspect."

He looked at Sophie, and she gave a rueful shrug before turning back to look at their parents. "When I stumbled across the bag that had been left behind filled with stinky crab and threw it away, I had no idea that any of this was going on. I guess Chambers came up one bag short and went back to his deliverer, who overheard me talking about my find."

Tonya asked, "Sophie, honey. Who? Who was the person?"

"Sue. The golf pro, Sue Connor."

The gasps from their parents ensued once again. "That woman helped me with my swing, and she was the thief who took a shot at my daughter?" David roared, his face red and his gaze snapping.

Sophie rushed over to her father and threw her arms around him. "Daddy, I'm fine. I'm fine. They got her last night, and Mitch has her in jail."

Still blinking in disbelief, Barbara looked at her son and asked, "Why? Why would she do that?"

Settling Sophie back on his lap, he said, "According to what she said last night, she hates it here, hates being under Travis, who she considers to be inferior to her. She's pissed at The Dunes Resort, hell, pissed at the world. From what I gathered, she just saw it as a way to make an easy buck. Purely motivated by the lure of money."

Sophie asked, "By the way, what gossip mill was already running this morning?"

"Your mother and I decided to do an early morning breakfast at the diner, and one of the servers always listens to the emergency band radio. She heard that there had been a shooting at the golf course last night. Someone else said that a female had been taken to the hospital, and we started trying to call your phone—"

"My phone!" Sophie's head jerked around, her gaze landing on her purse. "I must have the sound turned down." Looking back at her parents, she said, "I'm so sorry!"

"Well, we hustled over here. Barbara and Thomas looked out their window and saw us running, and they rushed out to see what was going on." David's eyes met Callan, and he added, "I know I should apologize for us barging in here this morning, but a parent never stops worrying about their child."

Smiling warmly, he replied, "You all are family. You're welcome in our home anytime."

Sophie shifted in his lap, her gaze boring into his, her lips curving in a smile. He knew she understood the meaning of his words and his welcome. His home was hers.

"I'm stunned. Absolutely, positively stunned," Roger said, leaning back in his chair, his gaze bouncing between all the people in the room.

Sophie nodded and said, "She fooled everyone. And I feel terrible having suspected Ann last night."

Travis was leaning forward, his forearms resting on

the table. At her statement, he spread his palms wide and said, "But how could you not suspect her? You had just found out about the investigation, and she suddenly shows up, starts telling you that her father was a crab fisherman from Maryland and her brother works for a seafood company. Your car suspiciously doesn't start, and she's driving you all over the golf course near where you'd found the bag! I think I would've leaped from the moving golf cart at that point!"

A giggle slipped from her lips, and she nodded. "You have no idea! I considered doing just that. But when she actually turned in the direction of the restaurant, I thought maybe it was all my imagination." Sobering, she said, "Until the shooting started."

"I still don't understand," Carlotta said, her finger-nails tapping on the desk. "The Dunes Resort is a beau-tiful golfing community, located in an unspoiled area of our country. It brings in valuable tax dollars to a very poor county and offers employment opportunities. I just don't see why her hatred of us was so strong."

Shifting in her seat, Sophie nibbled on her bottom lip in indecision, then choosing to be honest, she said, "It really was all about money. From what I understand, Chambers was raking in a ton of money with his illegal seafood scheme. He paid Sue very well to be on his payroll. On top of that," her gaze shot nervously toward Travis, "she said that she was sick and tired of always getting paid less than the male golf pros."

Brows lowering, Travis said, "I've been at The Dunes Resorts since before it opened. I was getting paid more because I have more years of experience than she did. But we were on the same pay scale."

Roger reached over, patting Travis on the arm in a calming manner. Sophie observed that not only did Travis take a deep breath and settle, but Roger's hand stayed comfortingly on Travis his arm. Looking up, she could tell that Roger had been watching her watch them.

"Yes, we're a couple," Roger said. "We're not ashamed, but we'd decided to not let it be known. We feel that most people in Baytown would be very accepting, but we don't want to do anything that would bring undue attention to us and not The Dunes Resort."

Breathing a sigh of relief, she confessed, "You don't know how glad I am to find out that's what you two must've been talking about the other day." Seeing their heads tilt in unspoken questions, she explained, "After our meeting the other day, I overheard the two of you talking. It sounded suspicious and made me wonder if perhaps you weren't part of the scheme."

Carlotta sucked in a quick breath, her mouth pinched, and Sophie wondered if she was one of the people who was not accepting of Roger and Travis' relationship.

Carlotta opened a folder in front of her, saying, "Moving on to business, I've checked on Ann, who will be discharged from the hospital in a couple of days. Roger has temporarily promoted the assistant chef to take Ann's place until she can return." Turning her gaze to Sophie, she continued, "We know that there is no way to keep this out of the news, so we are going to need the Southern Living Magazine article to really showcase how wonderful we are. Sophie, before our meeting, I went by the house and the condo, and I just have to say that your work is exquisite. I know that your time with us will soon be over, but if you ever want any recommendations for work, I will certainly be glad to send prospective clients your way."

It was on the tip of her tongue to let them know she was not going to be leaving Baytown, but first, she had someone else she needed to talk to.

33

She heard the door on Callan's truck slam closed, and Sophie stood in his kitchen putting the final touches on dinner. Smoothing her hands over her dress, she tried to still the fluttering of nervous butterflies in her stomach.

Before she had a chance to rehearse what she wanted to say for the millionth time that day, the door opened, and he stepped through. Her heart never ceased to beat faster when her eyes landed on him, even when they were children. His gaze moved about the room, his face breaking into a smile when he saw her.

He stalked over, his arms enveloping her. As he pulled her close, she lifted on her toes, and with her arms wrapped around his neck, gave him her mouth. It may have started as a kiss of greeting after a long day, but it only took a few seconds for it to flame hotter. Breathing him in, she felt as though she were inhaling his very essence, something she not only craved but needed.

He lifted his head and said, "Damn, baby. That's the way I'd love to be greeted every day."

"I'm glad I decided not to move back to Richmond. I want to wake up with you every morning also." She watched as his smile widened.

Meeting his smile, she added, "I just had to let you know that seeing you walk in, you're every dream I've ever had since I was a little girl come true."

He pulled her in tighter, his hand cupping the back of her head and pressing it to his chest. With her arms wrapped around his waist, she heard his heartbeat pounding against her cheek. After a moment, she whispered, "Please, say something."

"I've officially filled out the paperwork to be discharged from the Coast Guard at the end of my enlistment. I've also officially applied to and have been granted provisional employment at that time with the Virginia Marine Police. I want to keep living in Baytown. I want to be with you."

Pushing back against his hand, she tilted her head so that she could look into his face. "We're going to stay here?"

At his nod, she squealed and jumped up, wrapping her legs around his waist. He began to twirl them around the small space, managing to get them dizzy while only bumping into one end table and a chair. Kissing her soundly once more, he said, "I think we're gonna need a bigger place."

"I don't care where we live, as long as we're together," she vowed.

She uncrossed her legs from around his waist, and he slowly lowered her feet to the floor, keeping his arms banded around her. Never taking her eyes from his face, she said, "I think Philip would be happy for us."

His eyes warmed, and he nodded. "All Philip ever wanted was for you to be happy. All I ever wanted to do was have your heart."

Whispering, she said, "You've got my heart, Callan. You've always had my heart."

Kissing her lightly, he murmured against her lips, "And I'll guard it forever."

Sophie sat in the pew near the front of the church and watched as Lia and Aiden exchanged their vows. The ceremony was beautiful, but it was the little girl standing up with her mother that had tears in everyone's eyes.

Lia's daughter was dressed in a pink dress, a silk ribbon in her hair that matched the silk ribbon around her mother's waist. Emily grinned widely up at Aiden as he kissed her mother and then knelt to place a little necklace over her head. Swooping the little girl into his arms, the three of them hugged to the applause of the congregation.

Shifting her gaze, Sophie caught the eye of Callan, standing proudly as one of Aiden's groomsmen. He winked at her, and her fingers automatically rubbed the engagement ring on her left hand. Callan had not wasted any time...he asked her to marry him shortly after she decided to stay in Baytown. They both realized that having known each other since their early years they did not want to wait, so one night on the town beach, he dropped to his knee and proposed.

As the reception was in full swing, Callan's arms were wrapped around her. With her head resting on his chest, she watched as other couples moved about the floor. Finn MacFarlane was dancing with little Emily, her giggles ringing out. Aiden and Lia were in their own little world, eyes pinned on each other. The other Baytown Boys and their women were snuggled together, as well as their parents.

As her parents danced nearby, her mother whispered, "I can't wait until we get your wedding planned!"

Her dad rolled his eyes, but he chuckled, twirling her mother around again.

Callan said, "She's right, you know. Looks like we'll be next."

She lifted her head, her heart full, and whispered, "I love you."

His smile met hers and he kissed the top of her head, murmuring, "Love you, too."

Hours later, the gathering stood outside with sparklers in their hands and the sound of cheering ringing out and watched as the couple ran to the limo to whisk them away to their honeymoon.

Sophie could not help but think how much Philip would have loved this night. She smiled to herself, startling when Callan said, "Hey, what are you smiling about?"

Looking around at their friends celebrating, a light giggle slipped from her lips, and she said, "It's good to be home."

She felt the deep chuckle rumble from his chest as he replied, "Yeah, Sophie, it is. Everyone together...it's good to be home."

Seven Years Later

Sophie sat on the beach, the summer visitors gone but the fall sun still warm on her face. She peered through her sunglasses out toward the water, keeping an eye on the children running and playing. Most of the Baytown Boys and her girlfriends surrounded her, their children involved in the game of tag, having lost interest in their sand buckets and castles.

Callan dropped onto the towel next to her, snagging her attention whenever he was around just like he always did. There were a few sprinkles of silver hair amongst the black, giving him a distinguished appearance. He leaned over, placing a kiss on her lips.

"Hey, babe," he said, his gaze making her as warm as the sun had.

Smiling, she reached over and cupped his jaw, rubbing her fingers over the stubble. "Hey, sweetheart."

He nodded to their friends lounging on blankets

nearby before his gaze turned toward the water and he asked, "Everyone okay?"

She watched as a little girl, whose blonde curly hair was flying in a tangled mess, fell as she tried to run faster than her legs would allow. Sitting up straight, Sophie was about to jump up when a dark-haired boy, a few years older than the girl, ran to her and gave her a hug. He took her by the hand and led her toward Sophie and Callan.

Tears hit her eyes as she watched the scene in front of her, and Callan reached over and grasped her fingers, giving them a squeeze. "Philip's a good big brother," he said, his eyes still on their children coming closer.

Swallowing past the lump in her throat, she agreed. "Yes...yes, he is."

Reaching them, the little boy looked up and said, "Lisa fell down in the sand, Mom."

Callan had risen from the beach towel and scooped up the little girl, whose tears quickly dried as she giggled. "Pwiwip helped me," she said, beaming at her dad as he kissed her tummy.

Sophie reached her arms out to her son, and Philip immediately ran to her, allowing her to cuddle him. *How long will it be before he doesn't let me do this?* Ignoring the sadness that thought brought, she kissed his forehead and said, "You're the best big brother in the world, Philip."

As those words left her mouth, she smiled at the truth of that statement...both for her son and for her own brother. The children soon ran back to their friends, a new crop of Baytown boys and girls in the making.

Callan dropped back to the blanket and took her lips in a sweet kiss. "Happy?"

She nodded and said, "You were right, you know… all those years ago." Seeing his questioning look, she said, "You still guard my heart."

He moved in for another kiss, her lips still in a smile. Leaning back, he turned his head as she whispered, "He would be happy, Callan. He would be so happy for us."

A warm breeze blew over the beach, the gathering below enjoying the best Baytown had to offer. A few white fluffy clouds passed overhead, unheeded by most of the humans below.

Old friends. New friends. Parents. Grandparents. Children. The sound of laughter. The scent of sunscreen. Colorful blankets dotting the sand. A scene replayed over and over in history.

Former kids, now grown up with children of their own.

Another delightful breeze blew off the bay, as though someone had sighed in pleasure.

Be well, Squirt. Take care of her, Callan.

The cloud passed, and the gathering below continued to enjoy their day. Except for one curly-

haired, little blonde girl who looked up into the sky…
and smiled at the breeze.

Don't miss other the next Baytown Boys
Sweet Rose

Sleeping with the competition? Maybe not Rose's best
move.

Rose Parker wanted to open an ice-cream parlor in
Baytown, but life kept handing her one setback after
another. As for her annoyingly handsome neighbor
Jason? He always seemed to get everything he wanted.

Jason Boswell didn't mean to start off on the wrong foot
with the beautiful Rose, but something about her always
throws him off kilter.

When Rose finally manages to get the space for her
Sweet Rose Ice Cream Shop and upstairs apartment…
right across the street from Jason's shops… she makes a
discovery: letters from a former resident and a skeleton
in the cellar.

Thrown into a mystery from years ago, Rose has to call
on her neighbor for help. While Jason's determined to
keep Rose safe and uncover the truth, it appears that
someone in town wants to keep secrets buried…

Please take the time to leave a review of this book. Feel

free to contact me, especially if you enjoyed my book. I
love to hear from readers!

Facebook

Email

Website

Jaxon

Jayden

Asher

Zeke

Cas

Lighthouse Security Investigations

Mace

Rank

Walker

Drew

Blake

Tate

Hope City (romantic suspense series co-developed

with Kris Michaels

Brock book 1

Sean book 2

Carter book 3

Brody book 4

Kyle book 5

Ryker book 6

Rory book 7

Killian book 8

Saints Protection & Investigations

(an elite group, assigned to the cases no one else wants...or
can solve)

Serial Love

Healing Love

Revealing Love

Seeing Love

Honor Love

Sacrifice Love

Protecting Love

Remember Love

Discover Love

Surviving Love

Celebrating Love

Follow the exciting spin-off series:

Alvarez Security (military romantic suspense)

Gabe

Tony

Vinny

Jobe

SEALs

Thin Ice (Sleeper SEAL)

SEAL Together (Silver SEAL)

Letters From Home (military romance)

Class of Love

Freedom of Love

Bond of Love

The Love's Series (detectives)

Love's Taming

Love's Tempting

Love's Trusting

The Fairfield Series (small town detectives)

Emma's Home

Laurie's Time

Carol's Image

Fireworks Over Fairfield

Please take the time to leave a review of this book. Feel free to contact me, especially if you enjoyed my book. I love to hear from readers!

Facebook

Email

Website

AUTHOR INFORMATION

USA TODAY BESTSELLING AND AWARD WINNING AUTHOR

I am an avid reader of romance novels, often joking that I cut my teeth on the historical romances. I have been reading and reviewing for years. In 2013, I finally gave into the characters in my head, screaming for their story to be told. From these musings, my first novel, Emma's Home, The Fairfield Series was born.

I was a high school counselor having worked in education for thirty years. I live in Virginia, having also lived in four states and two foreign countries. I have been married to a wonderfully patient man for thirty-seven years. When writing, my dog or one of my four cats can generally be found in the same room if not on my lap.

Please take the time to leave a review of this book.

Feel free to contact me, especially if you enjoyed my book. I love to hear from readers!

Facebook

Email

Website

Made in the USA
Columbia, SC
29 March 2021